Three Genie Brothers

Three Genie Brothers

Christian Roulland Kueng

iUniverse, Inc.
Bloomington

THREE GENIE BROTHERS

This is a work of fiction. All of the characters, names, incidents, organizations, and dialogue in this novel are either the products of the author's imagination or are used fictitiously.

iUniverse books may be ordered through booksellers or by contacting:

iUniverse
1663 Liberty Drive
Bloomington, IN 47403
www.iuniverse.com
1-800-Authors (1-800-288-4677)

Because of the dynamic nature of the Internet, any web addresses or links contained in this book may have changed since publication and may no longer be valid. The views expressed in this work are solely those of the author and do not necessarily reflect the views of the publisher, and the publisher hereby disclaims any responsibility for them.

Any people depicted in stock imagery provided by Thinkstock are models, and such images are being used for illustrative purposes only.
Certain stock imagery © Thinkstock.

ISBN: 978-1-4759-6185-0 (sc)
ISBN: 978-1-4759-6184-3 (hc)
ISBN: 978-1-4759-6183-6 (ebk)

Library of Congress Control Number: 2012921985

Printed in the United States of America

iUniverse rev. date: 12/19/2012

Contents

To my family who holds a special place in my heart,
To my friends whom I love like family,
You deserve the best this world has to offer.
God bless all of you.

Acknowledgments

I would like to give special thanks to Dr. Walt Pleasnick, retired teacher from the Hemet Unified School District, and Ms. Katie Bradshaw, special-education teacher in the Cucamonga School District, for their skills in proofreading, editing, and making suggestions for this book.

Chapter One

A Family of Jinn

Aristede and his wife, Cassidy, lived in a gray stucco-coated house in Ontario, California. Actually, their home was in an expensive bottle made of amethyst that sat unnoticed on a shelf between picture frames and other knickknacks. Every afternoon, the sunlight beamed through the windows of the French doors and bounced off the purple bottle's surface.

The bottle house was spacious and didn't show the true size of the living area. It was more like the inside of a round tent. In addition to a large center room, there were sleeping chambers, an eating area, and a sunken retreat with many pillows strewn around. Silky curtains draped down from the bottle spout, which served as the portal to the outside *human* world.

Aristede and Cassidy were jinn. *Jinn* was actually the old word for *genie* and is now used most often in formal conversation and on official documents. Aristede was a tall, muscular genie with hair cropped

1

short and a goatee. Cassidy was a slender woman who wore a thin, see-through veil that draped across the front of her neck and pulled back tightly to the crown of her head, tied off by a golden band. Her wavy blonde hair flowed down the middle of her back.

They had three ten-year-old sons: Justin David, Morgan, and Blake, who were triplets. When the boys were younger, it had been extremely hard to tell them apart. They had learned early on that triplets could create confusion just by answering to each other's names. But they also had capitalized on their identicalness. One time Justin David (whom everyone called JD for short) had replaced the mirror in their room with a glass pane; Morgan hid behind it so when Cassidy walked in on them, JD's mirror image didn't seem to follow the same movement as JD.

Another time Blake had pretended to be hit by a wooden block that had supposedly zoomed across the room, like an arrow, and hit his forehead, causing a bloodied injury. His shrill scream had brought Aristede and Cassidy running to see what the commotion was all about. When their parents weren't looking, JD had switched places with Blake. With a twist of her hand, whipping up a wash towel, Cassidy had found JD sitting there, smiling as if nothing had happened. They certainly enjoyed confusing their parents with their playacting.

Like most genie boys, JD, Morgan, and Blake wore loose-fitting, baggy pants and vests over their white button-down shirts. Although there was no question that these sibling brothers were identical—with dark green eyes, straw-colored hair, stubby little noses, and dimpled smiles—they were also different in many ways.

JD had a sense of adventure, which was enhanced by his fascination with the human world. He was also the first of his brothers to show his genie powers. It had happened when he was five and had wanted his stuffed griffin one night. He put his arms straight out in front of him, and the griffin began to flitter its wings back and forth before floating to his waiting arms.

Morgan, on the other hand, had an extensive vocabulary, using words like *preposterous*, *meticulous*, and *furthermore*, which made everyone consider him the *smart* brother.

Finally, Blake was the youngest triplet by ten minutes. He was sweet-natured and loved animals. But unlike JD, who neatly brushed his short hair up in front, or Morgan, whose eyes were almost covered with his parted hair that hung down, Blake could go for days without combing his hair at all.

One morning an official-looking parchment appeared in a dented and dimpled mail jar. Not only did the parchment have a red ribbon tied around the rolled-up paper, but also it had a gold seal that could be broken only by Aristede and Cassidy. It was a typical security measure by the Academy for Jinn Studies. This is where our story begins.

Aristede ushered JD, Morgan, and Blake into the sunken retreat.

"What's going on?" JD asked.

"You're coming of age when you can be *summoned*," Aristede said to them. "Do you understand what that means?"

Before JD had a chance to answer, Morgan stepped forward and eagerly shared what he knew.

"In the life of genies, usually beginning the tenth year, and in accordance with jinn law, genies must leave their containers, whether it is a bottle or a lamp, and go to the outside world, where they are forced into the service of a human master who receives three wishes," he said.

Impressed with his son's understanding of a genie's life, Aristede then asked, "What happens after a human's wishes are granted?"

"A genie returns to the life in his or her container until another person takes possession of it," Morgan added. "If the portal remains open, genies can come and go into the human world."

JD sneered at his brother and whispered coolly, "Show-off."

"Because of that, the masters from the Academy for Jinn Studies are coming to evaluate your powers. That's what this letter is all about," Aristede said. "They'll be here tomorrow."

Early the next morning, the triplets sat on the hearth of the fireplace. JD and Morgan were performing magic tricks for each other. JD blew into his hands, and when he pulled them apart, a pink hummingbird appeared, twittering from one part of the room to another. Quietly Morgan pointed at the bird, making it disappear, leaving behind only one pale red feather that glided to the floor.

Blake, on the other hand, played with a marble-like sphere called an *orbular*. It was the size of his fist. The swirls of tan-colored shapes let

JD and Morgan know their brother was watching a camel race. Unlike an ordinary camel race in the human world, these camels had wings, and they flew around a long oval track.

Usually the only sounds came from the low gurgling of water in the oblong reflecting pool in the center chamber of the bottle and from water splashing out of a copper sphere fountain in the sunken retreat. But today, at precisely nine o'clock, a low rolling sound trembled underneath them, interrupting their activities. The noises continued to grow louder. And there they were—their examiners. They were sitting on large elephants, three of them, linked together from trunk to tail.

On the lead elephant was a burly-framed man with short brown hair and long sideburns that were neatly trimmed. His height and his muscular body created an awesome impression to most people when they met him for the first time. Up close, the most unusual feature of the genie master was his eyes: one was an ocean blue and the other was a hazel-brown.

"It's Jindrake," Cassidy said.

He gave her a kind smile.

Jindrake was a highly regarded staff member to the viziers on the Supreme High Council of the Jinn (more commonly referred to as just the Jinn High Council, a group of very powerful genies who enforced the laws and ruled all aspects of genie life). Also, he had been Aristede's supervisor when he, Aristede, worked for the council himself.

Atop the second elephant sat a woman wearing a green outfit and whose hair went in all directions. On the last elephant was another woman, squinting her eyes behind her round, full-moon glasses. The guests floated up and out of their coaches, all in sitting positions with their legs under them.

JD, Morgan, and Blake moved from the fireplace and made a wide circle around the elephants. Their guests followed the triplets down the three steps into the sunken retreat where Aristede and Cassidy were. The elephants disappeared with a sudden *pop*, leaving behind a trail of green smoke.

"I didn't know they were coming by elephant train," JD whispered to his brothers.

Aristede and Cassidy didn't seem surprised at how they had arrived. In fact, it was almost as if they had been expecting it. Cassidy patted the place next to her on the sofa, indicating that she wanted the boys to sit next to her.

Jindrake opened his long, firm hand with his palm facing them. He pressed it first against Aristede's hand and then against Cassidy's, as this was the acceptable greeting in the jinn world.

"We should have known you'd be coming. We can always expect the unexpected with you!" Cassidy said.

"I thought I'd have a little fun surprising you. Besides, I have a special interest in these young genies, and it has given me a chance to see my favorite godsons."

The fact was that JD, Morgan, and Blake were Jindrake's *only* godsons.

"Now, let me make introductions," Jindrake said. He extended his hand to the taller of the two women. "This is Miss Florine."

The wild-haired woman bowed.

"And this is Miss Jinane," he added. "Both are instructors at the Academy for Jinn Studies."

Miss Jinane, through the bangs of her long, streaked-colored hair, gave them a scrutinizing look. She lifted the hem of her light-colored blue skirt and sat down on a large cushion.

The triplets already had been in the novice program, learning such things as elementary wish granting, enchanting objects by bringing them to life, and basic vaporization and smoke movement. Depending on the results of a formal evaluation, they would move on to a more rigorous course of study that included spending a week at the academy after the completion of a sequence of instruction called a *module*.

"There will be two parts to the examination," Miss Jinane said. "A composite score will determine the next phase of your education. Do you understand?"

The three boys nodded nervously. They had never had three teachers from the academy in their home before.

"Good. Let us begin."

The first part of the assessment was a written component. It had questions on jinn lore ("Where did the original jinn create their world?"), flying carpets ("What is the purpose of the number of knots in the fringe of a flying carpet?"), and the Supreme High Council of the Jinn ("Identify the differing roles of the viziers").

Morgan did extremely well, finishing in less than an hour. His answers succinctly explained how the twelve original jinn had come together in the Majlis-al-Jinn cave, one of the largest cave chambers in the country of Oman in the human world. The Garden of Wegelius was the place of origin of their world, and the knots determined the altitude a carpet could reach. He correctly identified the seven viziers of the Jinn High Council (one each for flying carpets, magical beasts, history and artifacts, currency, the Academy for Jinn Studies, Outsider relations, and enchantment laws). Blake could identify only five viziers, whereas JD could name only four. However, they both received extra credit on the exam, Blake for including historical background on previous Jinn Cup Derby races and JD for telling the proper way to land a carpet. Morgan did not have these details in his responses.

After a short break, the triplets were tested on their actual use of genie magic.

The test began with a simple warm-up activity, in which they had to levitate objects like stuffed toys, blocks, and parchment rolls, moving them back and forth in midair between the lady examiners and themselves.

Next, JD, Morgan, and Blake were asked to make illusory sounds that would come from some other part of the bottle. They could do this in their sleep, JD thought.

JD began by stomping his foot. A few seconds later, Morgan snapped the fingers on both hands in sync with his brother's foot stomping. Then Blake clapped his hands. When they stopped the sound making, the same sounds—stomping, snapping, and clapping—in the same synchronized rhythms came from the eating area.

JD let out a sarcastic yawn to show how simplistic (and boring) these tasks were.

Because of JD's rather insulting gesture to the first task, Miss Jinane whispered something to Miss Florine, who then smiled widely.

"Since it is obvious that what we have asked of you seems to be beneath your genie level, we have something else for you to show us," she said.

Aristede and Cassidy shook their heads in tandem as Miss Florine waved her palm from right to left, and each triplet held a scrap of parchment that gave him a random but unique task.

JD's assignment was to create a dancing wisp of light, emanating from his fingers. He held up his left hand, and lights shot up from his fingertips. No problem.

Morgan received a nearly dead single-stemmed rose. His task was to revive the wilting flower. With a quick wink, the peach-colored petals regained their color, and the stem strongly supported the blossom.

Blake was happy that all he had to do was cool a warm liquid in a chalice that appeared in his hand. He made it easy by twirling his finger around the chalice mouth. Suddenly four or five cubes of ice dropped out of the air and into the beverage.

"Not bad," Miss Jinane said to him.

For the final test, each triplet received an ordinary inanimate object and had to enlarge it. JD got a sand timer, Morgan had three pieces of cutlery shaped into a small sculpture, and Blake found he was holding a triple-decker sandwich. The boys were so anxious that all felt the adrenaline race through them. Making the sounds repeat elsewhere in the bottle was one thing, but enlarging a three-dimensional object was something else. They would be graded on how long it took to change the object, with extra points given for ingenuity.

JD excelled here, and Morgan managed to make the sculptural object four times its normal size. Blake leaned forward, and only the slices of tomato got bigger.

Blake got extra points for creativity for his selective enlargements.

"There. That concludes our assessment," Miss Florine said. She jotted down the last of her observations on her clipboard. "They are progressing nicely. A complete report of findings will be sent to you, along with the placement for their next instructional module."

"So we're done?" Blake asked. Aristede and Cassidy nodded smilingly.

"That wasn't so bad. I thought we would have been asked to *blend*," JD added.

Jinane and Florine turned quickly.

"Blend?" Miss Florine asked. "You can blend? I mean, a complete blend at your age?"

"Remarkable, isn't it?" Jindrake said with the same smile, which was crooked on one side of his mouth, the smile that Cassidy liked so much.

Blending meant taking on the colors, shapes, and textures of whatever was behind them in the background. Blending didn't really make them disappear; it only made them hard to see.

"Of course we can blend," Morgan said.

The boys stood in a straight line. JD dropped his head and loosened his arms. He rotated his head back up and around before he inhaled a deep breath. He looked as though he were warming up for a sporting event.

Within seconds, they blended into the background. The only way anyone could tell they were still there was by the blinking of their eyes. Without any warning, they unblended.

"I believe this information should be included in your observational report, don't you agree, ladies?" Master Jindrake said.

Jinane and Florine moved to the open space in the center chamber to confer privately with each other. They quickly scribbled some more.

"We will leave you now!" Miss Jinane said. "Will you be going with us, Jindrake?"

"No. I want to spend some time here with my godsons."

An updraft of smoke came from the floor. When the smoke cleared, the ladies had disappeared, off to assess another young genie.

Jindrake turned back and said, "Now that we're done with that, and to celebrate your outstanding performance today, I have something for each of you."

From another puff of purple smoke, a wicker basket materialized near one of the center chamber's many urns. Then the basket lid popped up and dropped just as fast, followed by a low growl from inside.

Hesitantly, Blake lifted the lid, and three furry tiger cubs were trying to climb out. Two of the cats were orange in color, and the other was all white. The only thing the white cat had in common with his brother and sister were the black stripes on his body.

"What do you know? *Panthera tigris*," Morgan said.

JD folded his arms in front of him and shook his head.

"Oh, peacock feathers! Can't you just call them *tigers*?"

Morgan lowered one eyebrow and sneered.

"That *is* the proper name for the species," Morgan replied.

"Only you would know that, Mr. Know-It-All!" JD retorted.

"Stop arguing and move over," Blake said. He squeezed between Morgan and JD and picked up one of the orange tiger cubs. He looked at his brothers curiously and said, "This is how to take care of animals."

While Blake bent down to play with the only female cub from the trio of tigers, JD and Morgan moved to the other two.

Now that each had his own little tiger cub, what were JD, Morgan, and Blake going to name them? That was where Jindrake helped.

"I can tell you the female enjoys citrus fruit, and the white cub drinks a lot of yak's milk."

"What about this one, sir?" JD asked. He grasped the cub tightly before the squirmy little thing could get out of his arms.

"That one is a handful. He's very active. It's almost like he's dancing a tango," Jindrake told them.

"Then that can be his name—Tango," JD said. He followed up with a chuckle. "Calm down. I'm not going to hurt you."

Blake and Morgan thought for a moment about possible names for the other two cats.

"I think I'll call you Tangerine," Blake said. He remembered what Jindrake had said about the citrus fruit.

She gave out a baby-like wail before licking his face.

"Both are interesting names. What about the other one?" Jindrake asked.

The white cub rolled his head as his tongue darted out of his mouth before he let out what sounded like a baby's yawn. He growled to make sure no one would forget about him, because he wanted the same attention his brother and sister were getting. So Morgan gently rubbed his head.

"He looks like a lump of snow, and he has a cold nose. I shall call him Sherbet, like the ice cream," Morgan said. Little Sherbet growled again, as if to express his satisfaction with the name choice.

"Where did you get these tigers, Jindrake?" Aristede asked as he stroked the thin goatee around his strong chin.

"Upon returning home one day, I found a little surprise waiting for me. A mama tiger had given birth to the cubs and left. I haven't seen her since," Jindrake told them. "I couldn't very well take care of them, since my work schedule takes me away from home far too often,

I'm afraid. I had to find them a new home. That's where you come in. Three tigers and your three sons—do you know what that means?"

"Triple trouble," Cassidy groaned.

Aristede was delighted at the idea of having tigers as house pets, but it only made Cassidy anxious. There was a rumbling in the pit of her stomach. She wasn't sure about having the little animals run around in her home, even if they were only cubs.

"You're concerned. I can't blame you," Jindrake said. "But please know that having tigers as pets can bring great pleasure. They'll be there whenever you need them."

"Yes, I know," she said. "But tigers . . ."

"Maybe this will help. If they become a nuisance, let me know. I'll find another home for them, perhaps with one of the viziers."

She thought that a better home would be with Jasper, Aristede's brother.

Jasper owned a camel farm, but the problem with that was camels didn't do well with tigers around. He wouldn't be able to train the camels, because of how nervous and skittish they were around tigers, even if the cats were small.

Aristede's voice was calm and reassuring when he said, "Dear, I had a tiger when I was a child. Remember, for genies, tigers are safe pets because they always mind their masters." The tigers began sniffing at his feet, and Aristede looked sternly at them.

"Watch this," he said.

He ordered them to sit on their hind ends. The spindly cats stopped in their tracks and did as they were told.

Aristede then clamped his right hand into a fist and stared into their marble-sized eyes. The three tigers instantly rested their heads on their front paws.

Cassidy conjured up a cup of sweet lemongrass herbal tea and stirred the beverage. Lemongrass, with its zesty citrus flavor, would be good for her anxiety about the animals.

"Curious," she said under her breath as she sipped her tea.

Aristede then turned to Jindrake and asked, "We didn't know you were back. Finished your business for the council?"

Jindrake let out a deep sigh.

"Yes, finally. We'd received reports that some genies living among the humans have been doing some strange things. They were interviewed, but alas, they had no recollection of their actions," Jindrake explained.

Aristede knew quite well that Jindrake couldn't say much more and had a feeling that Jindrake had said more than he should have.

"Pomaberry beer or plum wine?" Aristede offered.

"Wine, if you please," Jindrake replied. He didn't particularly care for beer made from pomegranate and berries.

As Aristede snapped his fingers and a glass of plum wine appeared before them, Jindrake turned and watched the triplets with their new pets.

"I'm glad these little cats are welcome. I had a feeling that this would be the right home for them," Jindrake said.

Blake lay on his side as he watched the tigers tumble down the steps. JD and Morgan flopped down on a pile of pillows with them. Eventually, Sherbet, Tangerine, and Tango tired of playing, so they moved over on either side of Blake, while the third lay down on his belly. Before long the tigers were purring as they slept, and Blake cradled them in his arms.

As they snoozed, the three cats rolled around, and the boys gently stroked their bellies. The cubs stretched their stubby front legs and made grumbly noises when they yawned before vanishing. Sherbet left nothing behind but his nose and whiskers, and only Tango and Tangerine's stripes were visible. Blake was still able to snuggle his warm cheeks against the cubs' invisible little round heads. Feeling the warmth of the boy's arms, the cubs eventually reappeared.

Aristede invited Jindrake to stay for the evening meal. Jindrake hesitated at first, but when he found that Cassidy was planning a menu of roasted ostrich and bird's nest soup, he graciously accepted.

While Cassidy excused herself so she could prepare the meal in the eating area, Aristede escorted Jindrake down three steps to the sunken retreat. It was probably one of the most comfortable areas in the bottle house, smaller and cozier than the center chamber. They sat down on one of the two sofas so they could sit and talk.

JD quietly moved to the big window through which the bottle dwellers could see into the outside human world and where they could occasionally see the Outsiders who owned the house where their bottle resided. *Outsider* was the term the genies used for the humans who lived *outside the bottle*.

"You seem to be lost in your thoughts."

JD nodded politely when he looked up to find Jindrake standing over him.

"It looks like a really wonderful place. I've wanted to go out there for as long as I can remember," JD said.

"Perhaps someday you will, when the stopper is out of your bottle," Jindrake said.

"Sounds like a plan to me," JD said. He puffed out his chest to show how ready he was for that time to come.

But it didn't look like that was about to happen anytime soon. Living in a bottle that had a glassy stone stopper fixed in it kept them from visiting the human world. So long as the bottle opening was closed off, so was the portal between the human and jinn worlds, and visiting the human world was impossible for this family.

"Be careful what you ask for," Jindrake said.

"One day I hope to take you boys to the outside world for a visit," Aristede said.

"Really, Dad? You mean it?" JD exclaimed. "That would be great!

He then looked up to the top of the curved bottle and added, "Too bad for *that* thing."

"Well, you're going to have to wait. We can't go to their world, but we can still move around in ours," Cassidy said as she returned to the sunken sitting retreat. "Ari, don't tease them like that. Who knows how long the stopper will remain in the bottle opening."

That didn't stop Blake from asking his parents a question. "What's it like out there, anyway?"

Cassidy thought for a moment.

"It's a great big place. The people always seem to be in a rush, and they get around in things called automobiles or airplanes. The biggest difference, though, is that Outsiders don't have magic."

"No magic? I can't imagine anyplace like that." Blake sighed.

"So until then, the only way to learn about what's out there is to watch from the window," Aristede said.

JD pushed one of the many fabric window coverings aside to get a better view.

"So the Outsiders don't know we're here?" he asked.

"And they may never find out—not until they uncork the bottle," Jindrake explained. "It's been like that from the beginning of the jinn. Sometimes an Outsider unknowingly opens the doorway between both worlds, and when his wishes come true, the human thinks it's *luck*."

Blake rose from his seat and moved to the large window, pressing his hands and nose against the thick glass. Although today they could see into the human world where their bottle was, it wasn't always that way. The view changed periodically. Sometimes two humans were there in a room; sometimes the view was replaced with a large tree on a grassy knoll in the genie world. None of the genies could explain why it was this way, but they were in a world of magic where anything could happen.

Blake looked first to his left and then to his right at the splendid wide view. It was a fairly large room painted in rich green, with floor-to-ceiling bookcases along the walls, stained in a reddish finish. The shelves were brimming with books on many subjects and many classic pieces of literature. There was a tall floor lamp behind an overstuffed, maroon-colored chair used for leisurely reading and a smaller one that matched it sitting on a cherrywood desk. It was difficult for any of them to see beyond the windows at the far side of the humans' room.

When they did spot an Outsider, it usually was an older gentleman with dark hair, peppered with gray around the temples. He would sit at the desk, thumbing through magazines. Sometimes he would scribble madly in a notebook. When he tired, he took off his wire-framed glasses and laid them on papers spilling over the edge of his workspace.

Once in a while they would see the other Outsider, the man's wife, when she came to let her husband know that dinner was ready or to remind him that it was time for bed.

Today they watched as the Outsider took a book off a shelf and made himself comfortable in the leather chair. He began to read.

Before too long, he fell asleep, his book perched on his lap, open somewhere in the middle. Every couple of minutes he let out a snort. Blake tapped the glass pane—tap tap . . . tap tap . . . tap tap tap.

"Because we are so small, any sound we make is inaudible," Morgan explained.

"In-what?" JD asked.

"Inaudible—he's unable to hear us," Morgan clarified.

JD crossed his arms again and sighed. "Oh, peacock feathers. More big words!"

Soon the man was in such a deep sleep that his snores made the bottle tremble. Blake didn't like it and pulled away from the window, closed his eyes, and covered his ears.

"There he goes again," Blake said as the floor shook.

"His snores are as loud as Dad's," JD said. He couldn't help but let out a short giggle.

In addition to the yummy bird's nest soup and roast ostrich sprinkled with sesame seeds, Cassidy had prepared steamed vegetables mixed with scorpion tails, and cinnamon kumquat tarts for the evening meal.

After finishing the last drop of plum wine, Jindrake said, "May the fortune of the twelve jinn be with you," before he turned into purple smoke and vanished.

JD, Morgan, and Blake wasted no time moving into the sunken retreat, and they sank down into the sofas. Each of them leaned back against the pillows behind him.

It wasn't long, however, before JD briskly jumped to his feet and pointed to the window.

"Look!" he exclaimed. "Who's she?"

Morgan and Blake didn't know either. All they could do was shrug their shoulders. But there she was, an Outsider girl. They watched her every move and found her intriguing. By all appearances, she looked to be about their age.

Chapter Two

Meet the Outsider

The genie triplets watched as the girl, who had dark brown hair, carried a tall glass of cold milk in one hand and a plate of homemade chocolate chip cookies in the other. She set the glass and the dish down on the table. She went to the built-in bookshelf and pulled a hardcover book before sitting down in the plush leather chair. Picking up her first cookie, she gently dunked it into the milk and then took a bite. The cookies disappeared quickly. In between sips of milk, she read. Cookie crumbs sprinkled across her pale yellow cotton shirt.

"I'm happy to see that you've made yourself right at home," the man standing in the open doorway said. It was the man the triplets had seen countless times.

"Of course, Granddad. I love it here with you and Gramma," she said. "You know, I can't believe you have so many books."

"Nearly all of them are from my teaching days," the man said. "So you enjoy reading."

"Yes. I read a lot back home," the girl said before changing the subject. "Since it's vacation time, will we get to go places while I'm here?"

"I have some ideas for trips that I think you'll enjoy, like going to Marine Gardens. There are lots of whales and dolphins to see. There are shows where the animals even perform for the audience," he told her. "How does that sound?"

"That'll be great," she said. "I can't wait."

"We'll make plans in the next few days," he added. "But now it's time for bed, Brianna."

He reached for the empty plastic plate and drinking glass, and they walked out of the room together.

Blake turned to his brothers and said, "We know that her name is Brianna, and those Outsiders are her grandparents."

"To be sure. She could not have been here very long," Morgan said. "I wonder when she got there."

Brianna Carruthers had just arrived to visit her grandparents, Christian and Isabelle. Her plane had landed at Ontario International Airport from Denver at nine thirty-five in the evening. The flight attendant had cheerfully escorted her off the plane and down the escalator.

"There they are! Gramma and Granddad!" Brianna shouted.

The escalator step hadn't reached the ground floor of terminal two before she jumped off and dashed to the waiting couple.

Brianna stood there glowing as the flight attendant happily said, "She was the best passenger we had."

"I wouldn't expect anything less," Christian said proudly. He had pushed his wire-framed glasses firmly back to the bridge of his nose.

"That's our Bree," Isabelle said.

Isabelle was a slender woman with light brown hair that sparkled in the sunlight, making her hair look almost blonde.

Brianna threw her arms around their waists and greeted them with a great deal of affection. She could smell Isabelle's peppery lilac perfume. She clutched her grandparents' hands snugly as they moved through an endless crowd of passengers to the baggage claim area located on the other side of the information station.

"Mommy and Daddy wanted me to give you a message. They said to tell you they'd be flying in after the Fourth of July," she said as they waited for her luggage to come around on the baggage carousel.

It was late when they got back to the house, where Christian and Isabelle had lived for the past thirty years. For much of that time, Christian had worked long hours as a teacher and as an elementary school principal. His wife, Isabelle, had taken a job in the children's department of the public library right after they had gotten married. It had been in the house at 1341 Euclid Avenue where the Carruthers raised their three children.

When Brianna woke at about eight o'clock in the morning, she unpacked the rest of her clothes and put them on hangers in the guest room closet. On the dresser, in a black case, was her Game Kid. She moved some of her stuffed animals aside and lay on the bed. She pushed the buttons on the handheld electronic video game. The brightly colored shapes moved into different places on the screen. After playing three games of Drop Down, she made her way to the kitchen, where she watched Isabelle take pancakes off the griddle and put them on the oval serving platter on the table.

Brianna forked one pancake and then a second, which she promptly dropped onto her own plate. She couldn't help but show her delight to see a ceramic plate with a handprint pressed into the center at Granddad's place. It was the same one she had made for him when she was in kindergarten.

"Did you sleep well?" Isabelle asked as she shifted the bangs away from her forehead.

"Pretty much. I was really tired," Brianna said. She poured maple syrup over the sliced pancake pieces.

"Not too much syrup, dear. I'll get you some milk," Isabelle said. As she took a jug of 2 percent reduced-fat milk from the refrigerator, she added, "I'll be doing laundry today. Put any dirty clothes in the hamper in your bathroom."

"Okay, Gramma."

Christian arrived at the breakfast table with the morning edition of the local newspaper in his hand. Only his eyes could be seen as he skimmed over the headlines.

"Here's an article about the Fourth of July festivities. Looks like Jerry and Sue will have their annual Breakfast on the Green before the parade begins."

Isabelle brought a glass of milk to the table. Brianna surely needed it to wash down her food.

"I don't know how they can afford to do that every year. Jerry invites so many people," Isabelle said candidly. She sat opposite her husband and dried her hands with the apron wrapped around her middle before taking one of the remaining pancakes. "Our invitation arrived yesterday."

"It gives him a chance to meet the voters. He's done it every Fourth of July since he became mayor," Christian said. He didn't even look up as he spoke.

"You know the mayor?" Brianna asked. She looked very impressed that her grandparents knew an important person.

"Yup. Sure do," Christian said.

"You see, dear, your grandfather taught school with Sue. They've been friends of ours for many years," Isabelle explained. "Speaking of friends, our neighbors have a daughter about your age. They live just across the street. You'll be able to play with her while you're here. I'll ask her and her parents over for dinner or something so you can meet her. That reminds me, I have some grocery shopping to do. Would you like to go with me?"

"Belle!" Christian said. He put his paper down on the table, looked across at his wife, and gave her one of those stern-looking stares. "You want the girl to die of boredom already?"

"I like grocery shopping," Brianna said.

"Yeah, it's like going to the dentist," he mumbled under his breath.

Brianna covered her mouth to keep from snickering, although it was funny to listen to her grandparents' friendly banter. It wasn't anything like how her parents talked to each other back home.

Christian decided that he and Brianna would do something else while Isabelle was out shopping. He then turned to his granddaughter and asked, "Brianna, do you like miniature golf?"

"I love miniature golf," she said.

"There's a place nearby called Golf and Fun. But it doesn't open until ten o'clock," Christian said. "We can get lunch afterward, too."

18

"I'd like that very much, Granddad," Brianna said politely.

"Any excuse to golf," Isabelle said as she shook her head. "Even if it is just miniature golf."

Christian closed his newspaper and set it next to his empty plate. He was a little tweaked by her comment, so he just ignored her. He would wait in the living room until Golf and Fun opened. Isabelle carefully placed her crumpled napkin on the table and walked to the back door.

"Don't forget your laundry," she said.

Isabelle picked up a basket and took a batch of dirty clothes to the washing machine in the garage.

Brianna, on the other hand, decided to get another book. After she finished licking the rest of the syrup off her plate, she moved to the family room. She heard a muffled voice from the TV in the front room.

There were many classic books from which to choose. Christian had some of her favorites. Brianna quickly scanned the titles, moving her eyes from one to another: *Little Women*, *The Wind in the Willows*, and *The Wizard of Oz*, and then she moved to Scott Turnkey's anthology, *Chronicles of the Caretaker*. It was a children's novel that had gained worldwide popularity in recent years. In fact, it had been published in many languages, and several studios were currently bidding to obtain the film rights to the stories. She took the book *Heidi* from the shelf, settled comfortably in the leather chair, and began reading.

As she got caught up in the story, the three genie brothers were sitting cross-legged playing a game called JinJi. JD rolled his pyramid-shaped dice and then watched as his playing piece vaporized and moved across the tattered edge of the faded game board. When his bottle-shaped piece landed on the same place as Morgan's, Blake plucked up the dice and laughed because it wasn't one of his pieces that had to be sent back to its home base. Morgan accused JD of cheating, as the dice were rolled in a questionable way.

Suddenly, Blake set the dice down carefully on the game board and looked up from the game itself. He uncrossed his legs and stood up, just staring over his brothers' heads. It was obvious to JD and Morgan that something had captured Blake's attention. They turned to see what it was.

"Look—there she is again," Blake said.

He pointed to the window just as Brianna straightened up in the soft chair. She quickly glanced to the door to see if someone was there. No one was. Her eyes narrowed, and she looked one way and then turned her head in the opposite direction.

"She sure likes to read. She has another book in her hands."

It was a boy's voice, soft and peevish, filling every corner of the room. This voice echoed as though she were deep inside a cave, and it sent a cold shiver down her back and through her arms.

"I would thoroughly enjoy being out there with all those books. It is a shame that the books are out there, and I am here."

This voice, also a boy's just like the first one, was different, very proper sounding.

"That figures, Mr. Smarty Pants."

This was definitely a voice of someone who was sure of himself.

Brianna heard what she thought were three sets of giggles. She put her finger into the opening of her left ear and rotated it back and forth. Yes, she had heard more than one voice.

"Oh, peacock feathers," the confident one said. "I think she can hear us."

"You honestly think so? H-how do you know?" The first voice spoke again.

"Preposterous! That cannot be."

"Just watch her. She's looking around for something. Let's try talking to her."

"N-n-no. We m-m-mustn't."

"Actually, having one of them with the ability to hear us has never happened with the other people we see."

Brianna put her book down on the table next to the chair and cautiously moved over to the bookcase. There she stood, turning her head again and gazing around the room. With her mouth twisted, she called out, "W-who said th-that?"

She was stiff, and her feet seemed to be cemented to the floor. She waited for some kind of response. It stumped her when the voices stopped talking. Finally, she walked back to the chair.

"Wonderful! Now I'm hearing people who aren't here," she groaned.

Resting her head on the back of the chair, Brianna closed her eyes and used her index fingers to rub her eyelids for a couple of seconds.

Then she felt a hand nudge her on the shoulder. When she opened her eyes again, a towering Christian was now there.

"Are you ready to play a round of miniature golf, Bree?" However, her frowning didn't go unnoticed, and he asked, "What's the matter, sweetie?"

"Um—nothing. Really!"

Christian squinted one eye more than the other. He put one hand across his chin.

"Go ahead. You can tell me."

Her mouth pushed to one side, and she said, "Did you hear them, Granddad?"

"Hear who?" Christian relaxed his arms before taking a seat on the cushioned footstool.

"The boys," Brianna replied as she looked back around the room again.

Seeing the look on his face, Brianna was certain that he didn't believe her, and she half-regretted having said anything at all. To her surprise, a smile grew on his face.

"I was watching a news clip about some young people in New York who are raising money for orphans in Darfur, Africa. Those were the voices you heard."

She thought about this for a moment and then said, "Well . . . I did hear the TV when I came in here."

"That's because the television set is against the wall, the one between the living room and this one. That's what you heard," Christian added.

"Are you sure about that, Granddad?" Brianna asked.

She was still unconvinced. The strange voices she had heard sounded different from those on the TV, and besides that, she had heard voices all around her.

"Yes, I'm sure. You said you heard boys' voices. The boys they interviewed were about eleven or twelve." Christian looked at his wristwatch. "Golf and Fun should be open by now. I think we'd better go before it gets too crowded." As they both stood up, Christian put his arm around Brianna.

Back in the bottle, the triplets couldn't take their eyes off them and watched as the Outsiders left.

"She heard us! H-h-how's it possible?" Blake asked. He rubbed his hands together nervously. "Why did you tell her you wanted to talk to her?"

"Why not? She's an Outsider, and I thought it would be fun," JD said. "Do you think she'll hear us again?"

"I cannot say for certain," Morgan said, shaking his head. "Your guess is as good as mine."

They would learn the answer to JD's question soon.

It was nearly one o'clock when Brianna and Christian returned home after having lunch at Giant Burgers. Isabelle had been relaxing on the patio, sipping iced tea, when she saw them emerge from the garage. She put down her drink and walked over to greet them.

"Did you two enjoy yourselves?" she asked as Brianna hurried over to her.

"It was great, Gramma," Brianna said. "We played on the Fairy Tale Land course, and I won."

"Congratulations! Your grandfather always tells me what a good golfer *he* is," Isabelle said. She looked at her husband and gave him a sly smile.

"That's *real* golf," Christian said. "Not the kind with castles and moats. Aside from all that, our little granddaughter cheated."

"I did not cheat!" Brianna exclaimed.

"I'm joking, young lady," Christian said. He then snickered and gave her a quick wink.

It was a sunny afternoon, and Isabelle fetched them something cool to drink.

Behind them was a pond with water spilling into it from a rock waterfall. Listening to the faint gurgling water was soothing. Christian went to get the canister of goldfish food and tossed several pellets into the water before sitting next to Brianna at the table. The orange-colored fish moved swiftly to the surface to scarf up the floating pieces.

Piled on the glass tabletop were three stacks of photographs. Brianna arched her head to look at the photos Isabelle had been organizing. She picked up a few from the pile closest to her, and as she looked at the old photos, looking at one picture and putting it behind the rest, she giggled.

"What's so funny?" Isabelle asked as she came out the back door.

"These pictures, Gramma."

Isabelle came with two glasses in her hands. One was filled with tea for Christian, and the other with orange juice for Brianna. She looked over her granddaughter's head.

"Hold that one up, dear."

Brianna obliged immediately and lifted the photograph so Isabelle could have a better look at it.

"You know who that is, don't you?"

"This is my dad," Brianna told her. "But what is *he* doing with a doll?"

"Not a doll," Christian said. He took a sip of his iced tea. "That was Joey."

Joey wasn't just any kind of doll. Joey was a dummy a ventriloquist would use. Brianna learned that when her dad was about nine or ten, he had wanted to be a ventriloquist and took Joey everywhere.

"Remember, Chris, how Kyle would get so upset whenever somebody referred to Joey as a dummy?" Isabelle said. "I had to make all sorts of clothes for that puppet. Joey even had to have its own place at the dining table."

This was one of the funniest things Brianna had ever heard, and she couldn't help herself from laughing out loud. It was hard to imagine her father acting so silly. The Kyle Carruthers in the picture was a 180-degree opposite to the clean-cut, proper Kyle Carruthers who wore suits with white shirts and bland ties.

"Casey and Carson teased him so much about it, too." Isabelle sighed. She closed her eyes and said, "Poor thing."

Christian picked up one set of photographs and thumbed through a few of them.

"What are you doing with these pictures anyway, Belle?" he asked.

"Since Brianna came, I started thinking about the time when Casey, Carson, and Kyle were younger," she began. "I found the pictures in a shoe box in the hall closet, so I thought about making a scrapbook for each of the children."

"Even Casey?"

Brianna knew Christian was referring to her father's older sister. One day many years before, Casey Carruthers had vanished. A stunned Christian and Isabelle had held out hope that she would be found. The police had investigated and even followed up on crackpot leads. Casey's picture had also appeared on milk cartons, but she was never found.

Isabelle began spreading out photographs, and she picked up one showing her daughter in a cheerleader uniform the day she had made the pep squad. Isabelle rubbed her misty eyes, and she then blew her nose, which sounded like a honking goose.

"She's been gone for almost thirteen years," Isabelle said softly. "Her scrapbook will be here if she ever comes back."

Christian took the photo from his wife's hand. There was something in the picture that he hadn't noticed before.

"Brianna looks just like her."

Isabelle grinned at him when she saw that what he had said was quite true, and she said, "Doesn't she, though. The only difference is the hair color, but they do look alike."

"Gramma, can I help you make the scrapbooks?" Brianna asked. It was her way of cheering up her grandmother.

"Thank you, dear," Isabelle said. "There are some scrapbooks I made in the family room. Take a look at them to get some ideas. It'll be fun."

After dinner, Brianna sat down on the rug in the family room and pulled her legs in close. On one of the bottom shelves was a stack of large, square-shaped books. *Isabelle's Garden* was carefully hand-lettered in curly letters across a floral wallpaper cover. She flipped through a few pages before returning it to the pile and then selecting another scrapbook.

Inside the second one she saw photos of Christian piecing houses together with wood, laying the railroad track down, and even trimming miniature trees for his model train landscape. Christian wore a train conductor's hat in nearly all the photographs. After she had gone through all the pages, she set the scrapbook back on top of the others.

Then Brianna picked up one book that looked like an old-fashioned photo album. Printed on the cover was *Carruthers Family History* in an old style of lettering. She got up from the floor and plunged into the cushy chair, looking closely at family photographs that went back over a hundred years. Pictures of great-grandparents, great-aunts and great-uncles, even distant cousins filled the book. She read the caption to each picture. A neatly hand-printed family tree showed the connected relations of people in the photos.

She was alone in the room, or so she thought. Little did she know that there were three sets of eyes watching her, and they were all inside the bottle.

Again Blake moved closer until he was standing right in front of the window. He could feel his heart pounding. If he hadn't put his hand over his chest, he thought for sure his heart would come bursting through his body.

Off to the side were JD and Morgan, both watching Brianna and wondering if she would be able to hear them again or if the time before had been one of those freaky occurrences. JD knew there was only one way to find out. He moved a little closer to the large windowpane.

As though he was ready to make a presentation to the Jinn High Council, JD stood erect and inhaled deeply, forcing his chest out. He coughed to clear the lump out of his throat, and then he paused briefly before he said, "Excuse me."

Brianna jerked her head and gasped. It couldn't be happening again. A prickly feeling ran down her spine, just as it had the first time she heard the echoing voices.

After a few seconds, she said, "Y-yes?"

"Then you really can hear us. We weren't sure if you'd hear us again. I'm glad you can."

She sat back in the chair, and the book she was holding fell to her lap. She put her fingers on the top of her nose, between her eyes, and caught her breath.

"Maybe I'm still tired from my trip. You're not real. It's only a dream. It's only a dream. You're not real. It's only a dream," she said to herself. "The last time I heard your voices, Granddad said I fell asleep. Maybe I'm asleep now."

She reached down to her left arm and pinched it.

"Ouch!"

"Obviously you *are* awake. You would not have felt the pain otherwise."

"If you're real, who are you? Tell me what's going on."

"E-e-even if we understood it all, we c-c-can't explain it."

"Can't or *won't*?" There was a little taunting in the way she asked.

"C-c-can't."

"Let us just say it is the way it is and just leave it that way, shall we?"

"I thought so." She sat there, shifting awkwardly in the chair, and took long breaths of air to keep from getting sick. "Oh, look at me. I'm having a conversation with figments of my imagination."

When she raised her head again, her eyes moved fast back and forth before finally settling on the door to the living room. The next thing the boys realized, Brianna pushed aside the footstool with both feet, and when she stood up, the book that had been resting in her lap dropped to the floor. She backed away as quickly as she could, nearly knocking over the floor lamp.

"Wait. P-p-please don't go just yet," Blake said.

She stopped, composing herself enough to ask, "Why not?"

"We like talking to you, Brianna. This is all new to us," JD said.

"How do you know my name?" Brianna asked.

"We have a great deal of knowledge about you," Morgan said.

"Yeah. We know you're visiting your grandparents. It must be a lot of fun traveling around like that," JD said.

Brianna said nothing, and before they knew it, she slipped out of the room and headed into her grandparents' living room. She walked past two chairs on either side of the fireplace and took an empty spot on the couch. It had been recently upholstered in a blue fabric with light diagonal lines. A large art print framed in wide dark wood hung perfectly on the wall.

"You're awfully quiet," Isabelle said. "Is everything okay?"

Brianna nodded timidly.

"Would you like some ice cream?"

"Mommy doesn't let me eat a lot of sugary desserts."

"I know, but now you're with Gramma. My job is to spoil you while you're here with us," Isabelle said. "I don't think it will hurt you this one time."

She went to the kitchen and returned a few minutes later carrying a bowl and a spoon. Brianna reached up with both hands for her dessert. Mocha almond fudge was her favorite.

"When you're finished, put the bowl back in the kitchen."

"Okay, Gramma," Brianna said.

She took her first spoonful as Isabelle sat next to her again. Brianna felt her grandmother's arms wrapped around her as she leaned her head against the woman's soft shoulder.

Christian had been enjoying the evening news, but he let Brianna choose what she wanted to watch. She chose a cartoon program about a hermit crab that lived on the ocean floor, and she laughed when Hermie's underwear appeared after he lost his shell.

As Brianna ate her ice cream, her arms got goose-pimply. At first she thought it was the cold dessert. The temperature in the room was a comfortable seventy-eight degrees. But the more she thought of talking to bodiless voices, the more she found it disturbing. Was it real or imagined? And if it was real, what did it all mean?

She quickly finished eating her ice cream. She felt the cold pressure building in her head and knew she was having a brain freeze from eating it too fast. She didn't care and rushed to put the bowl in the sink.

After the popular television show ended, Brianna went to her room and changed into her pajamas.

She lay on her pillow to play a game on her Game Kid. However, Brianna couldn't concentrate, and when the video device made a bleeping noise to show that the game was over, she tossed the plastic box aside.

She climbed under the covers and rolled over on her back. With her arms clasped behind her head, she stared at the white ceiling. The Carrutherses' vintage 1920s house was in an established neighborhood and not where anything out of the ordinary ever occurred. All she could think about was the voices she had heard.

"I'm not dreaming or imagining any of it, and I know I'm not crazy."

She reached for the table lamp on the nightstand and turned off the lights before rolling onto her side, and within a mere half hour's time she was asleep.

Chapter Three

Master Jindrake's Advice

JD dropped down onto a plush cushion right in front of the window. Talking to the Outsider was all he could think about. But there it was, the outside world without the Outsider. He sat for a long time until out of the corner of his eye, he saw his brothers.

"Has she returned yet?" Morgan asked.

"No," JD said. "It's late and she's probably asleep, like we should be."

"Probably. She was most likely having a nightmare about us," Morgan said.

"About us? We're not scary," Blake said.

"I know that, but she does not," Morgan said. "You must admit it is befuddling to suddenly hear voices and not know where they are coming from."

"She doesn't understand what's going on any more than we do," JD said.

"Why didn't we just tell her we're in a bottle in her grandparents' house and that we're genies?" Blake asked.

"We are not allowed to until we are released," Morgan told him.

"But this is different," Blake added.

"True, but it is still jinn law. But I have a feeling we'll see her again," JD said.

"What makes you say that?" Blake asked.

"We might have scared her for now, but she did talk to us before she left the room," JD said.

Blake stood there, shaking his head and looking fairly concerned. Morgan tried to assure him that Brianna would be okay and they didn't have to worry about her.

However, that really wasn't what had been bothering Blake. He tried to understand just as Brianna had wondered about hearing voices, and how this could be happening at all. As Blake thought about it, the more frustrated he was because no one else could listen in on them.

"Let's go to bed," Morgan said.

He and Blake moved toward the bedchambers. After a moment of just sitting there with his eyes frozen on the big window, JD turned his head around and called out, "Wait!"

Both brothers stopped.

"Remember Dad always said that one day, when the bottle is open again, he'd take us out there?"

"And you heard what Mom said, too. She doesn't think that will happen for a long time," Blake said.

"Exactly. So until then, Brianna can tell us more about what it's like out there. It's a great chance for us. I don't think we should pass it up," JD added.

"That would be dangerous. Should she discover who we are, she could end up being our master," Morgan said.

"Morgan's right. I think we're playing with fire!" Blake said.

JD, Morgan, and Blake didn't see Brianna for a couple of days. She had been spending much of her time helping Isabelle with the scrapbook projects by selecting the photographs and arranging them on construction paper backing. Brianna carefully pressed each piece into place on the page after swiping the glue stick along the edges of the back of the paper.

In the meantime, Aristede and Cassidy had received the report of findings from the Academy for Jinn Studies about the recent assessment of their children's current abilities. The officials moved the triplets into the advanced level of instruction, which was rare for genies this young. The teaching masters often sent practice material that would prepare them for the next set of lessons in their educational program.

Dear Young Masters Justin David, Morgan, and Blake:

The training at the Academy for Jinn Studies is designed for the improvement of all natural abilities of young genies.

Before meeting with academy instructors in September, all students must be able to perform a variety of skills with the theme for this term—transmogrifications. These activities focus on the theories and concepts associated with changing one object into another.

In preparation, you will need to do the following:

First, take an inanimate object and, based on the color of that object, transmogrify it into a fruit or vegetable. Then take the fruit or vegetable and turn it into an animal.

Finally, take two creatures and merge them into one. Please care for and feed this creature properly and bring it with you, along with your reflective journal, to the meeting at the academy.

Good luck.

Warmest regards,

Miss Jinane and Miss Florine,
Assessment Examiners and Senior Instructors
Academy for Jinn Studies

The first part of their assignment was simple for them to do, but they had to spend time to change the fruit into animals. It was challenging turning the green apple, the lime, and the banana into a frog, a turtle, and a canary.

After much thought about the merging part of the assignment, the boys decided to work with a frog and a turtle. These animals both were small, had four legs, and were green. They proceeded to create a *frurtle* and named it Timmy. It was quite amusing to watch Timmy jump around the spherical copper fountain.

Working on an assignment helped JD, Morgan, and Blake take their minds off the Outsider girl.

As they were documenting the results of their lesson in parchment journals, Brianna returned to the family room. She was an eager reader and had finished reading two books since she arrived. Now she was perusing the shelves for the next one to read. It was Blake who was the first one to see her from their vantage point inside the bottle.

"You're back!" Blake exclaimed.

Brianna didn't really want to hear any voices. If she did, it meant that there was something very odd and unexplainable happening here. She listened.

She didn't know how much time had passed—a few minutes perhaps, or maybe it was only seconds—as she tried to figure out from where, exactly, the voices were coming.

"Brianna, we were hoping to see you," Morgan said as he made his way next to Blake. "Are you all right? We did not mean to frighten you."

Brianna gathered up the courage to talk to them again.

"Well, to be honest, I was a little scared."

And why wouldn't she be? It was only natural when anyone has a conversation with a set of disembodied voices, even those sounding pleasant enough.

Her eyes wandered for a moment before she asked, "You said you could see me?"

"Yeah, we can see you," JD told her.

"You keep saying *we*. I counted at least three voices before. How many of you are there?"

"You are absolutely correct," Morgan said. "There are three of us."

Happily, Blake added, "We're brothers, and we're triplets."

Brianna knew twins back home. There were Mia and Monica King, who were identical twins. And then there were Wally and Sherry Sommers. They were fraternal twins, meaning that they happened to be born at the same time and were no more alike than any other siblings. But she had never met triplets.

She sat in the chair and did her best to relax. Brianna looked around in many different directions, since she didn't have any idea where the voices were coming from.

"I wish I had brothers or sisters. I'm an only child, and I get lonely a lot of the time, especially when my parents go away on their trips. They travel a lot," Brianna said.

Brianna was more at ease, as though she were talking to herself. She began talking about how, when her parents were traveling, she stayed with her cousins most of the time. It was fun, but she enjoyed staying with her gramma and granddad because they lived in California and took her on trips to local amusement parks and places of historical interest.

"Granddad took me to Golf and Fun after I heard you the other day. Do you like miniature golf?"

"No," JD said.

He didn't want to let it be known that he didn't know what miniature golf was.

"My grandfather likes regular golf better. Miniature golf is more for kids," Brianna added. "Granddad was a good sport about playing, but I think he let me win."

The triplets had no grandparents to talk about, and the only relative they had visited was their uncle Jasper. The other relatives were Aristede's aunts Majo and Saffire, who, according to the boys, were quite old and talked about themselves a lot.

The uneasy feelings began to subside and were replaced by sheer curiosity. She might not have understood what was happening any more than the triplets did, but she still liked talking to them. The triplets were only too happy to let her go on talking, since it allowed them to hear more about the curious human world.

Brianna started talking about her favorite animals—whales, sharks, and dolphins—and the trip to Marine Gardens her grandfather was planning so she could see them up close. She also had a black kitten named Midnight. Blake shared about their pet cats, Sherbet, Tango, and Tangerine. He left out the part that they were tigers.

But she was doing all the talking, and she wanted to know about them. The boys did not hesitate to oblige.

"We enjoy the same things you do, like reading books and playing games, just like any other kids your age," Morgan said.

"My age? How old are you anyway?" Brianna asked.

"We're ten," Blake said.

"Really? What a coincidence. I'm ten, too," Brianna exclaimed. "I've been thinking. You know what I think you are?"

It sounded more like a statement than a question.

Blake's body stiffened. How could she know? His ear gave a quick twitch.

"It's simple. I don't know why I didn't think of it before," Brianna said. "You're ghosts!"

"Ghosts! Oh, peacock feathers!" JD exclaimed as he scrunched his face. "You've got to be kidding."

Morgan knew immediately that JD shouldn't have reacted the way he had, and he elbowed his brother in the ribs. He clapped his hand over his JD's mouth with one hand and put his finger to his lips with the other to let JD and Blake know they had to be careful.

Morgan then pulled his brothers away from the window, not wanting Brianna to hear them. If the conversation continued as it had been, they could unwittingly give her enough clues to figure everything out. They probably had given out too much information as it was.

"She's a nice girl," Blake said. "You heard her. She doesn't think we're real. There's nothing to worry about."

"She is an Outsider," Morgan reminded them. "We need to be quiet."

There was a long, silent pause as the three of them kept watching her.

The silence was finally interrupted when Brianna asked, "What else could you be, anyway? It's that or you're all just figments in my head. Since only I can hear you, that's what you have to be, and that's why Gramma and Granddad can't hear you. You're making yourselves known only to me."

Regardless of what Morgan thought, JD still wanted to take this chance to learn about the outside world. He moved closer so he could tap his finger on the glass.

"What's beyond the doors?" he asked.

Brianna swiveled her head around to see what he was talking about. She strolled to the set of doors and turned the knob on one of them and gave it a slight push. JD stood on his toes to get a better view of a yard of beautiful flowers and plants, a fishpond, and a large climbing tree. But JD didn't seem impressed, even though he hadn't been sure what to expect.

"It looks nice," he said.

"*Nice*? Is that all you have to say about it?" Brianna said. She sounded a little put out by his reaction. "What did you expect?"

"I don't know," JD said.

"Look. There's even a swing Granddad made when my dad was a little boy."

While Brianna went on about just how beautiful the backyard was, JD still was more interested in what lay beyond the fenced-in yard.

"So how long will you be visiting?"

"Just until Mom and Dad get back from their trip. They're in Europe right now. I got here a couple of days ago."

"Tell us about that U-rup place where your mom and dad are," JD said.

"Europe?" a puzzled Brianna said. "You don't know much about geography, do you?"

She picked up a world globe standing in the corner and told them about the different countries, with museums and art galleries, the high Alps mountains with snow on them all year round, and all the old buildings.

Before they knew it, Morgan and Blake found themselves back by the big window.

"We went on vacation to Paris, France, last year. I got sick to my stomach when we went to the top of the Eiffel Tower," she said.

"Someday I'd like to see as much of the world as I can, too," JD said. "How far is U-rup from your house?"

"It's very far away. Here we are, in California," she said as she pointed to the West Coast of the United States. "My parents are in Switzerland, here. The people are friendly. It's surprising how many Europeans can speak English."

"English?" Morgan said. "What is English?"

"It's the language we're speaking," Brianna said. She found it difficult to cover up her confusion. How could they not know they were speaking English? What did they think they were speaking—Japanese?

She put the globe back in its display stand and returned to the chair. She closed her eyes and shook her head again. After letting out a muffled sigh, she said, "I don't get it. This is so bizarre."

Their conversation came to an abrupt end when Isabelle poked her head into the family room and asked for Brianna's help in the flower beds. Gardening was another one of Isabelle's favorite hobbies.

Before Brianna left, she wanted to know if they would talk to each other again.

"It is a remote possibility, but we cannot be sure about that. It depends," Morgan said.

"Whatever that means," she said under her breath. "Nice talking to you. Good-bye."

The triplets waited for a few seconds in case Brianna came back for something. When they heard the back door of the Carrutherses' house slam closed, Morgan spun quickly around, while JD and Blake remained at the window.

"I know who might have the answers about everything that is going on," Morgan said. "Follow me."

Before either JD or Blake realized it, Morgan was already out the front door.

With the exception of the top of the bottle, all other bottle exits led to an entire jinn society. The buildings of the city of Jinwiddie stood in the hazy distance.

Morgan passed a large tree shielding the grassy knoll as he started down the pebble pathway. His rushed footsteps sounded like hundreds of parchment pieces being wadded up into paper balls.

Just over the hill was a small round house in the shape of a perfume bottle. Flecks of orange with blue, purple, and yellow speckles stippled the smooth exterior glass. A soft yellow glow was visible in the window.

JD knocked on the door of the one person Morgan thought could help them. A minute or two passed, and no one answered.

"I don't think he's here," Blake said.

"Try again," Morgan said.

For a second time JD knocked on the door, this time harder. The door slowly creaked open. Blake took a step backward, and his ears twitched as soon as he saw their brawny godfather, Jindrake.

"Ah, Justin David, Morgan, and Blake. What a pleasant surprise. Come in. Please make yourselves at home," Jindrake said.

Crisp-looking satin pillows were piled on one side of the room. A stew was cooking slowly in the marble-framed fireplace, and a pleasant odor of charcoal scented the room. The last grains of sand filled the bottom of a large sand timer, and without any help from anyone, the timer turned upside down. The sand began flowing downward again.

Unlike the center chamber in their bottle house, Jindrake's center room was tiny and offered little seating. JD, Morgan, and Blake sat at the low table. In a metal stand that had long lost its luster rested a crystal ball. There was a storm moving violently inside it. Jindrake used it when he communicated with other sages.

"We're sorry to bother you, sir, but we have to talk to you about something," Blake said.

The man looked from one triplet to the others. They sat silent, not sure where to start.

"May I get you some snail stew to nourish you?" Jindrake offered his guests. He picked up the ladle and poured some into a bowl. They declined.

"You look deeply troubled. Go on, young ones," he said.

"Well, we have been talking to an Outsider," Morgan said.

"That's not unusual. Outsiders can be quite entertaining," Jindrake told them. "I have many Outsider friends with whom I communicate on a regular basis."

"Yes, but we talk to a human girl while we're in our bottle," JD said. "And you know our bottle is closed."

It was hard for Jindrake to hide the look of utter surprise on his thick-haired, goateed face.

"That's not possible. No genie can communicate with an Outsider like that."

"B-but sir, it-it's true," Blake said.

For a man who had such a presence, you would have thought he wouldn't be able to bend his legs at the knees and tuck his legs in close to his buttocks as he sat down. He listened to them as they retold their fascinating encounters with Brianna.

For the longest time he said nothing. Jindrake rubbed his chin thoughtfully. Finally, he said, "Remarkable. Are you the only ones she can hear and speak to?"

"I believe so. Mom and Dad have not said anything about Brianna," Morgan said.

"That's good. That way she doesn't overhear any conversation that would lead her to suspect you are genies," Jindrake said. "Have you told your parents about this?"

By the boys' silence, Jindrake knew they hadn't.

"I do believe your parents ought to be told so that they can closely monitor the situation. If other Outsiders begin to hear you, then I recommend contacting the Jinn High Council immediately," Jindrake said. It sounded like a command.

"Tell us, sir, why can this girl hear us?" Blake asked.

Jindrake stroked his beard again, only this time more quickly than before.

"An answer to that question, unfortunately, I don't have. There's no record of such a thing ever happening. There may be a connection between the girl and the three of you. Perhaps this girl is highly sensitive to sound, and that's why she can hear you. In due time, you will learn what the reason is. It will reveal itself sooner or later."

"So to find out, we need to keep talking to her?" JD asked.

"No! You shouldn't be talking to this human child. It could be dangerous, since you not only risk becoming her genies, but you also risk discovery of the entire genie world."

"Sh-sh-she's only visiting. What's the problem with that?" Blake asked.

"A great deal! You'd each have to grant the Outsider three wishes, and she could own you for a long time. Three wishes from each of you mean nine wishes."

"Plus our parents," Morgan began, interrupting the genie master. "That is six more. She would get fifteen wishes altogether."

"Yes. That's true!" Jindrake said. "Even after a genie has completed providing the wishes, and the human owner forgets he ever was in possession of one of our kind, it creates a major inconvenience."

Jindrake pushed himself up from the table. The old hoops dangling from his long earlobes twisted back and forth. The three boys followed his lead and got up, too. JD and Blake bowed their heads and nodded politely to thank him. Jindrake bowed respectfully in return and escorted them to the door, where he bowed one more time.

Once they were outside again, JD led his brothers away from the bottle.

"So when do we tell Mom and Dad about Brianna?" Blake asked.

One of JD's eyebrows jutted up.

"Oh, peacock feathers. Are you serious? You want them to know? Then we'll never find out more about what's out there. No, we aren't going to tell Mom and Dad anything."

Both Morgan and Blake had looks of uncertainty that told JD they didn't think this was the best thing to do.

Chapter Four

The Amethyst Bottle

Cassidy was kneeling in the flower bed, troweling the hard dirt so she could add more plants to her garden. She was hidden behind the lavender flowers on a large azalea shrub when JD, Morgan, and Blake got back to the house.

Unlike most genie women, who preferred not to work with their hands, Cassidy enjoyed working in the garden, and her soil-stained work clothes were proof of that.

She straightened up, holding her hands upright as the gloves she was wearing flew off. She clapped them, knocking off the leftover dirt. When she saw the boys, she made a teal-blue handkerchief appear and wiped the sweat from her forehead.

"Where have you been?" she asked.

"We went to see Master Jindrake," Blake said.

"That was nice of you. I'm sure he enjoyed the company," Cassidy said. "By the way, it's time to feed Sherbet, Tango, and Tangerine. I want you to go in and take care of them while I finish up out here."

The gloves covered her hands once more, and she stepped back into the flower garden, where she started to plant the tray of mums.

Back inside, JD, Morgan, and Blake were surprised to find a trail of pillow stuffing. The tigers were savagely pulling apart fabric with their sharp teeth. Each triplet picked up a tiger.

"Just look at this mess. How could they?" Blake asked.

"They're tigers. What did you expect?" JD said firmly.

Morgan winked his right eye, and a large bottle, the kind used to feed baby animals, appeared in each cat's mouth. Sherbet, Tango, and Tangerine sucked on the nipples, filling their empty bellies.

The triplets raised their arms and wiggled their fingers. Right away thousands of fuzzy pieces shriveled up, and soon the mess disappeared.

Everything had quieted down, with the cubs sleeping and wheezing softly. The stillness didn't last. Down in the sunken retreat, they heard a familiar voice calling for them. They let the tigers sleep and stepped over to the window.

"Hello. Are you here? I finished helping Gramma."

JD was excited to see her again. On the other hand, after what Master Jindrake had said, Morgan and Blake were more apprehensive about talking to Brianna now. Morgan shook his head in a way to let JD and then Blake know to be quiet.

There Brianna stood, staring at the bookcases on the north wall. Her eyes slowly moved up the rows of books and across those on the middle shelf. The silence had reminded her of the last time she sat in the chair reading, when she suddenly heard the voices.

She walked to her grandfather's desk, where she pulled out the rolling chair. She bent down to look under it.

When Brianna finished looking there, she stood up and brushed off the lint and dust from her knees. Tapping her finger to her mouth, she looked again at all the wonderful books. Then suddenly an idea came to her.

"Why didn't I think of that before?" she said. "It was over here."

Brianna moved over to the other bookcase. Some of the letters on the spines of the older books had rubbed off. Others had laminated dust jackets on them to keep the books from getting dirty or damaged. Then she saw the book she wanted, the one with gold letters on it. *Chronicles of the Caretaker* was one she had read before. Maybe there was something—a clue perhaps—from the adventures of the main character, Jamie Collins. In the story, an ordinary man by most appearances, Jamie was in reality a *protector* of witches and warlocks, fairies and leprechauns, and other good creatures from the evil wizards of the north, south, east, and west.

She took the book down from the shelf and eagerly flipped to the table of contents. Dropping into the leather chair and leaning against one of its arms, she began reading. The book was as interesting to read now as it had been the first time, and, like before, she found it difficult to put down.

But as she leafed through the cream-colored pages, a picture in the fifth story, "The Blue Jinn," captured her attention. When she looked more closely, there it was—a very familiar-looking bottle. It was partially hidden behind a small clock in the illustration, and if the reader wasn't careful, the bottle could easily be overlooked.

"What do you know? Look at that!" she gasped.

Setting the book face up on the pillow next to her chair, Brianna turned, and from where she was sitting, she honed in on the amethyst bottle on the bookshelf. It made her mouth drop open.

"That book!" Morgan whispered. "She has discovered something in it."

JD agreed with him and nodded his head. He knew the danger they were in, and it was time to start worrying. Blake was the most nervous of the three, with beads of sweat running down his forehead and his ears twitching. He tried not to breathe loudly and inadvertently bit his tongue.

With a keen eye on Brianna, they watched as she walked gingerly toward the amethyst bottle. She hadn't looked closely at it before, but now she couldn't take her eyes off it. She reached past family photographs in their silver and oak frames, and she gently picked the bottle up. Carefully holding on to the rim, she closely inspected the detail, from the full-body base, with curves that looked like a cut-open rubber ball, to the gold and green tassel. A coin-like object on the cloth ribbon dangled loosely around the bottle's narrow neck.

"The picture of the bottle in the book and the bottle on the shelf are identical," Brianna said.

She stroked the glassy surface before she pulled the smooth topaz stone stopper out of the spout opening. The bottle began to smoke. JD, Morgan, and Blake knew they had no choice. They stood still as their surroundings blurred, and the purple smoke swallowed them. Within seconds the smoke moved up and, like a flame sucked upward through a chimney, spewed out of the bottle. They had been summoned!

Brianna's hands shook so hard that she dropped the purple bottle. The rosy tinge in her cheeks drained, and her face turned eggshell white. As if in slow motion, she watched the vapor flurry in front of her.

She took two paces backward, catching her foot on the area rug's edge, and fell to the floor. The stone stopper fell from her hand, bouncing twice before it hit the baseboard. During all this, the girl just sat there, frozen to the floor as she continued her hard stare at the vapors through her silver dollar–sized eyes.

The purplish haze began to separate into blackened outlines of three figures. They were like shapes moving in a thick early morning fog.

Brianna sprang to her feet and scrambled out of the room, never looking back once to find out what would be there once the vapor evaporated.

With their hands pressed together, JD, Morgan, and Blake bowed their heads and chanted, "Your wish is our command; now make it so."

When they looked up, they found themselves alone in the room they had seen countless times from inside their home.

"C-can this b-be r-real?" Blake trembled. Standing in between JD and Morgan, he clutched hold of his brothers' arms.

"Oh, peacock feathers! Let go, you coward," JD said. He took Blake's arm and threw it off as though it were part of yesterday's garbage. "Just take a good look around."

It was true! The three genie brothers were in the Outsiders' house. Never in their wildest dreams had they thought they would ever get here. The world outside the bottle had always seemed so full of wonder, but actually being here was awesome.

Morgan moved closer to the amethyst bottle. A strange feeling spread through him as he picked up the bottle and cradled it in his hands.

JD began walking around the room. He touched the desk, the lamp, and even the globe Brianna had used to show them where Europe was.

Then something caught his eye in the book she had been reading. He snapped his fingers, and the book floated upward to hover before him.

"Amazing," JD said. He motioned to Morgan and Blake and beckoned for them to move beside him. "Come and look at this!"

Both Morgan and Blake peered over their brother's shoulder. But from the looks on both of their faces, it was obvious they didn't see what had excited JD about the picture. JD even turned the book sideways so they could look at it from a different angle and see what he saw. He impatiently tapped on the illustration, and it took them only a few seconds to see it.

"It's our bottle!" Blake exclaimed. His eyes almost popped out of their sockets.

"Brianna is an intelligent girl. With this book and then seeing us vaporizing out of the bottle, she will come to the conclusion of what we are," Morgan said as he shook his head.

There wasn't any time to think about it. The back door slammed.

There was only one thing the boys could do, and that was to go back into the bottle.

"Wouldn't it be better if we just showed ourselves and got it over with?" Blake asked.

"I must agree with JD," Morgan said. "Since we have been summoned, there is nothing in the law that says that is what we have to do. As long as we grant her wishes, we will have followed the rules."

JD pushed the front of the book closed and tucked it under his arm. He had decided to take *Chronicles of the Caretaker* with them. Without the book, Brianna would still be missing clues and therefore be unable to put all the pieces together to learn who and what they were.

Their time was running out. A low hum of voices was getting louder; the Outsiders were getting close. As they hurried from the back patio and through the house, Blake nervously looked toward the door.

Morgan raised his arms, and the smoky mist again wrapped around their bodies, like a tornado tearing across an open prairie. Just as fast as they had vaporized out, the smoke absorbed the boys as it flowed back into the bottle.

And it was without a second to spare.

"Good thinking, Morgan. The Outsiders almost caught us," JD said, breathing a sigh of relief.

They quickly shifted to the sunken retreat and watched as Brianna's hand was squeezing Isabelle's, desperately pulling her grandmother into the room. Christian was right there behind them. Brianna thought that once she showed them the book and they inspected the bottle, both of them would believe what she had told them about the strange event was true. It had to be more than just a coincidence about the bottles. But as she leaned down for the book, she stopped cold in her tracks.

"What book?" Christian asked. He looked around the floor.

"*Chronicles of the Caretaker*. It was right here."

She lifted up the pillows and then tossed them away. She glanced quickly around the chair.

"Where'd it go? The book was on the pillow here. Honest," she said. She sank down in the chair and rested her head in her hands.

Isabelle was now feeling very sorry for her granddaughter. She sat down on the edge of the chair next to her, took hold of Brianna's hands, and pressed them close into hers.

"I think I know what happened," Isabelle said.

Brianna perked up. Isabelle believed she was telling the truth. A feeling of relief filled her whole body.

"Yes, dear," Isabelle said. She tenderly patted one of the girl's small hands. "You probably fell asleep and had a dream."

Asleep? Dreaming? Was she kidding?

Brianna swiftly pulled her hand back close to her. Her body tightened, and her smile was replaced by an angry glare. Brianna forcefully leapt up from the chair with her hands clenched into fists. Her lips hardened before she let her pent-up anger loose.

"*It was not a dream. It really happened!*" she screamed.

Christian and Isabelle were taken aback. They had never seen an outburst like this from their granddaughter before. They straightened up, their backs firm in place and still. Tension between the elder Carruthers and Brianna was thick as Brianna continued her tirade.

"I *did* see that purple smoke!" Brianna snapped. "There *is* something strange happening here, and it has to do with *that* bottle."

"This bottle? There's nothing in here. It's just made of colored glass," Christian said as he tried to remain calm and rational.

He snatched the amethyst bottle, not as gentle about picking it up as Brianna had been when she held it. His face in the glass looked back at him; it was like a fun-house mirror distorting the features of his face. He flicked his finger against it to show her there was nothing out of the ordinary about the attractive knickknack.

Inside the bottle, however, was another matter. JD, Morgan, and Blake lost their footing and fought to remain standing on the quaking floor. They knocked into each other before falling backward. Fortunately for them the cushions softened their falls.

Then without warning, the rocking and twisting stopped. Christian had returned the bottle to its place on the deep shelf. As he had predicted, Christian found nothing out of the ordinary with the bottle.

Brianna didn't say anything more. She turned her back on them and stormed out of the room. To show just how angry she was, Brianna slammed the door behind her.

Slumping down among the cushions, a relieved Blake wiped his forehead and said, "That was close."

"Wow! Is she mad," JD said, raising his eyebrows. "I feel sorry for her, but I'm glad I took this book."

"You'd better have a strategic hiding place for it, too, because if Mom and Dad find it, they will know we were out there," Morgan said.

JD had the perfect place for it. He went behind the marble fireplace and shoved it between two parchment rolls. It would be safer there.

The triplets moved out from behind the fireplace. Morgan and Blake sat down on the hearth, while JD remained standing.

"Things are getting out of hand," Blake said.

"Oh, peacock feathers!" JD said. "Stop your whining."

"I just think it's time to tell Mom and Dad everything," Blake told them.

"We may not have to. All they have to do is look up. Once they see the stopper is gone, they're going to ask questions. Then we'll have to tell them what happened," JD said.

"Not necessarily," Morgan said. "Not if they *think* the opening is still closed."

With a quick wink of Morgan's eye, the bottle opening was clouded in blackness, like a black curtain that blocked any outside light.

Morgan walked with Blake to the reflecting pool and sat down on the marble rim. JD went to the wrought iron railing near the steps to the sunken retreat. He folded his arms and leaned on the railing, gently pressing down on his bottom lip.

"You know, with the stopper out of the bottle, we can leave anytime we want," he said with a grin on his face. He rapidly jutted his eyebrows up and down.

"You are a little ahead of yourself, brother," Morgan said. "There are still a few minor details to take care of. We still have to grant the wishes Brianna makes."

"She has the wishes coming to her," JD said. "We just have to be more careful now that she's our master."

That they couldn't forget. Brianna could hold on to them as long as she wanted and until her last wish was granted. And when she did make a wish, they would have no choice but to grant it, even if Aristede and Cassidy were around.

"And they won't be happy knowing their kids are genies to an Outsider girl," Blake added.

"Then how are we going to keep that from happening?" JD asked.

"We will just have to be ready for it," Morgan said. "We need to spend as much time as possible near the big window when the outside world is visible."

All this talk about summoning and wish giving gave Blake a physical pain in his stomach. It was the same feeling someone would have just before he threw up.

Chapter Five

The Neighbors
on Euclid Avenue

JD, Morgan, and Blake tried to get a few extra winks after spending hours waiting to see Brianna again. By the time they made their way to the eating area the following morning, they found Aristede and Cassidy were already eating breadfruit pancakes, bacon, and pomaberry juice. JD poured some juice and passed the pitcher to Morgan. The pomaberry juice made its way to each triplet.

Aristede gobbled the strips of browned, crispy bacon in three bites, followed by gulps of juice, much to Cassidy's embarrassment.

"I have to be in the office early. Mr. Shalimar moved up our meeting," Aristede said in between bites. "I'm running late as it is. I had better be going."

He took a last sip of juice and then leaned over to kiss his wife. Cassidy watched as he then patted the boys on their heads. Aristede stood very still and barely had a chance to think about what was about to happen when, within seconds, he became purple smoke. Instantly, the smoke shot across the room and out the door.

Cassidy waved her hand, making the plates, bowls, and eating utensils fly to a cleaning basin. With another wave, the dishes sank into a sea of cleaning bubbles.

She then turned to her sons and asked, "What will you be doing today? I certainly hope it isn't sitting in the center chamber. With the exception of visiting Jindrake, you've spent just about every waking minute indoors. What have you been doing?"

Blake was fidgeting, and his cheeks changed from pink to red. Both he and JD looked to Morgan, who commenced giving their mother an explanation.

"We have been working on our academy assignment and practicing transmogrifications. It is harder than it sounds, and we find it is much better to practice in a relaxed environment!"

If only JD or Blake could have come up with a story as quickly as their brother.

"That's good to hear. I'm impressed with how you aren't waiting to be told to practice. Good for you." Cassidy smiled as any proud mother would when her children realized how important it was to practice their magic. "I still have more work to do outside."

She waved her hands down around her body, and her clothing changed into garden work clothes. As she strolled toward the door, she looked back one last time.

"I could always use the help if you want to take a break from your studies."

Then she left them alone in the eating area.

JD nudged Morgan with his elbow, and they both got up. Blake continued sipping his juice while JD tugged on his shirt collar, and they made their way to the sunken retreat, where they plunged down onto the cushions. They were hoping Brianna would come back, but after what had happened the day before when her grandparents didn't believe her, Morgan and Blake had some doubts that they'd even see her again. Only JD believed she'd be back. She was curious. They'd just have to keep watch for her.

"But if she should come back, we must not encourage her to ask us questions," Morgan said. "I still say we should wait until she makes her wishes."

"She hasn't made one yet," JD said. "We would have known if she had, just like when we were summoned."

Without warning and whether he realized it or not, a curious look swept across JD's face. "You know," JD began as an idea came to him, "we have to get her to use all of her wishes without ever knowing she had them."

"How do you propose we do *that*?" Morgan asked. An intense scowl covered his face.

"We trick her into making them. Then when she goes home, she won't ever know it was genie magic," JD said. "Think of the fun we can have."

He then flicked his dark eyebrows up and down several times.

Morgan sat erect and just stared as he thought about this for a minute or two. It was an interesting idea—brilliant, actually—and Brianna would never have to know she was their master.

Blake had been awfully quiet as the blood pulsed at a rapid rate through his veins. It felt like several woodpeckers were hammering at his skin. It took a lot for him to ask, "And what if she does figure it out? What will we do then?"

He reached up to rub his wiggling ear.

"We'll be careful enough; I know we will," JD said. His confidence was as high as his pumped-out chest.

When they finally saw Brianna a few days later, she was looking for her grandfather. Christian was sitting behind his polished desk, poring through some of the most recent issues of *Contemporary Model Railroad Maker*. He noted features in the diagrams in his spiral-bound notepad.

Brianna stood on her tiptoes behind him and looked over his shoulder at plans for the backyard.

"I want to put in a garden railroad. I'm making plans for the trains to go around the fishpond and the oak tree," he said. He used his finger to outline the path of the railroad track in his diagram.

As he kept on working on his drawings, Brianna moved to one wall of shelves. She pushed her fingers across the spines of books while

Christian stopped what he was sketching. He removed his old glasses and put the end of an arm tip in his mouth as he watched her.

"Are you still looking for that book? I could help you find it."

"No thanks, Granddad." Then she turned to him and asked, "Are we still going to Marine Gardens?"

"Absolutely. In fact, your gramma asked when we plan to go, too. So I thought we'd go—"

"Yes. Yes! Tell me. When?"

He flashed a grin. Brianna thought she even saw a twinkle in the corner of his eye, like he knew something that she didn't.

"Tomorrow," he announced. The smile on his face was almost as wide as Brianna's. "How does that sound?"

"Oh, Granddad. You silly goose. I can't believe you teased me like that."

She threw her arms around his shoulders, hugging him tightly and smothering him with kisses.

"Thank you, Granddad. Thank you, thank you, thank you."

"Are . . . you . . . trying to . . . strangle . . . me?" Christian asked. He worked to lessen her grip by pulling at Brianna's arms.

Suddenly they heard a "Hump hum," from behind them. "Are you trying to kill him off, Bree?"

Brianna released her hands, and she turned quickly to face her grandmother, who was standing in the doorway. Standing next to Isabelle was a short, plump woman. With the two ladies was a young girl who Brianna concluded was the other woman's daughter, since they both had russet-red hair.

"Oh, no, Gramma," she began. "I was hugging Granddad. I wasn't trying to hurt him."

"You could have fooled me," Christian said as he rubbed his neck playfully. In a croaky whisper he added, "I'll never be the same."

"Granddad said we're going to Marine Gardens tomorrow. I'm so excited."

"Save some of that energy for the trip," Isabelle said. She then put her arm around the woman's shoulders. "Brianna, this is our neighbor, Lisa Bratt."

The lady brashly extended her hand to shake Brianna's.

"Hi. Glad to meet you," Lisa said. Her handshake was so brutal that the shaking hurt Brianna's arm.

"Very nice to meet you," Brianna said shyly.

Christian closed his notepad and straightened the magazines into a single neat pile. Before he left to go to his workshop to work on the trains, he said, "I'll leave you alone for a while. Are you still going with us to Marine Gardens, Lisa?"

With a big, toothy grin, Lisa replied, "Wouldn't miss it for the world, Chris." Along with Isabelle, she was one of the few people to call him Chris.

Lisa Bratt was much younger than Isabelle, but she was still older than other mothers with ten-year-old children. Her pulled-back hair, a dull auburn with streaks of orange, gave her a frazzled look, even when she wasn't. Lisa wore baggy clothes with the sleeves rolled up, but that didn't hide the extra pounds she carried.

"Ever since your grandmother found out you were coming to visit, she's been talking about nothing else," Lisa said. "I feel like I already know you. This is my daughter, Devyn."

"Hello," Brianna said softly.

"Hi," Devyn said. Her squeaky high voice made her just as outgoing as her mother.

Devyn was a head shorter than Brianna. She wore jeans, a T-shirt, and black-and-white sneakers. Her curly hair was pushed under a blue-and-white baseball cap, which made her look like a boy.

Isabelle wanted to show Lisa the new scrapbook she had recently finished about the Carrutherses' trip to Japan. She took Lisa by the arm, and the two women left Brianna and Devyn. Isabelle and Lisa chatted about Isabelle's scrapbooks and about how wonderful they were as they walked out the door. This gave the girls some alone time so they could get acquainted with each other.

Before Brianna could say anything, Devyn started asking many questions.

"So you're here for the summer, huh?"

"Not the whole summer, just three weeks," Brianna corrected her.

"Do you have any brothers or sisters?"

Brianna shook her head.

"Me neither. My parents said after I was born they didn't need to have more kids," Devyn said.

Brianna forced herself not to giggle at what Devyn had shared. It was one of those bits of information that should have remained private.

"I do have five cousins. Their names are Tanner, Eddie, Brayden, Makenzie, and Ava," Brianna said. "They're all younger than me—"

"Do you like video games? I do. I have a Y-Box, and my dad and I play it all the time. Sometimes we go to the arcades at Golf and Fun. Have you heard of it? It's not far from here."

"Uh-huh. My granddad took—" Brianna began, but Devyn's chitchat about how good she was at playing video games cut Brianna off a second time.

Devyn quickly changed the topic of conversation to school. She would be in the fifth grade in the fall.

"What about you? What grade are you in? I don't like school too much. They give us way too much boring homework. The kids at Hawthorne Drive—that's the name of my school—are okay. My best friends are Annie Gordon and Lizzie Masters. Our teacher, Mrs. Tomkins, called us the three amigos. That's Spanish for three friends. I hope that we're all in the same class this year. I asked our principal if she could arrange that for us, but Mrs. Reiter said she couldn't guarantee anything."

Brianna realized that she wouldn't be able to get a word in, so she just looked at Devyn and listened to her amusing babble. Devyn talked so fast that it made Brianna's head pound. The smile pasted on Brianna's face, along with an occasional nod, gave the impression she was listening while waiting for her chance to say something. Devyn didn't know the difference.

Eventually, when Devyn stopped to take a breath, Brianna got the chance to ask, "What do you want to do? You said you like arcade games. I brought my Game Kid. Want to see it?"

"Sure."

"Wait here. I'll be right back."

Devyn sat in the leather chair. She barely had time to get comfortable before Brianna returned. She handed the video game to Devyn, but the girl never even opened the game box and just started talking nonstop again.

Brianna rolled her eyes and even chewed on her bottom lip to keep from saying anything. But she released her bite right away when she heard an echoing voice say, "Hey, look. She has a new friend."

Brianna braced herself for the voices again. She began pacing around Devyn, who rotated around and watched Brianna look at everything but her.

Finally Brianna turned to Devyn and asked, "Did you hear that?"

"Hear what? I don't hear anything," Devyn said.

"Shh—just listen!" Brianna commanded, still scanning the room.

"Of all the people in your world, Brianna, why are you the only person who can hear us? It is completely unheard of, you know." It was the proper-sounding voice again.

Brianna shrugged her shoulders.

"What's going on?" Devyn inquired curiously.

Before Brianna had a chance to say anything else, the curly-haired girl just continued talking about school and the many times last year when Mr. and Mrs. Bratt were called to the principal's office to talk about how much trouble their daughter was in. There had been one time when she brought water balloons to school. During class, other children had jostled Devyn's backpack, and the water balloons broke, creating a puddle of water. Mrs. Tomkins had seen the mess under the desk, and the only thing Devyn had to say in her defense was, "All right. Who broke my water balloons? We needed those at recess."

"Oh, peacock feathers! That girl talks a lot."

"I shall take care of that," Morgan declared.

And then in an instant, all sound stopped coming out of Devyn's mouth. Brianna cocked her head, straining to hear. She was making sure she wasn't just imagining what was going on.

Devyn was still talking and completely unaware that Brianna couldn't hear her. Her lips were moving as they had for the last several minutes, but no sounds were coming out of her mouth.

JD thought it was much better this way instead of listening to Devyn's constant babbling. Brianna, however, didn't.

"To be sure that is better, is it not?" Morgan asked.

"No, not really," Brianna said. "I wish Devyn's voice would return to normal."

Inside the bottle, the genie brothers anxiously pushed against each other. There it was, as plain as day: Brianna's first wish!

Morgan took the lead and pressed his hands together. JD and Blake bowed and together, they said, "Your wish is my command; now make it so."

In midsentence, Devyn's voice returned and rambled about a dreamy-looking boy named Toby. She liked him a lot, but he was going steady with Jill, an annoying and snobbish know-it-all girl in Mr. Marino's sixth-grade class. Toby and Jill played tetherball at every recess.

Brianna blurted, "How'd you do that?"

"I didn't do anything," Devyn said. "What are you talking about?"

"Not you! Them!"

"Who?" Devyn asked, looking quite perplexed. "No one else is here."

"The boys!"

Devyn stared at her as though she had snails crawling out of her ears.

"I didn't hear anything."

Devyn went on about how only a crazy person would hear voices of people who weren't there. One of the voices Brianna heard tried to reassure her that crazy she was not.

Brianna didn't say anything. She only tweaked her mouth and said, "Let's go look at the fish in the pond."

She rested her hands on Devyn's shoulders and steered her toward the door. With a look backward as they crossed the room, Brianna said in a low voice so Devyn couldn't hear, "I'll be back."

And they left.

JD stood and stared, even when the view into the Outsiders' family room changed. The view now was the large tree on the knoll to the right and the distant skyline of Jinwiddie to the left. He had a strange glint to his eyes that prompted an "Uh-oh!" from Blake, who was suspicious of whatever wild idea was fermenting in JD's brain.

"Just listen to me, and don't say a word," JD said.

When JD spent the next several minutes telling them his idea, Blake moaned.

"I can't believe what you're saying." His ear was twitching rapidly.

"This is absolutely the craziest idea you have ever had," Morgan said. "You are kidding, right?"

"No, I'm not kidding. I think one of us *should* go," JD replied.

"L-l-leave the bottle! G-g-go out there! F-f-follow her?" Blake stammered. He made jabbing motions at the window.

"How else can we get her to make the wishes?" JD asked. "If things happen in other places and not just in that room, she won't connect them to the bottle."

Although it would be risky for JD, as he would be in alien territory, Morgan had to admit that their brother's thinking was sound. Blake did agree it was all very necessary. He was even happier since JD had offered to be the one to go to the outside world.

But leaving the bottle would be the easy part. They still had to make sure no one would find out what was going on. But how?

"We've begun our transmogrification lessons, haven't we?" JD said confidently. "I change into something and hide in Brianna's pocket. When she's not looking, I change back and follow her. I just wait to hear any wish she might make. It's a perfect plan, don't you think?"

"I guess, but there's a difference between changing a banana into a slipper and changing a person into something," Blake said.

"And what sort of plan have you formulated to keep Mom and Dad from figuring out that you are not here?" Morgan asked.

"I hadn't thought that far ahead," JD said. "Any ideas how you can cover for me?"

Morgan started pacing, gnawing at his fingertips and talking to himself. He moved quickly, not minding where he was going. He almost knocked JD and Blake over when he suddenly stopped. But he didn't care.

Finally he snapped his fingers and said, "We need a plan, and I think I have got it."

"Got what?" Blake asked innocently.

"Ostrich fever. What do you think?" JD said. He rolled his eyes before turning to Morgan and asking, "What's your idea?"

"Not here," he replied.

Before JD or Blake could ask any questions, Morgan ran up the short stair steps next to the fireplace and down the bedchamber hallway. JD and Blake followed him. Outside their bedchamber Morgan turned the doorknob, opened the door, and hustled into the room.

Once they were inside, JD and Blake made themselves comfortable on their respective beds. For the next ten minutes they listened as Morgan explained how they could implement his idea.

When Morgan was finished, JD said, "It just might work."

Chapter Six

Oh, I Wish!

It was a smogless summer morning in Southern California with a few white billowing clouds. A pastel strip of light fell across Brianna's bedspread as the sun crept over the eastern horizon. She was too excited to sleep, and by dawn, she was dressed and ready to spend a fun day looking at all sorts of sea life.

For breakfast, Brianna nibbled on rye toast covered with her favorite grape jam. She had just taken a few bites when the doorbell rang. It was the Bratt family, ready for the drive to the coast, which was nearly an hour from where they lived.

Marine Gardens overlooked the Pacific Ocean, where breezes swept inland, cooling the otherwise hot region. The aquatic park was soon crowded with parents and their children, who were all on vacation from school.

Lisa Bratt was dressed in a pea-green T-shirt and white shorts. She also wore a large-brimmed straw hat to protect herself from the sun.

The extra-large sunglasses on her face made her look like a giant bug standing upright on its hind legs.

Brian Bratt, Lisa's six-foot-tall, lanky husband, brought his digital video camera. He directed community programs for cable television, so he would be very skilled at capturing clips of their day.

"Just look at those girls. They sure are enjoying themselves, aren't they?" Brian said.

Their first stop was at the Sea Animal Encounter tank. Several younger children had rolled up their sleeves and were touching crabs, sea urchins, and starfish. Small, colorful fish scurried in and out among the rocks. Lying at the bottom of the pool were coins that had been thrown into the water.

"C'mon, Brianna. Toss in a quarter," Devyn said.

"I don't have any money. See?"

Brianna started digging through her shorts just to prove to Devyn nothing was there. When she turned the pockets out, a coin dropped to the ground.

Devyn gave Brianna a sneery kind of look and said, "I thought you said you didn't have any money!"

Brianna didn't know where the coin had come from and was just as surprised as Devyn to find it. She crouched down and picked up the round, flat metal object, turning the odd coin over and examining both sides of it. It looked like it was a coin from another country.

"Go on," Devyn said.

Brianna smiled before flipping the coin with her forefinger. It hit the water and sank down in the shallow tank.

"I'll save my wish for some other time," she said.

After Brianna and Devyn explored the tide pools, they followed the map on the brochure to the dolphin tank. Christian went to a vendor selling packs of dried fish so the girls could feed the bottlenose dolphins. They wasted no time finding spots along the edge of the tank. The frisky animals swam up to them right away, knowing that anyone there would have tasty treats for them.

"You can pet them," one of the attendants said. "That one—Splash—was stranded on a beach a few miles up the coast, and we treated him in the Rescue and Care Center."

The dolphins popped their heads up and made clicking noises as they bobbed up and down in the water. Brianna raised her arms and waved at the dolphins. It wasn't like waving to a friend from across the way. She extended her arm out toward the dolphins and in an exaggerated way, moved her hand up and down. As the girls rubbed the dolphins' noses, they enjoyed the marvelous creatures' lighthearted character. Neither Brianna nor Devyn noticed that a boy had found a clear space next to them until he asked, "May I touch them, too?"

Under a baseball cap similar to the one Devyn wore was a boy with sandy-blond hair and dark eyes.

"Sure. They're very friendly," Brianna said.

Although the boy was reluctant at first, he slowly approached the tank. True to his name, Splash slapped his tail on the water. The boy jumped back, but the smile on his face showed that he didn't mind. Splash came to the edge, close enough for anyone to pet him.

The children continued feeding the dolphins. That was until Lisa, who looked at her wristwatch, announced they had to take in a few other exhibits before lunch.

"Maybe we'll see you later," Brianna told the boy. She and Devyn moved away from the edge of the tank.

"You probably will," he said.

Brianna was starting up the concrete steps when she stopped cold in her tracks. As she turned, a puzzled frown spread across her face. There was something familiar about this boy. Goose bumps appeared on her arms. Without thinking about it, she rubbed her hands up and down her bare arms, making the pimples melt back into her skin.

"Do I know you?" she asked.

She leaned in forward to get a closer look at him, as it was hard to see his face under the baseball cap. But before he could give her an answer, Devyn came back, grabbed Brianna's arm, and off they went.

The placard at the manatee exhibit told park visitors that the gentle animals were lovingly called sea cows and gave information about the efforts to protect the endangered species from extinction. The manatees moved slowly, swimming to the warmer water to revel in the sunlight.

True to Lisa's schedule to get to see as much as they could before lunch, they quickly went through the shark and sea turtle exhibits.

The Carruthers and Bratt families had time to catch one more show before lunch, and they hurried to the Sea Lion Arena. The three sea lions tooted out silly songs on a set of horns. As their performance ended, Brian laughed the loudest when one of the sea lions, named

Maurice, belched into the microphone before scampering after his costars.

"Let's give a round of applause to Lola, Loomis, and Maurice, and their trainer, Denise," the announcer said.

"That is just what we needed to hear right before eating," Lisa said. The smirk on her face matched well with her rolling eyes.

When they got to the Island Grille Restaurant, a delicious aroma of smoked ribs greeted them as they walked through the door. Brian griped about the prices the park charged. But he stopped complaining about how it was all one gigantic rip-off when Christian said that he was paying for the hamburgers, sandwiches, and soft drinks.

After lunch, they went to the lower observation level of the main tank. It was nippy and dank, with a bit of glimmering light coming down through the blue water from above. Through the viewing window, orca fans watched in awe as two adult whales and their calf swam by.

Looking at the show schedule in her brochure, Lisa said, "The Orca Show begins at two o'clock. We'd better go up to the Aquatic Coliseum so we can get decent seats."

They had just started up the steps when someone said, "They're so big, aren't they?"

Brianna and Devyn saw it was the same blond-haired boy they had met earlier when they were giggling at the playful dolphins.

"Oh, it's you," Devyn said. The scowl on her face showed how much she didn't care for this intruder.

He smiled and dismissed Devyn's rudeness. He just told them, "I said you'd see me again."

"We're going to watch the Orca Show. Want to come with us?" Brianna asked.

"Sure."

There wasn't much time to find good seats to see the show. It suddenly occurred to Brianna that there was something about their new friend that she had to ask.

"Where are your parents?"

The boy was caught off guard by the question, almost embarrassed really.

"They're not here. I-I came with friends."

"They won't mind your coming with us?"

"No, not really. They're over there," he said. He arched his neck and pointed over her shoulder.

The children made their way past what seemed to be scores of people to the top level. The blue sky paled in comparison to the water, an azure shade of blue. They sprinted to the rim of the large tank. Blasts of air shot out of the larger whale's blowhole as it skimmed and plunged through the water. Everyone howled.

"We had better find places where we can all sit together," Isabelle said.

"That's fine," Lisa said. "But look at the warning on the sign."

The sign caused some concern. It read:

THE VERY WET SPLASH ZONE
People Who Sit in the First Thirteen Rows WILL Get Wet!

"Perhaps we should sit up higher in the stands," Christian said.

"Oh, Granddad! It'll be fun to sit close. How wet can we get anyway?" Brianna asked.

"Let's see—*soaked!*" Brian said.

Just the thought of mature killer whales splashing them was as exciting as plunging down the vertical waterfalls and into a cavern on the Wild Tsunami Rapids ride on the other side of the park.

"I don't think I want a whale to splash water on us either," Isabelle said.

"You girls can sit there. We'll go up many more rows and away from any splashing," Brian said as he started up the steps.

"Oh, Brian, it'll be fun. Don't be a wimp," Lisa said mockingly.

"I know we probably shouldn't," Christian said, looking at the girls. "It goes against my better judgment, but I want to sit here in the front row."

Isabelle and Brian gasped. Had Christian lost his mind? He was brave-hearted now, but how would he be at the end of the show?

"Chris, I swear, if we get one drop—*one drop*—of orca splash on us, I won't speak to you for a week," Isabelle said.

They all knew she meant it, too.

"Promise?" Christian replied. Then he looked to Brianna and Devyn, giving them a wide grin.

"Oh, you!" Isabelle said. She slapped him across the back of his shoulder.

Brian backed down the steps and sat on the stadium bench. He securely stowed everything in the watertight camera bag so that the expensive equipment would be safe and dry. He then folded his arms, stared skyward, and shook his head.

"I just know we're going to get sopping wet," he said to himself.

"I hope they sell towels here," Isabelle mumbled as she sat down next to Lisa. "I think we're going to need them."

Lisa chuckled, which sounded more like a series of hiccups than actual laughing. If they hadn't known better, the others would have thought that perhaps she couldn't wait to be splashed.

Brianna and Devyn squeezed between Isabelle and Lisa on one side and Christian and Brian on the other. Their blond friend sat behind them.

Soon the several-hundred-seat Aquatic Coliseum filled with people. It was a full house, with several hundred people squeezed tightly on the bleachers. The show was about to begin.

The announcer introduced the two orcas, telling everyone that killer whales were the largest members of the dolphin family and that they rarely ever attacked humans.

A man was standing off to the side with a bucket. He was the trainer, and as he tossed dead fish, he gave more information about the large creatures: how much fish they ate per day, how long they were, how much they weighed, and how long they had resided at Marine Gardens. He described their training routine as well.

The Orca under the Ocean Show included whales, exotic birds, and human performers. Handlers first released birds that circled above the pool. Aerialists then dove gracefully off a twenty-five-foot platform and into the tank. Their multicolored swimsuits matched the red, orange, and green colors of the parrots' feathers. A musical score and special effects enhanced the storytelling about the young swimmers making friends with the killer whales. A large projection screen showed close-up shots of squealing kids.

Next, the orcas rolled over and waved to people with their flippers as they propelled themselves through the water. The trainer put a whistle in his mouth, and when he blew into it, both whales performed on cue, slapping their tails on the water surface and splashing the crowd.

A black-haired teenage girl on the other side of the stadium was selected to be a participant in the show. She seemed nervous as she climbed up the ladder attached to the rim of the tank. The trainer blew the whistle again, and the larger of the two killer whales jumped straight up above the water's surface. A park photographer took a picture of one orca kissing her on the cheek so she would have a souvenir to take with her. The girl yelped and pulled away quickly, wiping her cheek on her white T-shirt before she returned to sit with her parents.

Devyn tilted her head toward Brianna and said softly, "I wish they had chosen me."

An attendant ran up the steps, calling for another eager volunteer to come onstage. Both Brianna and Devyn waved their arms in hopes of being selected. They were disappointed when Brianna's new friend was chosen instead.

"What is your name, young man?" the trainer asked.

"It's JD," he said into the microphone.

"Are you enjoying your visit today, JD?"

"Yes! It's my first time here, and I'm excited to see everything."

Another attendant took JD by the hand and guided him onto the tank deck.

The adult whales slid out of the water, curling their tail flukes. JD got the rare opportunity to rub the two orcas between the eyes and down the noses. The attendant stooped down and whispered something in the boy's ear and made him smile. A low hum began through the audience as they imagined what she had said to him. JD pulled back when one whale opened its mouth, and he slowly reached in, but he pulled his hand out quickly. When he looked up at the attendant, she nodded. This time, JD reached in to pat the orca's tongue. When he was finished, he got to give each of the killer whales a fish, and then he eagerly made his way back to his seat, skipping every other step as he scaled the bleacher stairs.

"Oh, that was gross," Devyn said. Her expression made her look like a shriveled-up prune.

No matter what Devyn had thought about JD's adventure, Brianna was impressed with his courage to put his hand into the large animal's mouth. She turned around and said, "That must have been so cool!"

He smiled back at her.

Another voice came on the public address system, speaking about the finale. He warned everyone that the large animals would leap up from the water and then come down with a lot of force. He added that anyone who made the unfortunate choice of sitting in rows one through thirteen would be soaked by the splashing.

"Uh-oh! I don't like the sound of that!" Christian said with a sigh.

"Relax, everybody. Both whales are swimming way over there," Lisa said as she directed everyone with her eyes.

Lisa spoke too soon. The orcas were careening through the water. The trainer blew into his whistle again and, for dramatic interest, gave a fast hand command, first pointing one arm down and then quickly extending his arm straight up. The killer whales dove downward into the tank.

"Here they come!" Devyn cried out.

Brianna started to have a queasy feeling creep throughout her body. After a few long seconds, she came to the realization that getting wet was the last thing she wanted to happen to her. She closed her eyes tightly and pulled her head down in between her shoulders.

"I wish I wasn't sitting here."

What happened next happened quickly. The two whales leapt up, leaned to one side, and slammed onto the water's surface. Mounds of water splashed the unlucky audience in The Very Wet Splash Zone. Laughter broke out among the shrieks of those who were soaked to the bone.

At least one spectator was not amused.

Brian Bratt let out a piercing screech as he jumped up from his seat.

"Look at us. Even my underwear's soaked through!" Brian cried.

He took off his black horn-rimmed glasses and wiped the water off the lenses. *They could have gotten this wet over on the Wild Tsunami Rapids ride*, he thought. That was one ride they didn't need to go on now.

Isabelle, Lisa, Devyn, and Christian sat there, waterlogged from head to shoes, like half-drowned rats, stunned and motionless. Everyone that is, except for Brianna, who found herself sitting several rows behind her family and dry as the desert sand. It was as if she had never been sitting between Devyn and Christian. Brianna blinked a few times to make sure what she was seeing was real.

Christian called up to her, "Bree. You were smart to sit where you did. See how much water splashed on us."

He laughed as the water dripped from his flattened hair down his face.

Why did Granddad say that? I was sitting with them, and he made it sound like I was up here the whole time. How did this happen?

Soon hundreds of satisfied spectators emptied the Aquatic Coliseum at the conclusion of the show. Brianna went looking for JD. She had an eerie feeling that he had something to do with the change in seating she had just experienced. She quickly moved down the bleacher steps, but JD was nowhere to be found. It was as if he had vanished into thin air!

The Carruthers and Bratt families waddled down the stairs with their arms arched out. Brian stopped near the bottom step, reached behind him, and tugged at the backside of his shorts so that he could pull his wet underwear out of his butt cheeks.

The Summer Nights Parade began when the sun went down, and it featured park employees dressed in character costumes. There were all sorts of sea character mascots who were singing, dancing, and waving flashlights with colored lights shining. Smaller children delightedly screamed when the characters came over and hugged them. It was a fantastic way to end the day, and everyone laughed about getting drenched. Even Brian Bratt was amused.

It was late when they got back to Ontario. As Brianna changed into her pajamas, she threw her clothes onto the floor of the guest bathroom. She brushed her teeth and then slipped into bed.

But as she lay there, she was having trouble getting to sleep. Suddenly she shot straight up and covered her oval-shaped mouth with both hands. What if it was magic that had moved her from her family and kept her from getting wet? Just like the magic in *Chronicles of the Caretaker*.

She had to find answers. The next chance she got, she would do research on Granddad's computer. She would do an Internet search and see what came up.

If she had been a little more observant, she would have seen clues right under her nose.

When her shorts hit the floor in the bathroom, a coin fell out and rolled to the wall. It was the same coin she had tossed into the wishing pool at Marine Gardens. After JD had disappeared, another coin magically slipped back into the depths of Brianna's pocket. It lay on the bathroom floor for a short time before transforming into a purple vapor. The mist hung low along the floor, moving swiftly from the bathroom through Brianna's bedroom. It continued its path down the corridor, and under the first door on the right into the family room. The vapor moved quietly, slowly, and deliberately into the amethyst bottle.

Chapter Seven

The Fourth Genie Brother

Morgan had trouble sleeping, finally slipping out from under his bedcovers and pulling on a robe. A soft blanket of silver from the moon served as his night-light, and he could see that JD's bed was still empty. Eagerly waiting for JD to return, Morgan decided to watch one of Blake's orbulars to pass the time.

First, it was camel racing through the ages. There had been many memorable Jinn Cup Derby races over the years. It was scandalous that Brown Emperor had eaten oats soaked in rum the year before last. The rum, banned food for racing camels, gave added strength to the camels' wings.

Five years earlier, a three-way tie had been broken with a runoff race. After the judges had spent several hours reviewing racing orbulars, they were unable to declare the final winner. The second race had ended when Starry Eyes barely beat Bellowing Mama to secure the coveted crown.

When Morgan got bored with that orbular, he got another one, which contained the first dricketts match of last season. Dricketts was another popular sport in the genie world. This game was played on flying carpets, with nine players on each team hovering over a shallow rectangular pool. They would throw a melon-sized ball across the line of scrimmage, attempting to oust players by knocking them into the water. This would go on until only one team had a player left in the game. The team that won three games in a row won the match.

While Morgan stayed awake all night, Blake, on the other hand, had been asleep for hours. Exhausted from a hectic day, Blake had dropped into his warm bed and had fallen fast asleep right away.

Morgan tiptoed to Blake and began rapidly waving his fingers up and down, levitating him off his bed to the middle of their bedchamber. With a quick wink of Morgan's eye, Blake fell to the hard floor.

"Wake up," Morgan said harshly.

Blake made a quick movement and let out a drawling yawn.

"What is it?"

"He should have been back by now," Morgan said impatiently. "We need to see if everything is okay."

Morgan looked as though he were about to take a step. Instead, he grabbed hold of Blake's arms, and they both turned into purple smoke. Like fog in a marsh, the vaporized duo flowed silently down the hallway, past the reflecting pool, and slowly down to the sunken retreat. The position of the crescent moon in the clear night sky showed it was already well past midnight.

Two days earlier JD had come up with the idea to leave the bottle and follow Brianna to Marine Gardens. The dilemma the triplets had faced had to do with explaining JD's absence.

At first Morgan had thought he and Blake could cover for their brother by telling their parents JD had come down with a severe case of ostrich fever, not a serious disease, but contagious nonetheless. That way JD would be confined to his bed. Then either Morgan or Blake would vaporize under JD's bedsheets before Aristede or Cassidy entered the bedchamber to check up on him.

The boys had nixed their idea quickly. It reminded them of the time when they had tricked Aristede and Cassidy by pretending to be one another.

67

"No. That won't work. They're too smart to fall for anything that simple," JD said. "We have way too much to think about, like changing our clothes and hair."

"We'd better come up with something if you want to sneak along with Brianna's family to that Marine Gardens place," Blake said as he sat on the bed's edge with his legs crossed under him.

Morgan had leaned against one bedpost, tapping his finger across his closed mouth.

"We must have a JD here for this to work."

"I know. I know," JD said. "I need to be in two different places at one time."

"Too bad you just can't divide into two people," Blake said.

Morgan straightened up, threw his legs over the side of his bed, and looked over at Blake, who hadn't any idea how important what he had said was.

"To be sure" Morgan said. "A doppelganger for JD would eliminate any suspicions about a missing brother."

"There you go again, using words nobody understands," JD said as he rolled his eyes.

"You do not get it. A doppelganger is a duplicate . . . double . . . a dead ringer for yourself," Morgan explained.

"He already has that," Blake said. *"Us!"*

"As it happens now, when JD leaves, there will be only two, not three, brothers in the house," Morgan said. "If you want to go, we need to make a copy of you."

Morgan jumped to his feet and paced, deep in thought. "But how do we do it?" he mumbled.

Their transmogrification skill was really not great enough to do what Morgan had suggested. Taking an ordinary object and changing it into a living, breathing genie would require tremendous magic. At least JD and Blake had been willing to try just about anything.

Morgan had picked up JD's stuffed toy griffin, saying it would be better to start with a three-dimensional object if they were going to make a three-dimensional being successfully.

JD had volunteered to try first, since it had to be his look-alike. He had squinted and stared intently at the stuffed animal. There was a short crackle and one loud *pop!* Now, facing them all was a four-foot, yellow-haired, fuzzy griffin. Instead of plastic eyes and a sewn threaded mouth, the griffin's face had looked just like JD's.

Next, Blake had decided to take a set of JD's clothes to create a copy of his brother. He had laid them out on the floor and waved his hands over them. The articles of clothing had inflated, rose up in the air, hovered, and began to swell. It had looked like an invisible person sleeping. Then, without warning, the satiny pants, slippers, and white shirt with red vest had zipped around, making crude bodily noises. It had sounded like helium-filled balloons ripping open.

When these efforts had proved to be unsuccessful, Morgan had wondered whether they needed something living to create JD's twin. Blake had eagerly offered to get Sherbet, Tango, or Tangerine, but JD was horror-struck. Imagine seeing a giant tiger, with stripes, a tail, and blond hair standing upright. A frightful thought, indeed!

JD had plopped on his bed, feeling dejected when it looked as if there was no way to cover his absence, and the opportunity to leave the bottle had quickly slipped away from him.

"It's no use. Unless we think of something fast, I'm not going anywhere," he said.

Morgan had been pacing around the bedchamber, nibbling at a fingernail, when he stopped and looked into the full-length mirror across from JD's bed. Without a second thought, he had moved in closer and stared at his reflection in the tall mirror inside a wide, freestanding frame.

"JD. Blake. Come here, and stand next to me," Morgan called. "I have an idea. It just might be the way to do it."

Morgan had stepped to one side so JD could be in the middle, and all three stood as the reflections looked out at them.

"Perhaps if we concentrate and focus, we can combine our powers to create a duplicate," Morgan had whispered.

JD and Blake both gave him a two thumbs-up to show Morgan they had decided to do as he, Morgan, had asked. They knew it was most likely their last hope.

JD had brought his arm down to his side, and he felt his brothers' hands take hold of his. It had started slowly and grew with such force that they began to tremble. It had felt as though an electric current was moving through their bodies. An orangish glow had surrounded JD, Morgan, and Blake, as well as their duplicates in the mirror.

"We need one of you to come out and join us," Morgan had said.

JD's reflection had smiled at them as if he were a close friend. He had winked once and made his way toward them. The boys had withdrawn from the mirror as the reflection stepped out of the wooden frame!

None of them had said a word to the guest. JD had stepped in front of his pasty-faced look-alike and examined him from head to toe. The two were basically the same: the short straw-colored hair, the dimpled smile on the left cheek. It was like having a third brother. As Duplicate JD stared back, his dark-colored, glassy eyes had a faraway look in them.

"This is *so* weird," Blake said.

Although there had been no question that this duplicate was JD's copy, they were still different people. Yet this doppelganger had been missing one thing that JD had, and it would create a potential problem for them. The duplicate JD had lacked the power of speech, and this baffled the triplets. Morgan had concluded that since Duplicate JD was a reflection, he wasn't real.

Yes, it had been a remarkable feat for the three genies to pull off.

"How did we ever do it?" Morgan said as he yawned. There were only a few dim flames flickering in the urns, providing barely enough light to see.

Morgan and Blake spent nearly an hour in front of the window. Blake now fought to stay awake. His shoulders sagged, and his eyelids began to droop.

Morgan crouched with his knees pulled to his chest as he looked into the outside world.

"What a day we had with that doppelganger, too," Morgan said softly to himself.

In between Blake's high-pitched snores, Morgan began thinking about all that had happened to them while JD was away.

Aristede had flown off to work at the usual time that morning. Cassidy had gotten up from the low table to clean away the dishes. She had asked JD to feed Sherbet, Tango, and Tangerine.

Duplicate JD had placed saucers of milk in front of the cubs. They had grown a little each week since Jindrake gifted them with the little creatures. Sherbet and Tangerine had lapped from the dish immediately, but Tango had been more interested in Duplicate JD than in filling his empty belly. His black nose had sniffed around the boy's feet, and he knew right away that it wasn't JD standing there. As Duplicate JD had begun reaching out toward him, the startled cub scampered out between the impostor's legs and promptly disappeared.

Sherbet and Tangerine, on the other hand, had whimpered and followed their brother, even to the point of disappearing as well. Morgan and Blake had swiftly scooped up the nearly invisible cubs, and after some tender petting, the tigers had reappeared in their arms. Before their mother had asked any questions, both boys had grabbed hold of Duplicate JD and scuttled outside so the tigers could play in the cool, shallow pool nearby.

Like scolding a small child, Blake had given firm verbal warnings to JD's all-smiling duplicate. Nevertheless, the admonishments had made no difference. It soon became apparent that another problem had emerged, one that Morgan and Blake hadn't anticipated: the *unexpected magic*.

The game of JinJi wasn't a particularly ruthless activity. Duplicate JD had sat with Morgan and Blake on the floor in the sunken retreat. The colored playing pieces vaporized from one square on the game board as Morgan and Blake commanded. Duplicate JD had eagerly taken to the game, and when it was his turn, he pointed, and his piece silently advanced. When he had tried to cheat by adding a few extra spaces, Blake objected. Duplicate JD had turned his back on him, but not before some of the pieces grew a hundred times their usual sizes.

At that point, Duplicate JD had narrowed his eyes and glared at Morgan and Blake. With a firm look, he had sent the two shocked boys flying. Morgan and Blake had slammed roughly against the playing pieces and, like flies trapped on sticky flypaper, they were unable to move.

The upheaval that followed had been heard in the farthest end of the bottle house. Cassidy had stormed down the hallway, only to find the two boys struggling to free themselves from the bindings. Their squirming had been exhausting, and when Cassidy waved her hands, Morgan and Blake slumped to the floor.

"Tell me," she said, still panting from running through the house, "what on earth is going on in here?"

"We were playing JinJi. And—" Blake stopped and looked over at Morgan.

"Go on."

They had to think of something, and fast. It would be better to downplay the situation if they were going to convince their mother it had been typical brothers playing around, and nothing else.

"JD got mad because he was losing," Blake said. "He got back at us for calling him a cheater. He thought it was funny."

"He is always using his powers to play jokes on us," Morgan said.

Cassidy had scowled at her careless son. It certainly hadn't sounded like anything he would do. Duplicate JD, on the other hand, had just grinned innocently back at her.

The rest of the day had been relatively calm, as long as they kept Duplicate JD away from their mother. That was, until Aristede had flown home from work. He had rolled his flying carpet up and put it under his arm.

Morgan had been drawing pictures in his parchment sketchbook, while Blake was playing with his miniature–winged camel figures. They put down their belongings, jumped to their feet, and sprinted to their father.

Duplicate JD, however, had taken a keen interest in the carpet roll Aristede had dropped. As Aristede hugged his boys, Duplicate JD had stooped down, unrolled the carpet, and run his finger across the threaded textures. They had no idea until everyone had heard Blake's "Uh-oh!" that something was amiss.

Everything happened so quickly it was hard to imagine how Duplicate JD had jumped on Aristede's carpet and begun flying around the room. Aristede barely moved out of the way to avoid a collision. Duplicate JD had leaned back, tilted the carpet, and flew around the contour of the bottle. The gushes of air made the tapestries along the curved wall ripple. His lean to his right guided the carpet in a circular turn, first behind the fireplace and then over the heads of Aristede, Morgan, and Blake.

Like a bat coming out of a bat-filled cave, Duplicate JD had dive-bombed them. He had clutched the carpet edges so he could swoop upward and then plunge again. The one thing that remained constant was that through it all he had that same dopey-looking grin.

Aristede had raised both hands and flicked his fingers, immediately stopping the runaway carpet (although Duplicate JD didn't stop). Instead, he had tumbled off the carpet, head over heels, landing at Aristede's feet.

Aristede had grown tense. His voice had bristled with displeasure as he managed to say only, "To . . . your . . . room . . . *now!*"

That had been the best thing to happen for Morgan and Blake. Their father was so angry that he hadn't been willing to talk about his son's bizarre behavior. Aristede and Cassidy wouldn't have to see JD until morning, when the real JD had returned. It also gave the boys the time they had needed to get rid of Duplicate JD by sending him back into the mirror. This had proved easier to do than creating him had been.

"It took all three of us to make him," Blake had said as Morgan moved the smiling Duplicate JD to the mirror.

"That is correct!"

"Then don't we need our JD with us to make it happen?"

"Remember. This is JD's double. So long as there are three of us standing in front of it, the mirror cannot tell the difference."

The orange aura had outlined their bodies again. The tight feeling in their chests had forced Blake and Morgan to clench their teeth until the throbbing got to an unbearable level. Morgan had struggled to breathe. All he could manage to say was, "Go back!"

Still with a smile on his face, Duplicate JD had stepped back into the glass. The second he let go of Blake and Morgan's hands, the aura had been broken, relieving the pressure on their bodies.

There was a sudden *thud* when Morgan's head hit the windowpane. As he looked around, there still was no sign of JD. Blake had slumped to his side and dozed off again with his mouth dropping open. It wasn't until Morgan decided to go back to bed that a purple vapor poured in through the bottle opening.

"He is back at last!" Morgan exclaimed as he grabbed hold of Blake by the shoulder. The quick, sudden motion startled him.

Once he got his bearings, Blake began rubbing his eyes, just in time to see the smoke pull itself together and re-form.

"Wow! That was amazing," an exhilarated JD exclaimed. "You won't believe what I saw."

"Shh! Mom and Dad are asleep," Morgan said.

"We've been waiting hours for you to come back," Blake added.

"It has not been easy around here. Your duplicate caused a great deal of chaos," Morgan said, clicking his tongue a few times.

"Did Mom and Dad figure out it wasn't me?" JD asked as he grimaced.

"No, but you are going to be punished for all the things your duplicate did," Morgan said. "Furthermore, Mom made a list, and you have to do everything on it without magic."

JD sighed and rolled his eyes. He stared back at the bedchambers and asked, "Where is he, anyway?"

"Don't worry. We sent him back into the mirror," Blake told him.

"Whatever happened here with the duplicate will be worth the punishment for going outside," JD said excitedly. He couldn't wait to tell them everything.

In the low light of the room, JD had a tough time containing his excitement about his day—about how he had been waiting in Brianna's pocket, about changing from a coin to his real shape after being tossed into water, and about how he had followed her, never too far away.

"There were so many humans, too. I tried to fit in with all those Outsiders."

Blake pointed to the JD's cap, denim shorts, and T-shirt. "I can see that. What are you wearing, anyway?" he asked.

"This?" JD said as he looked down at his attire. "This is what the other kids were wearing."

"You look like a gleeb," Morgan said flatly.

JD should have been mad at Morgan for calling him a name. *Gleeb* was not a very insulting term, but it was something they called each other as a way of showing how silly they were being.

Morgan reached over to take the cap off his brother's head.

"How could you wear this silly hat?" he asked. "Why does it have this?" He tapped his finger on the brim.

"It keeps the sun out of your eyes." JD quickly grabbed the hat back. "Some older kids wore it like this."

This time he put the hat on backward. Morgan and Blake looked at each other and tried to bury the laughter erupting deep inside them.

"Yeah, that really looks better now," Blake said.

"We were walking around so much that my feet started hurting," JD said.

"Funny that you say that," Morgan said, looking down at JD's footwear. "Those do not look comfortable."

Blake crinkled his nose like putty, and in a tone like he had just stepped into tiger poop, he asked, "Do those hurt your feet?"

"They're called 'tenny shoes,'" JD explained. "They're very cushiony. It's like walking on air."

"Tenny shoes? Why are you wearing something that belongs to someone named Tenny?" Blake asked.

JD just ignored him. Now that he had spent time with the humans, he was worldlier. No response to his brothers' comments was necessary, since their ignorance really held no merit.

"By the way, did Brianna make any wishes while you were out there?" Morgan asked.

"She did make one when we were at the orca show. She didn't want to get splashed, so I moved her to a new seat away from the water," JD said. "She wasn't sure what happened to her."

Morgan combed his fingers back through his hair. He looked again at the sand timer and said, "It is almost one o'clock. We had better get to bed."

"You should both go out there and spend time with Outsiders. They can be so funny," JD said, now arching his brows up and down.

"I am sure of that," Morgan said. He took the cap from JD again and put it on his head—backward.

Chapter Eight

The Boy on the Flying Carpet

Attached to the garage, Christian had built a workshop many years ago for his model train layouts. It had become his favorite place to relax. It wasn't uncommon for him to spend time working on his model railroad system until late in the evening.

One morning after breakfast, Brianna found Christian in his workshop. It was a long, narrow room divided into two distinct sections that included a worktable and several tool cabinets. The train layout sat on a piece of thick plywood, which was set against the wall on the other side. Patches of artificial grass with foam mountains, painted in shades of brown, made up the entire landscape. A control panel contained the on-off switch and several knobs to perform many tasks, such as running the trains forward and backward, making steam come out of the engine smokestack, and turning on the lights of the houses along the tracks.

Brianna jumped onto the maple stool next to Christian and sat quietly so as not to disturb his work. The girl stared closely at her grandfather's hands as he cut small pieces of wood.

A small light brightened the work area. A movable magnifying glass mounted to the table made it easy for Christian to see the delicate pieces as he worked. He let Brianna glue the support beams that he had cut out of wood with a knife (he dared not let her use the knife to make any of the cuts herself).

"How does it look, Granddad?" She was eager to hear his opinion about her work.

She held it steady as he lowered his eyeglasses below the bridge of his nose and squinted his right eye. He threw in a "Hmm" before giving her two thumbs-up. "Very well done, young lady."

By half past eleven Isabelle came to tell the model train building team that lunch would be served on the patio overlooking the fishpond. It was just in time, too, as their stomachs had started to grumble. Three places were set at the table. Brianna thought Isabelle had a warped sense of humor when she saw that some of the sandwiches on the tray were tuna on toasted white bread.

Later in the afternoon, Isabelle came back to the workshop, only this time with an envelope in her hand.

"Bree. A letter arrived for you."

Brianna slipped off her stool and took the letter from her grandmother's hand. She stared at the envelope. It was a thin letter (only one or two pieces of paper inside). The stamp was a strange one, and it was postmarked from the country of Liechtenstein. She recognized the handwriting immediately.

"It's from Mommy and Daddy!" Brianna exclaimed.

She tore the envelope open, and when she unfolded the paper, a photograph dropped out. Once she began reading, however, the smile on her face faded.

Brianna looked at the photograph. It was a picture of her parents standing in front of a palace. The disgust in the girl's eyes didn't go unnoticed by her grandparents. Her cheeks were turning tomato red before she angrily tore the picture into a hundred pieces. Along with the letter, she crumpled up the paper scraps and threw the wad to the floor before fleeing the workshop.

Christian bent down to recover the discarded letter and smoothed out the stationery. Isabelle tucked her head next to her husband's to read what had upset Brianna so much.

Dear Brianna,

We hope you are enjoying your time with your grandparents. This trip has been relaxing and just what we needed.

While in Switzerland we ran into some old friends from college, the Deans. They have asked us to join them on a cruise of the Greek islands, and we have accepted their invitation.

Although you had expected us to be back in the United States right after the Fourth of July, we will see you at the end of the month instead. We are sure that you will enjoy having more time in Ontario with your gramma and granddad. Give them our love.

Hugs and kisses,

Dad and Mom
P.S. Here's a picture of us at the prince's palace.

"Oh, how selfish of them! Chris, how can they do this to her?" Isabelle asked. She tried hard to curb her desire to let out a scream.

They left the workshop and hurried back into the house. The family room seemed empty when they got there, but grumbling noises gave Brianna away. She had found a quiet place on the floor behind the leather chair. As soon as Isabelle sat down in the chair next to her, she gently began brushing the girl's hair.

"I know you're disappointed, dear, and you have every reason to be upset with your parents," Isabelle said. "The time will go by quickly, and everything will be all right. You'll see."

Brianna glanced up at Christian and Isabelle, rubbing her eyes. The anger in her eyes melted away, and she looked like a lost little orphan with her tear-stained cheeks.

"They said they'd be back in three weeks, Gramma," she said. Her voice cracked as she spoke.

Brianna moved to the footstool and saw the crumpled-up paper in her grandfather's hand. She got up hastily, went over to Christian, and took the letter from him.

To make her point, she waved the paper near their faces and said firmly, "Why, Gramma . . . why do they need to be with their friends more than me? I feel more like a puppy than their little girl. Why are they doing this?"

The more Brianna expressed her feelings about her parents, the more upset she became. She went facedown in Isabelle's lap. The gentle woman took hold of her shoulders, pulled her in close, and cradled Bree's head against her bosom.

"I know it seems that way, but—" she said.

"It's true!" Brianna said. "I hate them for what they're doing."

"You don't mean that?"

Isabelle was horrified at Brianna's declaration. She pulled out a handkerchief from her dress pocket and gave it to her.

"Yes, I do. I just hate them! Hate them! Hate them! Hate them!" Brianna exclaimed. She buried her face into Isabelle's lap again and sobbed.

Isabelle was grateful that they were alone and no one was there to witness the private conversation. The truth was they had an audience, and they were nearer than they could ever imagine.

From inside the bottle, Blake and Morgan sat watching as the drama unfolded. JD was outside completing the list of chores Cassidy had given him as punishment for *his* misdeeds.

"I wish all their plans for their trip would just go up in smoke, and then they would have to come back."

Blake jumped up from his comfy cushion. He hadn't been so excited since they had received the tigers.

"She made another wish! Let me grant this one, okay?"

Morgan extended his hand, giving him the go-ahead.

"It's all yours," he told his brother.

Blake closed his eyes, brought his hands together, and bowed. "Your wish is my command; now make it so."

With her arms wrapped around Brianna, Isabelle rocked back and forth. The girl had every right to be angry about her parents' selfishness, but Isabelle was more interested in comforting her granddaughter. She had an idea about what might help.

Christian leaned in close, and Isabelle whispered something to him. He slowly backed out of the room, putting the letter on the table near the door. He returned a few minutes later, with one hand closed around a small object. Like a magician's sleight of hand, the exchange to his wife went undetected.

"Perhaps this will help," Isabelle said.

Brianna looked up pathetically at Christian and Isabelle through her bloodshot eyes. When Isabelle opened her hand, the light reflected on a small heart-shaped locket at the end of a silver chain. An etched line ran diagonally, dividing the heart into two parts. The heart had a polished side, and set in the satiny luster of the other half were three gemstones.

"Oh, my!" Brianna said. She pulled away from Isabelle's soft arms, and her eyes grew wide. She sniffed again and wiped the drips away with her handkerchief. "This is beautiful. Look at the shiny jewels."

"Those are real rubies. The locket belonged to your aunt Casey. I kept it for all this time," Isabelle said. "You're the oldest granddaughter, and I think you should have it now."

This gesture not only was meant to cheer her up, but it also meant something else for Isabelle. When they were making the scrapbooks, Isabelle had time to think about her daughter and become reconciled with the reality that Casey would never return to them.

The delicate silver chain wrapped around Brianna's fingers as she held it up to the light. She then pulled her hair back, and Isabelle opened the clasp so she could place the locket around Brianna's neck.

"Now let's go get some ice cream," Isabelle told her as she stood up and began walking to the kitchen door. "Ice cream always makes things better."

She was right about that. The sweet taste of the flavored iced cream would sweep away the horrible feelings Brianna had for her parents.

As Morgan watched the Outsiders leave the family room, Blake's stomach gave him a sudden twinge. It was pitiful to watch her go through the pain, especially when it was caused by people who professed to love her. His parents would *never* treat their children like that. He was feeling very sorry for the girl.

"I wish we could do something for her," Blake told Morgan.

Morgan must have felt the same way, because he had an idea about what that could be.

"What are you going to do?" Blake asked.

"You will see," Morgan said.

He put his arm around Blake and guided him toward the center chamber, stopping directly under the bottle opening. "It is time for something else to happen."

Morgan had decided it was his turn to go out and spend a short time among the humans. Blake went to get JD, and by the time they got back to the sunken retreat, it had been empty for many minutes. They knew where Morgan had gone.

Brianna spent the rest of the afternoon in the backyard sitting on the swing, which Christian had made for his children many years ago. It was a wooden plank that hung by thick ropes from the large tree. It was the same swing on which she imagined her father, who as a young boy had bent his knees and leaned forward to pump his swing higher with each pass. When he had reached the greatest height possible, he had launched himself off the swing. The curved path of the jump was probably steep so he could land as far from the tree as he could.

The swing was spinning slowly while she toyed with the piece of jewelry around her neck. Then a baby-like whimper, as if someone or something was in pain, made her twist the old-fashioned swing. Hearing the sounds again, she jumped off the seat and walked over to the rear gate. There, hiding behind a planter barrel, was a tiny honey-and-white-colored Pomeranian.

Brianna bent down, and when the puppy squeaked again, she put her hand around his head. The cute puppy immediately jumped up on her chest to lick her face.

"I think he likes you."

She had heard that voice before, and when she turned, she saw Morgan standing and smiling. He was dressed in the same clothes JD had worn when he came back after spending the day at Marine Gardens, only this time the baseball cap was backward.

Brianna stretched her neck to see the street beyond the gate.

"Where did you come from?" she asked.

"I was walking out there," he said. He pointed to the concrete sidewalk on the other side of the Carrutherses' fence. "When I put my dog down, he came into your backyard. Sorry about that."

A pulse of shivers shot through Brianna's thin-framed body while goose bumps rose on both forearms. Even her hair seemed to tingle a little bit.

Stroking the little dog's head and back, Brianna finally blurted, "I know you. Your name is JD. We met at the dolphin tank."

Morgan gave her one of those sour looks as though he had just taken a spoonful of bitter medicine.

"I believe you are mistaken."

Morgan gently took the puppy from her, but the little animal fought his way out of his hand, eagerly trying to get back into Brianna's warm, comforting arms.

"His name is Winston."

"Winston?" she said. "He's adorable. I wish I could just keep him."

There was Brianna's fourth wish out of the nine she was entitled to have (three for each triplet who was summoned when she uncorked the bottle).

While Brianna was cuddling the small, wiry animal against her cheek and talking to him in baby talk, Morgan stepped back, just out of her line of sight. Bowing and bringing his hands together, he whispered, "Your wish is my command; now make it so."

"I've never been allowed to have a pet," she told him as she looked up.

"Now you have one. He is yours."

"What do you mean, he's mine? To keep?"

Winston continued squirming, the same way he did when Morgan was holding him just a minute or two before. When she looked up at Morgan, she was surprised to find the blond-headed boy had gone. All that was there was a vapor flowing through the screen door of the house.

She blinked her eyes a few times and shook her head as the purplish mist separated into nothingness. Was her imagination playing a trick on her? Cradling the puppy with both hands, Brianna stepped up on the flagstone patio to the back door. With her free hand, she threw the screen door open and swiftly went inside to find Christian and Isabelle.

The boy, who Brianna said looked like the boy from Marine Gardens, didn't sound like anyone Christian or Isabelle knew. Christian thought he might be new to the neighborhood.

Isabelle scratched the little puppy behind the ear, which the puppy seemed to like, as he made soft whimpering sounds. Until the boy returned, Brianna would have to take the responsibility of caring for the little dog. She snuggled Winston closely, careful not to crush his tiny body.

But the boy didn't come back, and this secretly pleased Brianna because it meant she really might get to keep Winston for herself.

What happened the next day was an even stranger surprise than the appearance of the odd boy and the little dog. At midafternoon, the doorbell rang. On the front porch stood a man in a dark uniform, and on his pocket was the emblem of a telegram service. After Christian signed for the letter, the deliveryman tipped his hat and left. The yellow envelope had Brianna's name on it, so Christian handed it to her. She tore it open, quickly read the telegram, and rolled her eyes.

With her teeth clenched, Brianna said, "I don't believe it."

"What does it say, dear?" Isabelle asked.

Brianna walked over to one of the two armchairs by the fireplace and sat down.

"Mommy and Daddy are on their way here. Their trip got canceled," she told them, staring down at the yellow paper. "The cruise ship had a fire."

"I'm sorry. I hope no one was hurt," Isabelle said. She stepped closer and put her hands on the back of the chair. "You should be happy to know they're coming home. It's what you wanted. Perhaps the fire was a blessing in disguise."

"A blessing? I wished something to happen, and it did," she said. More anger began erupting in her stomach once again.

After dinner, she went to her grandfather's computer and began tapping her fingers on the keyboard. She waited impatiently for an Internet connection to be made. As soon as she could, she typed a few letters in the search engine. The screen filled with entries. During the next couple of hours, she selected the best choices to read.

Several times Brianna stopped and closed her tired eyes, putting her hand on the back of her aching neck. At the same time, she rolled her head to one side, then back around to the other.

Brianna typed in a different set of key words and continued scrolling down the list of entries. One looked promising—the one about genies.

> The jinn, also known as genies (derived from the Latin word *genius*, which means a guardian spirit), are endowed with supernatural powers. They occupy a parallel world to that of humankind by living in bottles, lamps, or other objects. Once freed from captivity, they will grant wishes on the person who freed them.
>
> The earliest jinn stories are found in the book *One Thousand and One Arabian Nights*. The French translation of the Arabian Nights stories used *genie* as a variation of *jinni* because of the similarity.
>
> Because genies can be ill-behaved and mischievous, they have been known to twist a wish, and therefore mortals must be careful for what they wish.

Her mouth was parched, and she hoarsely said, "I wish—" But then she stopped. "No, wait. I've already made several wishes. I don't know how many more I get."

The three brothers watched nervously. Blake's ear twitched like never before—three quick twitches followed by two long ones. Then the other one began twitching as well. Now that she knew about genies, what would they do? It was important that they not panic!

Brianna shifted in the chair and held her breath for about three seconds before letting out a shivering gasp. If the amethyst bottle had captured her attention before, it was nothing compared to how important it looked to her now. She pushed back her chair and moved closer to the bottle. She saw the stone stopper along the wall and realized that it had been lying there since she pulled it out of the bottle. She had forgotten all about it until now, when she picked it up and turned it in her hand before she gently laid it on the shelf alongside the bottle.

JD knew that something had to be done, and fast.

"Watch this—" JD said with a bit of mischief in his eyes as he raised both hands in front of him and extended his fingers. His eyebrows darted up and down. He looked actually gleeful at what he planned to do next.

"Brianna, the Outsider. You opened the door, and we need to reward you. We've visited your world. Now it's your turn to visit ours."

Brianna bolted backward until she knocked her shoulder against a bookcase. Half a dozen American classics and a few pretty knickknacks fell to the floor. She dropped to her knees next to Winston's doggie bed. Petting the puppy, she whispered, "I-I think th-there are genies in this house."

"What are you doing?" Morgan said. "She has connected all the pieces and now knows we are genies."

"I did what I had to do," JD said.

"So how is that going to help us?" Blake asked.

"I'm not finished. I want her to use her wishes, at least one of them to come here, and this should clinch it," JD said. "And do you know what will happen once she's in the bottle?"

"No. What?" Blake asked.

"I know," Morgan said. "Not only will her power over us cease, but we can have her tell us what she would wish for, send her back, and grant the wishes. At that point, she will no longer be our master."

"Exactly."

"That is brilliant thinking, JD," Morgan said.

JD uncloaked the bottle opening and with his hands around his mouth, he taunted her further. "Are you ready, Brianna the Outsider?"

What does he mean? Brianna thought. Her grip under Winston's belly tightened. Her arms became all goose-pimply again. A purplish glow began filling the underlit room, and when the smoky mist evaporated, it left the oddest thing she had ever seen in her life: a tassel-knotted, richly colored carpet floating.

And there was more: a boy sitting in the middle of it. His eyes were closed, his arms were folded in front of him, and the bobbing of the carpet made his loose-fitting clothing flap in the air.

When he opened his eyes, he bowed and said to her, "I am your servant. Come with me."

Her throat narrowed, which made it hard for her to talk. She only managed to say, "Y-you're the g-genie?" Brianna squinted at him and said, in a second breath, "W-where d-d-do you w-want to t-take m-m-me?"

The carpet made a clear about-face and began circling in the opposite direction over Brianna. Watching all the zooming turns was dizzying, so she closed her eyes.

"You want to know everything. We know you do. Follow me. Come into the bottle."

His body began to dissolve into smoke, and like water sucked down a bathtub drain, the vapory smoke returned from where it had come.

"Wait!" Brianna called to him. She rushed to the shelf and seized hold of the neck of the bottle. "How do I do that?"

"Just make the wish, and we'll reveal it all," echoed from the bottle.

His voice screamed repeatedly in her head, *Just make the wish, and we'll reveal it all. Just make the wish, and we'll reveal it all. Just make the wish, and we'll reveal it all.*

She hoped the pounding would stop so she could think more clearly. Then without any thought, she finally said, "All right! That's what I want. I wish you'd just tell me everything!"

A strange feeling overcame her, and the space around her began to fill with the purple mist until she was entirely wrapped up in it.

Brianna's face went white. The spinning made her want to vomit. She felt her feet leave the ground, and after several long seconds, there was a thump that vibrated through the room! Her legs bent at the knees and bowed. She slipped sideways, reaching out to catch hold of anything she could. No matter how much she tried to maintain her balance, she still landed on her bottom.

Soon the smoke cleared, and when Brianna looked around, she knew instantly she wasn't in her grandparents' house anymore—sort of.

Chapter Nine

The Genies Belong to Me

Brianna found herself sitting on a pile of large silken cushions. There were more of them spread around on the floor. Other than the sofas, there wasn't much else to sit on.

She looked out into almost total darkness. Her eyes adjusted to the dim lights from the low flames in the polished brass urns. But it was enough for Brianna to see that it was a perfectly round room, and from what she could see, it was the most quirky room ever, at least of any she had seen in her short life.

She heard a light crackling noise and then what sounded like a tiny firecracker exploding. The flickering orange remains of a smoldering fire came from the fireplace opposite where she was sitting.

Then she saw the triplets standing in front of a window. One by one, they carefully approached her. Morgan reached out to help Brianna back to her feet. Touching his flesh-and-bone hand made her realize that what she saw was quite real.

The boys watched unmoving as she slowly wandered to the reflecting pool, pushing her finger into the warm bubbles coming to the water's surface.

It took her only a few minutes to crisscross the center chamber. Although it still felt like a dream to Brianna, she found the place a fascinating one. It reminded her of an *Arabian Nights* movie, only this time it was like being on a movie set, and she was in the motion picture extravaganza.

By the low-flamed lights she saw the triplets standing shoulder to shoulder in the same place as before. She had almost forgotten they were there. Then she realized they had never taken their eyes off her.

"We're in the bottle, aren't we?" It was a question she didn't expect an answer to, since she already knew what their response would be before she asked. "And the three of you are genies. You're the voices I heard. Do Gramma and Granddad know you live here?"

"No. Only you do," Blake said.

"Of course they don't," she added. "I have to admit it is curious knowing that there are genies living in my grandparents' house."

Then it struck her that, although she knew some things about the boys, one question remained: "Can you please tell me your names?"

Little did she know that the answer would come from unlikely sources on the mantel. A whispery cough made her turn. She had to strain to see a well-dressed porcelain man on one of the picture frames. His green cape matched the parrot's feather on his wide, flattened turban. Brianna was startled when the man suddenly began providing a story about the framed photograph.

"This is a portrait taken last year of the charming family. Aristede and Cassidy have three sons: Justin David, Morgan, and Blake. They are descendants of the purple jinn, Mikayla."

The little man bowed when he finished and stepped back to his original spot on the ornate frame.

Brianna stopped to ponder what she had heard and looked at another frame, this one with wide, sleek silver borders. Just like with the first picture, another porcelain person turned to her. This time a pretty woman with long black hair who was perched on the bottom ledge of the frame prepared to speak. The woman put her fingertips

88

over her mouth to muffle a giggle. She lifted her skirt above her ankles and gracefully stepped down. The little lady waved to Brianna before reciting her part.

"Here the family is visiting a camel farm that Aristede's brother owns. As you can see, the children are feeding the young foals."

Brianna looked back over her shoulder at the three brothers. To the boy with blond hair brushed neatly in front, she said, "You're Justin David. I remember you from Marine Gardens."

"You can call me JD. Everybody does," he told her.

She turned to the boy with the windswept hair who stood between his brothers.

"And you're Blake."

His smile supported her conclusion.

Finally, pointing to the other boy on the left, she said, "And then you're Morgan. You're the one who brought Winston to me."

"Welcome, Brianna!" he said. The three of them bowed their heads.

Brianna moved over to the large window partially covered by a curtain. Blake moved one of the drape panels, and she was amazed at the view into the family room. This must be where they watched her.

"How did I get here?" she asked.

"You wished it," JD said firmly. "You're the Outsider who pulled out the stopper. We became your genies, and now we have to give you what you ask for."

"Actually, we have no choice," Morgan said. "Those are the genie rules when it comes to Outsiders."

"There you go again with that word, *Outsider*. Why did you call me that?" Brianna asked.

Morgan nodded his head toward the large pane of glass and said, "Because you live *outside the bottle*."

At that same moment, a faint light spilled through the big window. The door in the family room had opened, and someone had flipped the light switch. Christian was wrapping his bathrobe around his middle and tying the belt.

Brianna pounded her fists on the glass and cried out, "Granddad! I'm in here, Granddad."

It took only seconds for her to understand that he couldn't hear her, for the glass was very thick, and she was, oh, so small.

So she watched as Christian went down on one leg and picked up the Pomeranian. Winston wriggled his head and body with all his strength, nearly slipping out of Christian's gentle hands. The puppy popped up his little head and let out a muffled bark.

Christian seemed privately agitated. "Where is that girl?"

Winston barked continually, as if he had something very important to say. Christian's eyes fell on the neat rows of books. The children watched as he moved toward them. As he got closer, his face got larger and larger until it filled the entire window. Brianna knew by the determined look that he must have known that she was inside the bottle and he now was coming to get her out.

Suddenly the floor trembled, swelling louder until all of them began to vibrate, and the bottle began to teeter. Brianna grimaced. Was it one of those California earthquakes she had heard so much about?

"Your grandfather is picking us up. Hold on!" JD said. He tried hard to keep his footing.

Within seconds, their whole world had, quite literally, turned upside down. Water in the reflecting pool sloshed over the marble rim. Pillows tumbled, brushing against the children's legs. The porcelain people were knocked off their frames when the pictures on the mantel fell over. The porcelain man rubbed the bruise on his head where he hit the wall. The porcelain woman from the next frame lay twisted, her arm in the shape of the letter S. Blood flecks stained her sleeves.

Just as suddenly as the movement began, the rumblings stopped abruptly and with a thump.

For a split second, they could hear an Outsider's breathing at the bottle's opening. Then, just as gushing air came into the bottle, a smoky tornado of pale purple vapor whisked from behind the fireplace past them and seeped out of the bottle.

"What was that?" Blake asked.

"That Outsider must have inhaled some of our air and sucked it out," Morgan said.

The urns were barely lit, and it was hard for any of them to see.

A subtle dimness passed over them even after Morgan lit a few candles. A shadow slowly crossed over them and darkened the entire center chamber. A giant eyeball eclipsed the patch of light in the bottle opening, and it looked down at them.

Since the opening had been cloaked by JD to hide the fact that the stopper had been removed (and uncloaked for them to leave or enter the bottle without anyone suspecting anything), this was the first time that a sliver of light made its way in from the outside.

Brianna jumped up and down, waving her arms in hopes of gaining his attention. Alas, she was too small to be noticed. The light coming into the bottle when JD uncloaked the opening to go out to taunt Brianna was now blocked again.

"Look!" Blake said.

They arched their necks, and JD confirmed what they saw. "The Outsider put the stopper back in."

At that moment, they could hear a pattering noise. It came from the corridor by the fireplace—brisk footsteps coming from the bedchambers.

"Boys?" Aristede called out from the top stair step. He squinted his eyes to see into the center of the bottle. "Are you there?"

JD and Blake each grabbed hold of one of Brianna's arms. As her feet shuffled across the floor, she squirmed to break loose from them and didn't care who knew she was there. JD and Blake lifted her off the floor as they thrust her behind one of the curtains by the big window.

"Stay here and be quiet," JD said. "We can't tell Mom and Dad you're here with us."

"You mean you can't have them discover an Outsider here in the bottle, don't you?" Brianna snapped before JD pulled the curtain to hide her.

Out of the corner of her eye, the view of the family room dissolved, like fog rolling in from the ocean. It was difficult for her to grasp the genie magic that changed what she saw: Christian's desk, the chairs, the computer, the bookcases, even the French doors behind the desk. The moonlight reached its way into the genies' house, and Brianna froze, hoping the light didn't reveal her presence.

"There you are," Cassidy said. "We got worried when we went to check on you and you weren't in your beds."

The place was a mess from all the movement, and Cassidy moved over to the mantel.

"Poor things."

She snapped her fingers, and the picture frames propped upright into their original spots. The porcelain man had taken off his cape and bandaged the woman's wounds. Cassidy waved her hands, and this time, the two little porcelain people were as good as new and back on their platforms ready for their next presentations.

"The shaking scared us," JD said quickly, "so we came here."

Cassidy made her way over to them and pushed the curtains aside. "Did you see anyone before the bottle began to shake?" she asked.

Brianna gasped softly and covered her eyes, opening her fingers slightly to see how long it would take for the adult genie to discover her. Cassidy stared out the window and gave a hard, sorrowful look.

While Blake tried to conceal his panicky feeling behind a blush, JD made an effort to look innocent to send a different message. What would they tell their mother? Perhaps the punishment wouldn't be so awful if they explained they didn't intend to keep Brianna in the bottle. After all, it had happened so fast.

"I'm glad that's over. We can go back to bed," Cassidy said.

Aristede and Cassidy crossed the center chamber to the steps leading to the bedchamber corridor. They had expected their sons to be following them. However, JD, Morgan, and Blake hadn't moved and instead were standing in place.

"What are you waiting for? It's late," Aristede said.

That was when Morgan drew a breath before he said, "The stopper was taken out, and we were summoned."

"Summoned?" Cassidy asked. "Just now?"

Morgan shook his head.

"Not now, but when we came back from Master Jindrake's," he said. "You were working in the garden. We knew we had no choice but to go." He added that they had cloaked the opening so they, Aristede and Cassidy, wouldn't figure it out when they left the bottle.

Aristede was baffled and could only look to his wife, but she was speechless.

"And who summoned you?" he asked. "Was it that Outsider man or his wife?"

"Neither one," Morgan said. "It was the Outsider girl, their granddaughter."

Cassidy gasped.

"But when Brianna saw the smoke, she ran from the room and never saw us after our bodies took shape," JD added.

"Brianna?" Aristede said. "How do you know her name?"

Blake lowered his head. "W-w-we talked to her."

Aristede was now as dumbstruck as his wife.

"You—talked to her? You actually talked to her?" Cassidy finally asked when she found her voice. "How? She never saw you. I-I don't understand."

"Neither do we," JD said. "But it's true. She can hear us from out there."

Aristede cleared his throat and then exclaimed, "Impossible!"

He sounded just as surprised as Jindrake had been when the triplets told the genie master. Obviously, this bizarre situation had a greater importance than the triplets had realized.

"That isn't all," JD said.

"You mean there's more?" Cassidy said. "I can only imagine what that might be."

He turned to the curtains, and a shadowy figure stepped out and showed herself.

Aristede and Cassidy had been stunned enough, but now their peach-colored faces turned white. Through their round eyes, the size of sand dollars, they couldn't believe what they were seeing.

"Good gracious! Are you—" Cassidy said.

"Brianna? Yes, I am."

Cassidy turned to her sons and asked, "This is the girl you now belong to? How did she get here?"

They didn't answer. It was Brianna who spoke up.

"I made a wish because I wanted to find out what was going on with the amethyst bottle."

In the shocked silence that followed, Aristede eyeballed each offending triplet. He put his hands on his hips and took several deep breaths. It took every ounce of strength he had to control himself, especially while the Outsider stood there watching.

Deciding what should be done as a punishment, and so they wouldn't have time to think about the outside world, Aristede turned.

"I ought to send you to stay with Uncle Jasper. Working hard on a camel farm would be good for you."

"Really, Dad! You'd send us there?" Blake said to the appealing offer.

It definitely was not the reaction Aristede had expected. Since sending them to the camel farm would be like sending them on a vacation, perhaps it would be better to send them to live with his never-married aunts. Aunt Majo and Aunt Saffire traveled extensively and popped up on their doorstep every few years when they least expected.

"Eww," the boys chorused.

"They're weird, and they smell funny," JD said. He then stuck out his tongue and blew a raspberry.

Aristede kept from laughing by turning his head and biting down on his lip. What his sons told him was true, but his aunts were his mother's sisters, and he did have a soft spot in his heart for Majo and Saffire. That would be a most horrible fate for them.

"It's just that we wanted to go out to the human world so bad and see what it's like," JD added.

The color was returning to Cassidy's cheeks as the shock of all the revelations was beginning to wear off, and she agreed that the boys deserved to be disciplined for what they had done.

"But what are we going to do about the girl?" she asked.

Aristede felt very odd, at a loss really, about what to do, since he had never encountered anything like this in his life. All he could do was shrug his shoulders.

Brianna had quietly listened to them talking about what to do with the triplets. She was growing weary of her little adventure. Now with a hush in the conversation, with only the fire crackling, she stepped forward and announced, "I'm ready to go back home. That's my wish."

The lull continued. Concern was written all over their faces, and Brianna sensed immediately that there was something they hadn't told her. The distressed expressions made them look as if they had upset stomachs after eating something that had disagreed with them, like a bad batch of bird's nest soup.

"Did you hear me? I made a wish. Send me back to Gramma and Granddad."

"I'm afraid it's not that simple," Aristede said. "You see, my dear, with the stopper in the bottle opening, you can't go home."

Brianna gasped. "You mean I'm trapped? Here in the bottle? But I want to go back *now!*"

Cassidy tried to be helpful. "We'll find a way to make everything right for you." She turned to Aristede with a helpless look and said, "We must find a way to send Brianna back home."

"Until the bottle is uncorked, there's nothing we can do," Aristede said. "Jinn Code, Outsider Decree Number One Hundred Thirty-Nine, specifically says that 'any Outsider who enters the jinn world must leave through the same route.'"

"I don't care what Jinn Code Outsider Decree whatever says. There has to be an exception in the law! Brianna is a child and didn't know what she was doing when the wish was made."

"None of that matters. The human girl made a wish. That comes before everything else. I'm afraid there's nothing we can do," Aristede said.

When he saw the distressed look on his wife's face, Aristede said he would contact the viziers when he got to the office the next morning. Maybe there was something they could do.

JD took a step and swallowed.

"We never meant for this to happen. All we wanted to do was get you to use up your wishes."

Hearing those words, a confused Brianna turned her head swiftly.

"What did you say? What did you mean by that?"

JD didn't answer her. As her brain was processing it all, she finally shrieked, "I get it! As long as I didn't know that I was your master, you thought you could trick me! You tricked me into making wishes. I read on the Internet that genies twist wishes. Because of that, I'm trapped in here—maybe forever."

"Only because your granddad put the stopper into the bottle," Morgan said defensively. "We never imagined that would happen."

"But he did!"

Brianna started to hiccup and fight the tears from flowing.

"Now how am . . . I going . . . to go . . . home?"

More silence! Nothing they could say or how sincere an apology they could make would change anything.

Brianna used the back of her hand to push teardrops from her cheeks and then dabbed the corners of her eyes. The dreadful dream had become a nightmare. Her knees weakened, and she sank into an oversized cushion, pulling her body into a ball. Tears soaked the colorful fabrics on the pillows as she wept herself to sleep.

Cassidy leaned down so she could cover her with a blanket.

"Did you see how upset she was?" Blake said softly. "We've got to help her."

"How do we do that? Dad said he'd see what the viziers could do," JD said.

"We can't play any more tricks on her," Blake added. "It doesn't matter anymore."

"Don't we matter? We belong to her," JD said.

The other two boys looked at him. JD lowered his head and gave a quick head-jerk nod.

"You're right," he said.

"What will we do if she is trapped in here forever?" Blake asked his brothers. His ear gave a twitch.

"I just hope the Jinn High Council does not come and take us away," Morgan said with a sigh.

Chapter Ten

The Bottle's Prisoner

Brianna awoke the next day, jerking straight up. Fear swelled throughout her body, and she closed her tired eyes. Perhaps when she opened them again, she'd be in her bed at Gramma and Granddad's.

After a few seconds, Brianna opened her eyes, eagerly hoping that it really had been a horrid nightmare. But those hopes were dashed when she saw the hanging draperies, the fountain, the reflecting pool, and all the pillows. She was still in the amethyst bottle.

She rubbed the chill off her arms and was about to cry when she put her face in her hands. It felt cold and sticky. Then she heard voices on the other side of the arched doorway. She pushed the blanket aside and moved cautiously from the pile of pillows to the opening.

"Good morning," Cassidy said. Her tender smile eased Brianna's feeling of hopelessness. "Come. Sit down and have something to eat. You must be hungry. Do you like eggs and sausage?"

Brianna's nod was shaky and strained. She moved slowly to the table, where she quietly sat down next to Morgan.

"You will love Mom's cooking," Morgan said. "Her scrambled peacock eggs and camel sausage are great."

She slowly turned to him, as she wasn't sure that she had heard him correctly.

"What . . . kind . . . of . . . eggs . . . did . . . you . . . say?"

"Peacock eggs. They're delicious," Blake said. He put another piece in his mouth and chewed smilingly.

"And camel sausage?" Brianna asked. Her face shifted into a crinkly ball.

"What's the matter, Brianna?" JD asked. "Would you like breadfruit pancakes instead?"

There was another bashful gesture, and this time it was a shake of the head.

Cassidy brought over a bowl with the scrambled eggs, and the boys helped themselves by scooping some out, nearly filling their plates. She served the browned sausages from the pan. Some of the links were still sizzling.

"Boys, in the outside world, people eat eggs from chickens," Cassidy said. "They don't eat camel."

"Chickens. Yuck!" all the boys said, puckering their lips and creasing their noses.

"Would you like some toast, Brianna?" Cassidy asked.

Brianna looked around, but there wasn't a toaster in sight. She nodded nonetheless.

Cassidy put her hand up in front of herself, fingers pointing up. A second later flames ignited from her fingertips. It was obvious by her smiling face that although there was fire, she did not feel the burning flames.

A slice of bread lifted from a platter and hovered over the fiery fingers until it was lightly browned, and then it popped over to darken the other side. Cassidy offered her the toasted bread.

JD reached for some yak butter and spread it over his toast. Yak butter didn't look different from the butter Brianna used at home, so she spread some on her bread, too. JD told her how their parents had spent time traveling in the outside world, but Cassidy and Aristede didn't talk about it, since they weren't able to leave the bottle. JD leaned over to Brianna and said, "Your world was great to visit."

"Well, what you saw was special. Not every place is like Marine Gardens," Brianna said.

Cassidy reached for a pitcher and changed the subject. "Who would like juice?"

"I do! I do!" Blake said.

"Me, too, Mother," Morgan said.

Brianna said nothing as she stared at her glass while Cassidy poured the red liquid with green swirls. She glanced around, side to side, to watch the others slurp some down.

"Go ahead, Brianna, try it," Morgan said.

Brianna took a small sip. The juice had a sweet and sour tang to it. It reminded her of the taste of an all-day sucker that changed flavors with each lick. "It's pomaberry juice," JD told her. "Do you like it?"

There was something about the juice that Brianna had never tasted before. She smacked her lips and said, "It tastes pretty good. There's a unique taste of something else. I don't know what it is."

"It's a grasshopper mixed in with the berries," Morgan said.

Brianna's eyes bulged as she made a feeble attempt to smile. She just stared at the red liquid, but she couldn't get the image of a chopped-up and blended grasshopper out of her mind. It was easy to see she wasn't very excited about drinking a beverage with grasshopper in it.

Morgan offered something else.

"We have yak milk instead if you prefer."

"Like from a long-haired ox we have in our world?" Brianna asked.

Morgan nodded with a large smile on his face.

"No, thank you. I'm fine," Brianna said. She tried very hard to be polite to her hosts.

She pushed the camel sausage links around the eggs to make it look as if she were eating her food. While she just nibbled, the boys gobbled their meal and finished quickly.

Aristede thought that many of the magical feats his sons had done were rather clever. His handsome face beamed with pride, as he couldn't do some of the magic they did until he was much older.

Cassidy didn't pay attention to him. The only thoughts racing through her mind were about what they could do to help poor Brianna.

"The family must be frantic about her," she said.

Brianna sat slouching, her shoulders drooping. She could think only about going home.

"Isn't there another way to uncork the bottle, like through a window or something?" Brianna asked.

"Not really," Blake said out the corner of his mouth.

"Why not?" she asked.

"Because the top opening leads to your world," Aristede explained.

"I still don't understand. Why can't I go out another way into my world? You have a front door and a lot of windows. Can't you just go out another way and take me with you?" Brianna asked.

Aristede shook his head.

"Those other exits lead to places in the genie world."

"What about through another bottle's opening—one that doesn't have a cork in it?" Brianna asked. There was certain neediness in her voice, which only showed just how she was grasping at any possible way to get home.

"That's not an option either," Aristede added. "The Jinn Code doesn't permit that, since those other bottles could lead anywhere in your world."

"So it's hopeless! I'm never going home," Brianna said tearfully.

Before Aristede could answer, a faint whistling began to resonate in the eating area. He shifted his eyes and announced, "Mail's here."

One by one, three creamy-white round objects appeared in the wide-mouthed mail jar. They weren't there for long. Within seconds, the orbulars made their way out of the jar and hovered in front of them.

These fascinating objects caught Brianna's interest and, for a few brief moments, took her mind off finding a way home.

"What are those?"

"They're from *The Orbular Times*," Aristede said.

As the orbulars slowly began to spin, dazzling colors glittered from the filmy, glass-like material. Within seconds, the baseball-sized spheres filled with the images of people.

In the first orbular was the face of a woman telling them that the weather was going to be sunny. But by week's end there would be a strong chance of thunderstorms. A man in the second orbular gave the results for the winged camel races at Jinnetti Downs. The results of the fourth race excited Blake, and he cheered when he heard that Fire Ball Rider won, with his favorite cameleer, Nicolas, flying. The reporter added that it was Nicolas's thirteenth consecutive win of the season.

The announcement in the second report was about a dricketts summer practice between the Tessinari Twilighters and the Durainian Dragons. The match was scheduled before the official season, which began in the fall, at the same time the triplets would be spending a week at the Academy for Jinn Studies for further instruction and assessments on what they were learning this term.

Finally, the last orbular reported an appeal from a family who had been desperately searching for a lost family member. The untidy man had a mangy tangle of silver hair sprouting from under his turban. The man's deep-set eyes, fraught with terror, made him look like a jittery goat.

"Get him out. Help. Please. Help me," the haggard man begged once his face looked out at them.

A young woman came into view within the same orbular as the strange man. Her whitish complexion made her sharp blue eyes a striking feature on her face. Her eyes swelled with tears as she pleaded with everyone watching her for any information about her missing father.

"He isn't a well man, and I need to get him to Jingrey Healers for help," the young woman added.

The first orbular changed stories and reported that the Jinn High Council had begun discussing a minimum fiber weight on all new flying carpets.

As the orbulars dimmed and the images faded, Brianna announced, "I get it! They're like the different sections of a newspaper. News, weather, and sports."

Cassidy giggled and said, "Yes, Brianna. That's exactly what they are."

Aristede wiped his mouth of food debris with the napkin that had been resting in his lap.

"I'd better get going. With the viziers' new project, I need to get to the office," he said. "Bring the boys and Brianna into Jinwiddie later so we can have the midday meal together."

He put on a robe and grabbed what looked like a rug, unrolling it. The carpet hovered until Aristede jumped on and flew out the front door. His abrupt departure caught Brianna entirely by surprise. First with her eyes wide open and then with her eyes shut tightly, she shook her head quickly. When she opened her eyes again, she half-expected to see Aristede still in the room.

"Your dad just flew away on a flying carpet!"

"Of course he did," JD said. "It's a beautiful day to fly to work."

"I thought being a genie was his job," Brianna said. "What does your dad do?"

"Dad works at the DFC," JD said.

"DFC? What's that?"

"The Department of Flying Carpets," Morgan told her. "They are responsible for monitoring all flying carpets and issuing flying licenses when genies are old enough. All flying carpets must be registered to licensed flyers."

"One time, Dad was helping one old genie who landed her carpet in the palm tree in her yard," JD said. "She kept waving her arms, accidently changing the men from the Office of Genie Rescues into dung beetles. It took five other department officials to get her down."

When they finished the morning meal, Cassidy urged the boys to take Brianna outside. This gave Cassidy time to get the extra bedchamber ready for their young guest.

What a relief. Brianna dropped her fork and used the napkin on her lap to dab her mouth. At least now she wouldn't have to eat the camel sausage links still sitting on her plate. As the youngsters turned toward the door, Cassidy watched the foursome scurry away before getting up and busying herself with other work.

Brianna followed JD, Morgan, and Blake. The center chamber looked different in daylight than it had at night. It appeared much larger, as now she could see in every nook and cranny.

Once she was outside, Brianna quickly learned the bottle's front door led to an entire other community, and it was amazing to see. They took a stepping-stone path around the house to a yard with flower beds and a humble vegetable garden walled off by rocks. Brianna looked closely at the outer glassy walls of the genie house. It looked exactly like the bottle in the Carrutherses' home, down to the ribbon around the top.

JD led her to the grassy knoll. As they stood together, he pointed to a distant city. From this level, the buildings consisted of curves, round edges, and straight walls. The city sat alone, a wall all the way around, making it look like a fort in the desert.

"That's Jinwiddie, where Dad works."

Blake reached for her hand and led her to a tent by a small lake. He placed a finger to his lips and pulled up the flap of the tent's entrance. Straining her neck, she saw Sherbet, Tango, and Tangerine tumbling playfully with each other on a bed of straw.

"Oh, they're adorable," she squeaked. "C-can you play with them? Aren't they dangerous?"

"They're very tame," JD said as he picked up Sherbet.

The white cat stroked his long, silky whiskers and swished the top of his soft, brush-like tail across JD's cheek.

Brianna stretched out her arms and hoisted Tangerine into her arms and snuggled her face against the little cub the same way she had when she first got Winston. The tiger cub took to her immediately, licking at her nose playfully.

Blake took the cubs to a patch of the neatly cut grass. JD and Morgan were right behind. The boys rolled on their backs (with the tigers on their chests) and wrestled with the animals. The tigers growled as they pawed at their cheeks. Blake held Tango above him, and when he got tired, he set him down. The tiger's short legs took him across the grass to the small lake, where he sipped chilly water from the shallow end.

Brianna watched Tangerine jump over to Sherbet. She rested her head on top of his, and soon both were asleep. Brianna flinched when the three cubs disappeared, leaving behind noses, whiskers, and stripes, until JD told her they'd be back soon.

Cassidy stepped from the house, standing on the stone step, and began waving to the children. Brianna followed JD, Morgan, and Blake back to the house. Once they were inside, Cassidy took their guest up the narrow glass steps to a simple door behind the fireplace. Since the door was hidden in near darkness, it could be easily overlooked.

There was one window that provided the only light, allowing them to see that this bedchamber was on the small side.

A long, circular pillow rested against the bed's headboard along with several small square ones. The wardrobe was bulky and took up so much space that it was hard for so many people to move around without bumping into one another.

Just then, JD came over and said, "Hey, Mom, Brianna needs some clothes while she's here. She can't go around looking like *that!*"

Brianna made a face. "What's that supposed to mean? There's nothing wrong with what I'm wearing."

Although what he'd said sounded like an insult, JD really didn't mean it to sound like that.

"I guess it's okay. But not for here," he said.

Cassidy turned and stepped to the wardrobe. As she turned, her long, silky skirt swayed across the floor, like ocean waters washing in and out on a sandy beach. "I've already taken care of that," she said.

Cassidy waved her arm at the wardrobe, and the door swung open, displaying neatly in the cabinet clothing in Brianna's size. Cassidy even offered to sew sequins around the hem of the skirts. Several pairs of shoes, similar to the kind that Cassidy wore, were arranged in a single row on the bottom shelf.

"Now you'll look like a genie," JD said.

The three brothers' bedchamber was at the end of the hallway on the other side of the fireplace. Blake couldn't wait to show it to her.

It was larger, and it had to be to accommodate three beds, all unmade, which extended out from the curved walls, and a three-drawer dresser on one side of the door with a freestanding mirror on the other. Sports posters of winged camel riders adorned the remaining open spaces on the walls.

Clothing was loosely spread across the floor, and as JD sized up the bedchamber, he knew they had some cleaning to do if they wanted to avoid Cassidy's fussing about it.

The three boys raised their arms, and the clothes swiftly moved into the closet. Brianna watched their every movement. The young genie brothers looked as though they were controlling puppets on strings. Then the bedcovers, blankets, and sheets changed from a crumpled mess into smooth, freshly made beds.

"We usually are very meticulous when it comes to tidying our bedchamber," Morgan said.

Cassidy looked around as her children smiled proudly.

"Oh, really?" she said sharply. "Well, you missed a sock over there." She tilted her head toward the far end of the room to make sure they knew where to find it.

Blake quickly moved his arm, and the lone sock flew into the bottom dresser drawer.

Chapter Eleven

J Dream of Genie Life

Half an hour later, Brianna emerged from her bedchamber wearing the clothing Cassidy had conjured up for her. With her hands on her skirt, Brianna spread the fabric and pirouetted like a ballerina. Veils draped down her back from a pink hat. No longer did she look like a curious Outsider; she looked more like a typical young genie girl who fit in with this genie family.

Brianna followed the boys from the fireplace across the center chamber and down to the sunken retreat, where they had something they eagerly wanted to show her.

"Come play JinJi with us," Morgan said. "We will teach you how to play."

She thought it was charming how the colorful playing pieces were in the shape of genie bottles. As Morgan explained the rules, it seemed like an easy enough game to learn.

JD rolled a pair of multiedged flat dice. Brianna pulled back from the game board when one of JD's green-glassed pieces vaporized and floated above the game board. She couldn't wait for her turn to watch her piece materialize at the exact spot that matched the numbers on the dice. She was in for a disappointment. When it was her turn to move the piece, she waited breathlessly for it to vaporize. It took only a short time for her to realize she had to move it with her finger.

As the game progressed, Brianna made longing glances into the outside world. She didn't even notice Cassidy until she came over and whispered, "A fillion for your thoughts."

"A *what?*" Brianna asked.

"A fillion. It's our money. Like a penny in your world."

"Oh!" Brianna said.

It started to set in just how different life in the bottle was from that in her grandparents' house in Ontario and her home in Colorado.

"I don't understand, Miss Cassidy. If I'm in the bottle, I should be seeing my grandparents' house. The bottle sits on a shelf in their home. Why don't I see that now?"

"I can't explain it," Cassidy began. "All I know is that once you come into the bottle, you've entered another world."

Brianna scratched the side of her head. "And that doesn't make sense," she added.

"You're in the genie world. It's a world of magic where what doesn't make sense to you is reality for us."

"Sometimes we don't see your family for days," JD said. "It's your turn again."

Brianna rolled a five and a two, and they continued playing. Morgan finally won the game, and just like they had when the game was in play, the JinJi pieces vaporized and returned to the box.

"It must be fun to do magical feats. When did you know you could do magic?" Brianna asked.

Cassidy remembered the first time her sons showed their powers. She closed her eyes and could see the first time they moved toys without touching them as if it were last night. It had happened when the triplets were five years old.

One night, nearly six years ago, JD had wanted to sleep with one of his stuffed animals. He reached out his arms. Nothing had happened—at first. With further practice, his stuffed griffin had begun to wobble, its wings flittering back and forth. Within a second, the toy had risen to a hover before floating to him.

The next morning, Morgan had tried to make his toy move across the floor. JD had made it look so easy. It had taken some coaching from JD, but Morgan's toy panda slid from one side of the room across to the other. It caught him off guard, hitting him and nearly knocking him over.

"It was so easy," JD said. He was cocky about how he said it.

Morgan gave JD an annoyed look and said, "Now look who is showing off."

Brianna turned to Blake. "What about you?"

Cassidy put her arm around her son. "Blake needed a little more time. But he got the hang of it," she said. "He's very good at enchanting things."

"What are all the things you can do? Can you show me some magic?" Brianna asked.

Cassidy looked to her sons. JD, Morgan, and Blake's eyes lit up, and they knew they couldn't pass up an opportunity to show her.

Blake squinted his eyes and stared intently at a pear on the table and tried to wave it over to him. All he could muster was changing the yellow fruit into a brass bell.

"Can't you do any better than that?" JD folded his arms and snickered.

Blake looked angry, and then he rolled up his sleeves before picking up one of the many pillows. There was a determined look on his face as he set the pillow on the water's surface in the reflecting pool. Seconds later, a two-headed ocean turtle splashed the water with its front flipper legs as it swam toward them.

Not wanting to be shown up by his brother, JD picked up another pillow, flatter and slightly larger than the one Blake had used, and put it on the water. He had intended to repeat Blake's trick. The only difference with his turtle was that it had four heads.

"Mom, JD's copying me. Make him stop!" Blake whined.

"I'm not copying—exactly," JD sneered.

"JD, don't copy your brother. Be original," Cassidy said.

By this time, Brianna had become very interested in the genie world, much like JD had become interested in the human one. She had many other questions for the triplet brothers.

"How did you learn it all?" she asked.

"Like Mom said, there were some things we could do since we were little, but we cannot do everything—we are still learning," Morgan said.

"So you go to school," Brianna said.

"School?" Blake looked baffled.

"Actually Brianna, they don't go to *school* like you know it," Cassidy said. "The Academy for Jinn Studies sends lessons with skills to learn and practice. Right now they're in their transmogrifications unit."

"Trans—what?" Brianna asked.

"Transmogrifications. Changing one object into another," Cassidy said. "Once they finish, they will go to the academy for a week of colloquiums and examinations before they move on to the next module."

"Colloquium? What's that?" Brianna asked.

Cassidy had to think a minute.

"A colloquium is a type of meeting where they get to discuss their learning and share what they can do. In this case, the boys will meet with other genies their age and be put into groups to complete assigned tasks in real-life situations."

"We can play another game. It's called 'chameleon,'" JD told her.

"Chameleon?" Brianna sighed.

"Come on. Let's go outside, and we'll show you," JD said.

On the grassy knoll, JD covered his eyes and started to count. Morgan and Blake scattered. Playing chameleon was a lot like playing hide-and-seek in the human world, only genie children were visible one second, and then before anyone knew it, they blended into the background.

"Eight . . . nine . . . ten . . ." JD shouted. "Here I come."

After JD opened his eyes, he rotated around, and as expected, there was no sign of his brothers. Morgan and Blake kept still and watched to see which direction JD would go first.

Morgan quietly reached down to the ground, picked up a pebble, and lobbed it. The small stone rustled the leaves of a shrub, prompting JD to turn quickly.

JD was hoping to see one of them unblend, even if it was just for a second or two. As Blake took a few steps toward the big tree, Morgan remained perfectly blended and giggled. However, the giggle sounds almost betrayed him. Morgan slyly dropped to his knees and stooped low to the ground. He waited a few seconds before he started to crawl.

JD turned slowly and moved to the middle of the lawn. This gave him the best view to catch either Morgan or Blake. It was frustrating for JD to know that they were probably moving, yet he couldn't detect any movement. Morgan and Blake were playing the game quite well.

"Hey, Blake," Morgan called out as JD moved closer. "JD's right behind you."

His game plan was to make JD move away from him and, hopefully, fluster Blake into revealing himself. The crafty trick worked, too.

In his attempt to get to the tree, Blake stepped on a branch, cracking it in half. JD focused on his target, just as a cheetah would stalk its helpless victim in the wild.

Morgan now could move easily throughout the yard as he continued crawling toward the large tree. Before Blake knew it, Morgan pushed him aside. Blake lost his concentration and unblended.

"There you are!" JD said gleefully. "You're *it* now, Blake."

"No fair," Blake cried. "Pushing isn't allowed!"

"Quit your complaining. Cover your eyes, and start counting," JD said.

Following some argument about whether pushing violated the rules of chameleon, they finally came to an understanding that they would refrain from pushing in all future games.

Brianna was seeing firsthand how magic enhanced life. It was nothing she had expected based on what humans believed about genies.

"You know, we have stories about genies—" Brianna started. Morgan interrupted her.

"The proper term is *jinn*," he corrected. "But we have gotten used to *genie*."

Brianna hadn't meant to insult her hosts and quickly explained the word's origins.

"It's not a bad word. It comes from the Latin word *genius*, which means a guardian spirit. I read that when I was researching what you could be. Well, anyway, there are stories about genies who live in bottles and lamps. I've even read about one who lived in inanimate objects, like rings," she told them. "They stay in their confined spaces until their masters call for them. These stories never say what they do while they wait to be called. Who knew there would be all this?"

"There's a lot more to show you," Cassidy said. "I have to get some things in Jinwiddie before we meet your father for the midday meal."

"Jinwiddie!" Brianna said. "Oh, that's the city you showed me when we were outside. Is it far from here?"

"It's not too far," Cassidy said softly as she reached into a pocket and pulled out a small piece of yellowed parchment, adding things she had forgotten to include in her list. JD peeked at the list.

"What's this stuff?" he asked. "Hamburger? Hot dogs? Pizza?"

Just as Brianna was looking forward to seeing a genie town, she was relieved to learn that they could get *regular* food.

"You can really get those here?"

"If you know the right shop, like the Outsider Gourmet Foods Shoppe. You can get just about anything," Cassidy told them. "We'll have some of your favorites, too, boys. Like filet of dragon, phoenix tongue, and donkey brains."

"Mother!" JD said.

"Yuck! Those aren't our favorites. They're Dad's," Blake said. His lips pressed together as though he had just bitten into a plump caterpillar.

"Oh, yes. They are, aren't they? I forgot," Cassidy replied with a soft giggle. Then she said, "Come," and like a small puppy, a carpet with plenty of room to carry all of them came to her side.

She reached inside a dangling bag. It looked like a small mouse searching for an escape route. She pulled out a closed fist, and when she opened her hand, she counted some shiny coins. The different-colored metal objects spangled brightly across her palm.

"These are dibbins and doblers. They're our large currency. The smaller ones are fillions and fletts," Cassidy said.

She handed one to Brianna to look at closely. It was a dobler.

"This looks just like the one I found in my pocket at Marine Gardens," she said.

JD snickered, and Brianna looked at him.

"That was me—my way to hide until we got to that place," he said.

"So you *transmogrified*." Brianna was picking up the vocabulary quickly. "Cool."

Cassidy then took the dobler back, let the coins slide off her fingers into the sack, and pulled the drawstrings to close the pouch.

"Is everyone ready to go?"

The boys nodded and quickly stepped onto the carpet.

There was short tremor before the carpet lifted off the ground. It stayed there, two to three feet high at first. Then it pulled back, ruffling the rear part of the rug before shuttling away. Everyone quickly gripped the fringe tightly to keep from falling off as they became fully airborne. Before too long, they were flying over green-patched landscapes with the assortment of buildings of the city before them.

Cassidy leaned to the left, with the children doing the same, and the carpet turned. Through the dips in flight, the cool breezes brushed across their faces. The carpet began its downward movement and soon slowed down.

"Not long now," Cassidy said.

Chapter Twelve

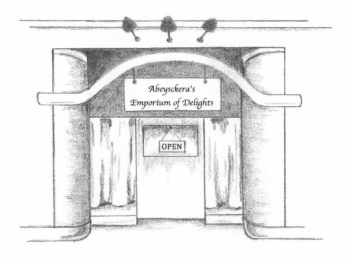

Abeysckera's Emporium of Delights

Sunbeams bounced off the pristine spires on either side of a wide, arched entrance. The carpet hovered on the outskirts of Jinwiddie, and everyone stepped off. Cassidy clapped her hands, and the carpet vanished.

Shoppers crowded Merchant Square. A variety of wares—brass jugs, baskets, and water jars—were being sold from small tarp-covered shops. Buyers were noisily bartering for vegetables, fruits, and spices. Sometimes people stopped at the tall four-sided obelisk with a pyramidal top and went through their purchases from the outdoor street vendors.

A peddler with a monkey perched on his shoulder stood on the corner. The monkey was jingling necklaces and earrings as his owner called out to passersby. The man bargained with anyone who showed any interest in the jewelry.

A short distance away, a tiny boy was receiving a firm scolding from his mother for levitating candy from a shopkeeper's hand. There was a woman with two little girls who were sitting on bobbing carpet squares. They were tethered to their mother's wrist so they wouldn't drift away from her.

In the center of the city was a vast indoor shopping mall. Cassidy and the children walked across a wide bridge that separated the building from the open-air marketplace. Inside chattering crowds were streaming into and out of the shops.

Brianna looked up at the three floors above her. A set of carpet squares moved continuously up and down by themselves to the different levels. Off the main thoroughfare were more shops, some large like Bottles, Lamps, and More and small specialty stores that sold things like books and parchments.

JD proudly pointed to one of the city offices, which included the Department of Flying Carpets, where Aristede worked. Across from the DFC, on the wide walkway, was a new Carpet Wash. Draped in front was a banner with UNDER NEW MANAGEMENT written across it. A line of genies sat patiently, waiting to get their carpets cleaned.

At the next corner, JD pointed to a sign.

"There's the Sweet and Sour Treats. Can we go there first, Mom?"

Cassidy smiled. "I think that would be a great place to begin. Don't count on eating a lot of sweets. It'll rot your tongues."

Brianna made a face that was part perplexed and part ready to laugh.

"Excuse me, Miss Cassidy, don't you mean rot our teeth?" she asked.

"No, dear. Sweets rot our tongues," Cassidy said.

"Yeah, you should have seen what happened to Morgan once when he had eaten too many chocolate-covered grasshoppers," JD said, laughing. "It took two weeks for his tongue to grow back."

"All he could do was mumble. We couldn't understand a word he was saying," Blake added.

Morgan pushed his giggling brothers.

"That is not in the least bit humorous, and it is not nice to embarrass me. What happened was awful."

"Morgan is right. Let's not bring the incident up again," their mother said.

Rows of scrumptious toppings and jars of brightly colored candies and lollipops filled the shelves of Sweet and Sour Treats.

The children placed their sundae orders and moved to the other side of the candy store. They had barely a few minutes to sit down when their ice cream dishes came to their table. Lists of toppings were posted on an attractive sign: iced goat-whisker shavings, chopped chocolate scorpions, lemon-flavored watercress, and creamy caramel dates. All they had to do was say what treats they wanted, and the topping of choice would fly onto the sundaes.

Random chatter was resonating through the shop. Over all the noise, the triplets heard someone call out, "JD, Morgan, Blake!"

The person calling to them was a rather tall, handsome boy with dark brown hair. He was looking over the smaller boys and girls. His name was Cody, and his sparkling white teeth charmed genie girls.

"Did you hear? Indra-Jindra's uncle's bottle got uncorked. He's now the property of an Outsider."

JD, Morgan, and Blake burst out laughing together, even though it was never a laughing matter when a genie belonged to an Outsider. But this was the uncle of Indra-Jindra. She was someone few people liked and who always looked down on other genies because she worked in the Jinn High Council office.

When Cassidy finished her sundae, she said, "I think it's time to go to the Outsider Gourmet Foods Shoppe."

"Do we have to go with you, Mom? Can't we just meet you at The Genie Café? We want to go to the Magical Music store first," Blake said. Chocolate grasshopper legs stuck around the sides of his mouth.

Cassidy gave a simple wave of her hand, and a handkerchief appeared.

"I don't know about letting you go unattended," she said as she wiped Blake's face.

"Please, Mom. We'll stay together," JD said.

"We solemnly vow nothing will happen," Morgan added.

Blake clasped his hands together and said, "Pleeeeeeeeease."

She relented, but only on one condition.

"I don't want you to go anywhere else. Do you understand? Don't forget we're meeting your father at noon."

They all darted toward the door, weaving through some other shop customers who had been waiting in line. Brianna was lost to them as she tried to keep up. She thought she'd been separated for good until Morgan came back and caught hold of her hand.

Outside the shop, Cassidy turned and strolled in the opposite direction and soon found herself at the Outsider Gourmet Foods Shoppe. Inside there were rows of meat and strings of sausage in a glass case.

The man behind the counter told her they were out of "pi—aa—zza," but they would have more ingredients by the end of the week. Cassidy then left the shop and walked from one store to another.

A few walkways away, as the four children were making their way to Magical Music, JD saw people gawking upward near Flynn's New and Used Flying Carpets.

"Hey, *Triplet One, Triplet Two,* and *Triplet Three,*" a brash and uppity older girl called out.

Surrounding her were two other younger genies. It was obvious she was the leader of the group, as she pushed them aside, making her way to them.

"Oh, no! Look who's here," JD said as if he'd just stepped into camel dung.

"*Indra-Jindra,*" Morgan said. He let out a groan from the side of his mouth. He turned to Brianna and added, "Let's not tell them that you are human."

"But why? I'm not ashamed to be human," Brianna said. She was a bit irritated.

"Because she loathes Outsiders, that is why," Morgan said.

Indra-Jindra was a skinny girl with black hair draped down her back almost to her waist. Her younger brother, Ian, and a larger boy stood near her, which made her feel very brave to bully others younger than she.

"Who is that guy with Indra-Jindra?" Morgan asked.

"His name is Martine," JD whispered back. "I think he's her boyfriend."

"Yuck. That's sickening," Blake said with his tongue out to one side of his mouth. He looked as though he had just swallowed a bug.

"Looking for a carpet?" Indra-Jindra said tartly. "You have to try one of the new automatic ones."

"I like the older ones better," JD said coolly.

He remembered that his father had talked about reports showing people flying the new carpets had more accidents than people who used the standard models. The thick-weaved carpets pulled to the left as they reached cruising altitudes. As a result, the new models were more difficult to control and caused a great deal of anguish for the DFC.

Indra-Jindra boasted that her father let her fly his carpet and that she had to be careful the authorities didn't catch her. "I can't wait until I get my license next month," she said.

She gave an added click of her mouth and a sneak wink, as she knew darned well that Aristede worked for the DFC. JD, Morgan, and Blake just sneered at her.

"Do you guys fly?" the spiky-haired Ian asked.

"Not yet," Blake said.

Ian prodded them further. "Surely you have taken a flying carpet out on your own at least once, haven't you?"

Blake retreated behind Morgan. JD couldn't squelch the craving to show up these snooty idiots. Morgan saw JD's reaction and placed his hand on JD's shoulder.

"Yeah. All the time. Haven't we, guys?" JD said.

Morgan and Blake nodded, even though it wasn't true.

"Can you think of any thrill greater than flying high in the open air and with such speed?" Indra-Jindra said. "Even the Outsiders don't have anything like this."

"Thank goodness there aren't too many of *them* around," Martine said.

He had a dopey smirk spread across his face. With his mousy hair parted down the middle and drooping limply, he looked like a scrawny rat. By all appearances, Indra-Jindra and Martine made unlikely companions. In reality, their attitudes made them perfect for each other.

"What do you mean by that?" Brianna asked as she scowled and put her hands on her hips. It was obvious she wasn't very happy with these genies.

"What Martine means is that our world is for us, and their world is for them," Indra-Jindra said. "I say there should be a law against them even being here. The least we could do is send all Outsiders back to where they belong, and I'm working with the viziers to see that that happens."

"And what if they can't leave because of a closed-off bottle?" Brianna asked.

"That just tells you how stupid Outsiders are," Ian said. He pushed his spiked hair upward in front. "My sister's right. Lock them up."

"That's not a nice thing to say. They're not stupid," Brianna said. "They control genies, don't they?"

"That's if they can figure out they have one," Martine said. He let out a little snicker as he playfully elbowed Ian in the side.

The lanky boy's offhand comment prompted Ian to give an earsplitting laugh, and with his mouth open, a gap between his two front teeth was revealed.

But Indra-Jindra wasn't laughing, as she didn't think Outsiders were funny at all. She harshly shoved Ian and Martine sideways and stepped closer to Brianna. She leered straight at her.

"Are you an Outsider lover or something? Outsider lovers need to have their heads examined."

"I'll have you know that I'm an—" Brianna said.

"You're a *what*?"

Indra-Jindra gave a nasty stare through her partially closed eyes.

JD jumped in to protect Brianna. "She doesn't know much about the Outsiders."

"They're so ugly," Ian said.

"Just like you," Indra-Jindra added.

Through the belly laughs, Brianna didn't say a word. They were narrow-minded bigots and didn't deserve the time of day. Instead of listening to their prejudiced opinions, she backed away from them and ran. She didn't even look back once.

"What's the matter with her now?" Indra-Jindra said.

"Brianna, wait. Stop!" Blake called to her.

"You're such an idiot, Indra-Jindra. Can't you ever stifle that mouth of yours?" JD asked.

"What did I say, Triplet One?" Indra-Jindra asked. She sounded almost angelic.

"I hope your uncle gets to be with his Outsider for a long, long time," JD said back to her.

By the time the boys caught up with her, Brianna had found an empty table in Magical Music. She sat there with her arms crossed and the scowl on her face etched deep.

"Do not let those baboons get to you. They are not very bright, especially that Indra-Jindra and her brother. She just thinks she is important because she works for the Jinn High Council. She actually works as a clerk for one of the viziers."

"It's okay to be mad at them."

They became quiet, and Cassidy moved out from behind a table and gently brushed the girl's cheek with the back of her hand. When she learned what Indra-Jindra had said about Outsiders, Cassidy said, "I'd be angry at them, too, Brianna."

"You know how Indra-Jindra can be, Mom," Blake said. "We tried to tell Brianna that."

"They're right, you know. Unfortunately, there are some genies who hate the idea of Outsiders gaining control over them," Cassidy explained.

Brianna turned swiftly and said, "Humans didn't make the rules."

"Of course not, dear. Too bad for them, because if they spent time with Outsiders like we have, they would see what wonderful people they are," Cassidy added. "Now let's forget about them and go have lunch, shall we?"

Aristede was already waiting for them at The Genie Café. It was a very noisy place. A few older men, who sat sipping a bitter brew, were engaged in a loud conversation about enchantment laws. The words and language they spoke were obscure and at times difficult to understand. But JD, Morgan, and Blake did recognize a few words and laughed. Sitting at another table nearby, several female patrons talked nonstop about the disgraceful events they had seen in an entertainment orbular.

After finishing his midday meal, Aristede bade them good-bye and returned to his office, while the rest of his family made their way down the walkway and veered to the right. Two doors in was a narrow, but long, store called Abeysckera's Emporium of Delights.

JD pushed open the door to the specialty shop, and as he did, the bell above the door frame made a dinging noise.

Brianna looked in all directions at the wondrous items. In the glass display case on the far wall were a variety of round objects made of metal. These talismans, engraved with different figures (usually animals) were worn for protection and to ward off evil. On the shelves next to the display were piles of paper parchment in every color imaginable. Most genies still preferred the traditional parchment for its thickness and texture.

There were some oddities that people were buying in the open-air shops outside the mall, but none as interesting as those found in Abeysckera's Emporium of Delights where not all the "delights" were delightful.

But the strangest items were on the other side of the little store. In an area segregated from the rest of the shop were creatures flittering their wings. What made them even more interesting was that they had heads, wings, and beaks of an eagle and bodies and tails of a lion. The sign over the entryway said GRIFFIN CORNER. Griffins had become popular household pets.

JD, Morgan, and Blake made their way past other genies to the homemade potion-making section, which had shelves full of very unusual items. Many airtight sealed jars contained parts of living creatures, like dung beetle shells and yak intestines, as well as some things they hadn't heard of before. It was there that a boy with two brown moles above his lips waved and hurried to them.

"Hi. What are you doing here?"

"Hello, Sammy," Morgan said. Whereas the triplets' friend Cody was tall, Sammy was a much shorter boy. "We are just showing—"

"Who's she?" Sammy asked. He definitely wasn't listening to Morgan, as his attention had shifted quickly to Brianna.

"She's a friend who's visiting us," Blake said.

"I didn't know you had someone staying with you," Sammy said.

Sammy edged forward. He tilted his round head with a pointy chin and moved in close until he was stooping under her face. Brianna could feel his breath across her cheek. He pulled back, eager to ask her a lot of questions.

"What's your name?"

"It's Brianna."

"How long are you visiting the triplets?"

She drew up her shoulders indifferently and didn't say anything.

His eyes stared at her until he announced, "You look like a nice girl."

"And you look like a nice boy," Brianna replied.

A boyishly handsome man waded through the people at the same time Cassidy asked, "You're not alone here, are you, Sammy?"

"No, he isn't," the man said.

Cassidy raised her head, and as the man turned, two dangling gold earrings swiveled from his earlobes. There was little doubt that he was Sammy's father, Alexander, who had the same pointy chin and peppermint breath as his only son. Along with Aristede, he worked at the DFC.

"What a surprise," he said. "Ari didn't tell me you'd be here."

"The boys have a birthday coming up, so I thought this store would give me some gift ideas, Alex," she said.

"We're here to find gifts for them, too," Alexander said.

Sammy jumped into the conversation. It was a bad habit of his.

"Wait until you see what we got. Mr. Abeysckera just took our order," Sammy said. He was hardly able to keep from exploding with his secret.

"There, there, Sammy. Don't give the surprise away," Alexander said. He began arranging his son's uncombed hair.

"We'll see you on the thirtieth. Say good-bye, Sammy. I have to get back to work."

Together they left the shop and walked up the thoroughfare.

On the back wall, an emerald-green drape hanging waved as the ceiling fan turned. The creases in the material formed shadows in the folds. It caught the children's attention, so they moved in for a closer look.

"Good afternoon, young ones." It was Master Jindrake. "I see you have an Outsider with you. What are you called, my dear?"

"B-B-Brianna."

"You're the Outsider the boys told me about. Fascinating situation," he said. "It's a pleasure meeting you, Miss Brianna. I wish you great speed in your return home."

"Th-thank y-you."

JD lowered his head.

"Then you know we belong to Brianna."

"I thought you might continue to talk to your Outsider. The temptation was too great to keep you from communicating with her," he said. "And meeting your friend confirmed that suspicion."

"We told our parents everything, starting with how Brianna could hear us," Morgan said.

"The mystery of an Outsider's ability to listen in on conversations inside bottles you'll still need to solve," he told them. "But it was best to let it all play out."

"What do you mean, sir?" Blake asked.

"Your powers are getting stronger. I saw that during your recent assessment," Jindrake said. "I believe you've been selected for something very important."

The bell at the shop's door dinged. Jindrake turned. It was obvious by the way he looked at the newcomers that he had been expecting them. He bowed to excuse himself.

"May the fortune of the twelve jinn be with you."

He walked over to the newly arrived customers. He talked for a bit with a man and wife with their two youngsters before leading them to another part of the store. It looked as though he knew these people well. Morgan recognized this man.

"You know who that is, do you not?"

JD looked and shook his head.

"No, not really," he said.

"That is the vizier for enchantment laws, Master Vartan," Morgan said.

"Master Jindrake knows everyone," Blake said in a whisper.

Brianna took a step and stared at the vizier.

"Do you think he could help me? If he's in charge of laws, perhaps he could change a few so I could go home through another bottle or something."

They reminded her that Aristede had already talked to the Jinn High Council, and if that were a possibility, it would have happened by now.

Brianna dropped her head and made her way to the parchment section, where she picked up a book of blank parchment pages. The bindings were stitched with sturdy threads, and the cover was colored with inks of different hues, in swirls like those found on a marble. There were different writing instruments on the shelf below.

"Do you like that book?" Cassidy said. "It would make a lovely journal to write about your time here with us."

"I guess it would," Brianna said. "Are they expensive?"

"Not really. Only a dibbin and a few fletts. I can get it for you if you'd like."

Brianna smiled and didn't say anything.

As they made their way toward the exit, Brianna wrapped her arms around the new journal, clutching it tightly. She was quietly happy for the gift and couldn't wait to begin writing about her experiences.

The last rays of light grazed the glass buildings as the sun began to duck beneath the horizon separating the skies from the earth. Streaks of color ranging from deep orange to blue and purple began filling the sky. The crowd in the open marketplace had thinned. The only ones left were the merchants who were packing up their wares and wheeling their carts away.

"If we want to get home quickly, we'll have to vaporize," Cassidy said.

Brianna frowned and whispered into Morgan's ear, "Aren't we flying back to your house on a carpet? What does it mean to vaporize?"

"Just watch," Morgan said.

"Everyone hold hands," Cassidy said.

JD, Morgan, and Blake grasped hold of each other's hands. Brianna reached over and slipped her hand into JD's palm. Their bodies all became pillars of smoke, purple in color! Within seconds, the smoke dissolved, and they were gone.

Chapter Thirteen

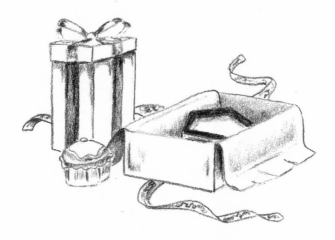

A Special Gift
for the Genie Brothers
(and More Surprises!)

The invitation read:

> You're cordially invited to JD, Morgan,
> and Blake's birthday party.
>
> Saturday, July 30th
> Two o'clock in the afternoon
>
> ### RSVP

Every year for the triplets' birthday, Cassidy threw a lavish celebration. Clearly she delighted in planning the event, putting up decorations, and organizing party games—basically rushing around frantically trying to make everything perfect. It was so hectic, and Cassidy counted on her fingers the number of tasks that still needed to be done.

Aristede was, in the meantime, cooking food for everyone. He saw himself a gourmet chef with a specialty in dragon meat—dragon burgers, dragon rump roast (which took several days to prepare), and dragon kabobs. He saved his cooking skills for special occasions. The boys' birthday certainly fell into that category.

Even the triplets chipped in (and why shouldn't they—it was their birthday).

JD waved his arms, and a tower of plush pillows appeared. He directed them around the room.

With the motion of blowing air from his mouth, Morgan had all the colored balloons inflated. With his arms outstretched and with palms facing upward, he gradually moved his hands upward; the balloons complied with his command.

Finally, Blake snapped his fingers, and rolls of narrow paper streamers appeared. He twirled around his finger as if he were painting a picture, making the streamers twist from one part of the room to the other.

Their home looked festive, and they were now ready for the party guests to arrive. Still, Cassidy had one more thing on her mind—getting all the party games set up.

Blake wasn't interested in the games. Rather he focused his attention on something more important.

"Where are our birthday presents, anyway?" he asked. He looked all around.

Aristede grinned devilishly as he stroked his goateed face. "You'll just have to wait until your party," he said.

"But, Dad, we cannot wait *that* long!" Morgan said.

"That's just too bad," Aristede said before he went back to basting the dragon meat.

At two o'clock, vapors started streaking through the walls. The party guests began arriving.

Darren and Chloe, two of the triplets' friends, who had been neighbors and now lived in Jinwiddie, were first. They were the same height even though Darren was three years older than his round-faced sister.

The triplets' best friend, Cody, was next, with his brother and sister. Brianna recognized him from her visit to Jinwiddie. Ryan and Faith had the same dark umber-brown hair as Cody. Freckles dusted Ryan's cheeks.

Outside two figures were flying on a carpet; one of them was large, and the other was small. There was a burst of laughter, then silence, and laughter again. When the carpet came into view, it was Sammy and his father, Alexander, who had been telling jokes ("Do you know how to drive a genie crazy? Put him in a round bottle and tell him to stand in the corner!").

Jindrake was invited too and made his usual flamboyant entrance via purple smoke from the glassy floor.

Aristede pressed his hand to Alexander's and then to Jindrake's.

"Where are Aristede's famous dragon kabobs?" Alexander asked.

Aristede smiled broadly. "Let's start with some dragon bruschetta."

With his bony-knuckled fingers, Alexander took a piece of toasted bread with tomato, basil, and dragon meat topping. A tasty sauce gave it that little extra flavor. Some of the diced dragon wedges fell into his lap. There was plum wine for adults and pomaberry cola with whipped cream for the children.

While Alexander and Aristede talked about work, Sammy followed Brianna, bombarding her with more questions about what she liked to do back home and who her favorite camel racer was. He was a lot like Devyn Bratt and was as uninhibited as Devyn (if not more so). The difference between them was that he wasn't annoying, and she found his interest in her flattering.

Cassidy gathered all the youngsters and hurried them to the oblong reflecting pool. Meanwhile, across from them in the center chamber appeared a zebra. Everyone knew right away they were going to play pin the tail on the zebra.

"You play this game with a real zebra?" Brianna asked.

"How else would you play?" Sammy asked.

The thin zebra tail he was holding swished back and forth, even slapping him in the face a few times. The zebra whinnied every time it did, too, and Sammy almost thought the animal enjoyed it.

Squinting one eye, Sammy put the tail at eye level, taking aim at the zebra's rump. Instead of walking toward the animal, he let go of the tail, which then floated to the zebra's striped body. Immediately the children began shouting at the animal.

As she watched the ruckus, Brianna asked, "What is everybody doing?"

"Distracting the zebra, so it will move. That way the tail does not land in the right place," Morgan explained.

The tail jiggled around in midair, and the zebra took a step, moving from its spot. As it did, it became more difficult for the tail and body to reunite. Sammy had to anticipate which way the zebra would move. All that mattered then was to concentrate until the tail reattached itself. The dangling black tail wound up behind the right side, near the rump.

"Not too bad," Darren said. "At least you got the tail in the same general area as the zebra's behind, Sammy."

Brianna clicked her tongue and moved away from the play area. It was very distasteful for her to watch the game any longer.

While JD played, Brianna quietly left the house and made her way up the hill. The patchy cloud cover eclipsed the blue skies, with the sun shining one minute and clouds drifting through the next. The weather had been unpredictable all week.

It was Chloe's turn, and as she aimed the tail, JD saw Brianna wasn't there. No one remembered seeing her leave the bottle house. He went looking for her and found her sitting under the giant tree.

"I got the tail on the back of the knee," JD said. "Not bad in this game."

"Hmm." She shook her head. "I think it's cruel—for the animal, I mean."

"It doesn't hurt it," JD said.

"Maybe not." Brianna sighed. "But in my world, we don't take an animal's tail and make it a game to see who can get it back on."

They sat staring at the bottle house and didn't look at each other for the longest time. JD looked up at the creeping gray-lined underbelly of clouds. Instead he said, "It looks as if it might rain."

"I guess we should go inside," Brianna said.

"Yeah. It's time for our cakes and presents," JD said eagerly.

They brushed the blades of grass off their clothes and hurried down the hill.

Cassidy had moved to the other side of the chamber after all the tails were dangling on the zebra's striped body. Cody was the winner, as he got the tail closest to its rightful place.

A silver tray appeared filled with small individual cakes frosted in dark chocolate. There was one for each party guest. On top of each cake, like a cherry on a chocolate sundae, was a colored candy. The candy for each cake was a different color. Within a few seconds a cake floated to each of the children.

"Oh, goody," Ryan exclaimed. "Changling gumdrops. I love those!"

"This should be fun," Alexander said as he waited for some extreme transmogrifications to begin.

Ryan put a green gumdrop in his mouth and began chewing. He dropped his head, turned sideways, and backed away from the others. His face squished; it was painful for him to swallow.

Shortly afterward, Ryan turned pale orange, and his lips began to pucker. Gills appeared on his neck, while three blue tail feathers grew on his behind. Before too long, Ryan became a bird-fish, and everyone laughed as he flapped his wings and jumped around trying to take flight, gulping for air at the same time. Within minutes, the transmogrification faded, and Ryan was back to his normal self.

"My turn," Sammy said.

During this change, Sammy's ears became pointy, black, and droopy. With the head of a bat, Sammy's body sprouted a long, tan-colored tail and a shaggy mane around his neck. His lionlike roar made the others jump.

"It's been a long time since I've seen a bat-lion," Chloe said. "I didn't think that change happened anymore."

Chloe and Darren tossed light blue-green gumdrops in their mouths at the same time. Their arms recoiled, and their noses became beaks. The other half of their bodies morphed into stallions. Each parrot-horse mimicked what the other said. Faith, Sammy, and Ryan shrieked with glee.

When it was Faith's turn, she picked the red gumdrop off her cake. Before putting it on her tongue, she took a look at it.

"Red is my favorite. I think I know what I'll become," she said. She didn't really know, since every gumdrop could make any transmogrification.

Faith's gumdrop took effect immediately as the clips that kept her hair pulled back on the sides of her head popped off. Her face became furry, and whiskers grew rapidly under her nose. Her legs became the tail fins of a goldfish. She became a very unique cat-fish, and even after returning to her normal form, she still meowed for several minutes.

Cody remembered the first time he had a changling gumdrop, and it hadn't been a pleasant experience for him. When he didn't return to his normal body shape for several hours, healers had to be called in to help end the transmogrification. Since that time, the genies manufacturing the changling gumdrops had refined the quality control process so the length of the change wouldn't exceed a minute.

Cody hesitated slightly before popping the gumdrop into his mouth. Antlers began protruding out of his head, and a scaly green tail grew on his backside. He became a deer-alligator.

The triplets threw their gumdrops in the air and caught the candies on their tongues. The room filled with anticipation as the boys scrunched their faces and gulped. Their transmogrifications seemed to happen much more quickly than any of the others.

JD's legs suddenly looked like long sticks, and he had the head of a bovine. He became a crane-bull. Morgan became part sea creature with a furry body that made him look like a dolphin-bear. Blake ended up as a walrus-scorpion with two front teeth that extended down his chin and with a curved lower body. His stinger flicked, startling Faith and Chloe, and making him more intimidating than his brothers. And like the others, the triplets reverted without experiencing any side effects.

Brianna tugged at Morgan's shirt and said, "Those candies are weird. Why would you want to do that to your bodies?"

"They are like toys. They are not dangerous, or anything like that," Morgan said. "It only lasts a few seconds. I mean, no one has ever gotten sick. Try one."

"B-but wh-what if I-I c-can't—" Brianna said. She was very apprehensive about trying one on her own.

Before she could protest any further, Morgan popped a gumdrop into Brianna's mouth. She gulped. There was no chance of chewing, because she immediately swallowed it! She hoped no one was watching as her head began to bob, and her waist began to expand. She developed a puffy tail, and before she knew it, she turned into a turkey-bunny. Fortunately for her, Morgan was right. Her experience lasted just as long as the others had, and she was no worse off for it.

Jindrake smiled and muttered under his breath, "Children's games." A muffled giggle followed.

After the children finished eating the little cakes, everyone gathered around the small pile of wrapped gifts by the fireplace. Blake picked one up and began rattling it near his ear. JD and Morgan did the same with other packages.

The three boys waved their hands, and the wrapping paper began tearing off. Torn strips and pieces flew in all directions. The presents from Brianna contained boxes of chocolate-covered grasshoppers. They quickly shoved several into their mouths.

"And what do you have to say to Brianna?" Cassidy asked. By the tone of her voice, she was disgusted with their manners.

"Dank ou," Morgan said.

Darren stepped toward the triplets with a cylindrical package. Once the wrapping came off the parcel, there was an odd-looking fat orange candle. But it wasn't an ordinary candle. This one had a carved face with chubby cheeks, and it looked as if it were asleep.

"I know what this is," Morgan said.

JD and Blake looked at each other and shrugged.

"And you do, too. Come on. Think! Remember, Ambrose had one, and it predicted his great-uncle Felix would become a genie to that fisherman," Morgan said. "It is a seer candle. You know—it predicts the future."

"Oh, yeah. I remember now," Blake said. "Felix smelled like tuna when he got back."

Blake dropped low so that he could get up close to the seer candle. His nose almost touched it. He put his finger under the candle's bulging chin and pulled his finger back and forth to get it to move. This proved to be a colossal mistake. In an instant, the candle snapped at him with its teeth, and Blake jumped back. With its eyes opening slowly, waking up from a deep sleep, the candle furrowed its eyebrows.

"Do you *mind?*" the snooty seer candle said. "I was having a marvelous dream about riding a sea horse across the oceans."

"I-I a-am s-sorry," Blake stammered. "I-I d-didn't kn-know s-s-seer candles h-had d-dreams."

"Why would we *not* have dreams?" the indignant candle asked. He then arched his neck and turned his head, as best as he could. "What a droll place this is. You do not intend to put me on that mantel there, *do you?*"

JD and Blake managed only to shake their heads. Morgan, on the other hand, found the seer candle quite amusing.

"I think we will call you Ebert," he said.

"Ebert!" the seer candle cried. He was highly insulted. "I will have you know that I already have a name."

"You do?" JD asked.

When the candle threw him an infuriated look, JD modified his tone.

"You do. Yes, yes, you do."

"My name is Silvestri," the candle said proudly. "Now let me get a good look around. Go on, pick me *up.*"

Morgan didn't say a word and did as Silvestri had ordered. He held him in his hands carefully, with the face pointing outward. No sooner did Silvestri scan the room than he let out a deep sigh and said, "I have no choice. This place will have to do. You may place me down again."

Morgan put him on the marble rim of the reflecting pool, and suddenly, Silvestri closed his eyes and began to sway. A flame erupted on the wick.

"Oooohhh. Oooohhh. I see something," Silvestri moaned. Then he said:

The time has come for the brothers three
To solve an unexpected mystery.
It all begins with an arrival today.
Let the pictures guide your way.

Silvestri yawned with a great, loud growl before going back into a deep slumber. Within a few minutes, he even began to snore.

JD crinkled his nose. "What's *that* supposed to mean?" he asked.

"Beats me," Blake said. "Let's open our other presents."

The triplets' next gift came from Sammy, who excitedly announced to everyone that he had picked out kaleido-bubbles. A telescope-like device, the kaleido-bubbles contained colored glass at the end of a viewing shaft. It provided multiple images of whatever was in the viewfinder. When twisted, the kaleido-bubbles expelled bubbles with those same images in them.

Next, Cassidy smiled as she handed three small, brightly wrapped packages to the boys. They couldn't weigh more than a few ounces. Aristede made his way over to his wife and put his arms around her. His smile was just as wide as hers. Together they said, "Happy birthday!"

JD and Blake quickly took the packages with their names and were halfway through unwrapping the presents, while Morgan took his time peeling the thin paper away. Inside, tissue paper still covered the boys' presents, which, when scaled back and completely unwrapped, showed velvet pouches. They opened the pouches and pulled out shiny metal objects attached to chains.

"Talismans! They are just like the ones we saw when we were in Jinwiddie," Morgan exclaimed.

"Why do you think we went there?" Cassidy asked. "I hope you like the ones I chose for you. In fact, Jindrake was extremely helpful with his suggestions."

Jindrake stepped forward and said, "A talisman is a wonderful tool for a genie." He picked one up. "Remember that there is power in sameness, as there is power in differences. The three of you together can make anything happen."

The triplets pulled the metallic objects over their heads and adjusted how they hung around their necks. Each talisman was different. JD's had a dragon. The animal on Morgan's was a unicorn, and although Blake was fond of camels, he liked the elephant because, as he said, the elephant represented strength.

As they fondled the engraved details, Morgan wondered about Master Jindrake's comment about their gifts.

"What do you think he meant—power in sameness, power in difference?"

"We are the same because we're triplets," JD said.

"What about the difference?" Blake asked. "What does *that* mean?"

"That is what I am saying. It is all very cryptic," Morgan added.

"Why doesn't he just come out and tell us what he means?" JD continued.

"That is just his way. Maybe he was warning us to be careful," Morgan said.

There wasn't a whole lot of time to think about it. Aristede pulled his hand out from behind his back to reveal an orbular.

"Now here's the gift from your uncle Jasper," he said.

"It's an orbular," Blake said in a low voice.

"Not just any orbular. Watch it and see," Aristede said.

Aristede released the orbular, and it hovered like a hummingbird. The children gathered around to watch tan and brown shapes turn into camels inside the milky white sphere.

"I already have orbulars with camel races," Blake said. His face showed just how disappointed he was. "I have a whole collection of them."

"You don't understand. It's not just any camel race," Aristede said. "We're going to the Jinn Cup Derby. Uncle Jasper got tickets for you. That's your birthday present from him."

Going to the Jinn Cup Derby caused a great deal of excitement, which was especially evident by the beaming expressions on the men's faces. They were acting like giddy boys.

"The Jinn Cup Derby! That's the most well-known and honored event of the year," Alexander said. "Those tickets are difficult to get."

He was right about that. To get tickets to *this* race would take knowing someone close to the racing association.

"Jasper has entered his fastest camel," Aristede explained.

Suddenly their attention shifted to a tinkling sound, like that of a table knife gently tapping the side of a half-empty water glass. The noises soon echoed all around them. Everyone looked quickly around in all directions.

JD was the first to spot something glimmer above them. It turned out to be a superbly wrapped box with a golden bow. Just like the orbular, the package hung there in midair. When Blake tried to seize hold of the parcel, it moved again and descended to the floor.

Scrawled across the notepaper attached to the gift was, "To Justin David, Morgan, and Blake." That was all that was written on the tag. There was no name of the person who had sent it.

Blake lifted the object and quickly discovered that it wasn't as heavy as it looked. Under the wrapping was a five-sided ebony-black box with carved symbols on the top panel. Inlaid on every side of the box were painted pictures that had faded over time.

"It's an old box," Blake said. He handed it over to JD.

Upon closer scrutiny, the boys saw that each painting showed the same young man wearing a pointed, twirly turban. His shirt was blood red. Attached to the light yellowish-green sash around his trim waist hung a mighty sword. The paintings didn't seem to be connected in any way. If there was a story to tell in the pictures, the connections were not readily seen.

Without any warning, JD let go of the box. He shook his head and repeated, "No! No! No! It's not possible."

"What's the matter? What happened?" Cassidy asked.

"I-I could have sworn the man in that picture just moved!"

Aristede picked up the box, handling it with care.

"Nothing's moving on it now."

JD was still skeptical.

Aristede handed the ebony box to Jindrake.

When Jindrake had worked for the Supreme High Council of the Jinn, one of his responsibilities had been overseeing the preservation of their culture's antiquities. He took his job quite seriously. If anyone could help them, he could.

Jindrake examined the relic closely and was delighted by what he saw. He just couldn't resist touching the wood edges, the ribbed markings, and the painting panels.

"It's an exquisite artifact. This box is very old, very old indeed. Look at how faded the pictures have become," he said. "The writings, however, are in the ancient jinn language. They go back to the time of the first jinn. I have seen drawings like this in the ancient parchments at the Library of Records and Antiquities, but I'm not sure what they mean. We can at least translate the markings and find out what they say. If you like, we can meet at the library in the morning."

Aristede nodded, and Jindrake took great care of the box as he handed it back to him.

There was a brief stillness in the room before they heard a loud shriek. It took a few more seconds for anyone to realize it was Brianna who let out the scream. She had been peering through the boys' kaleido-bubbles, intrigued by the images. This time the bubbles emitted the image of a dark figure.

There at the window in the door, a hooded man was staring at them. The shadow from the cloak's hood made it impossible to see his face. He pulled away when he realized that he had been discovered.

"Someone's watching us!" Brianna said as she felt her ice-cold blood run through her body.

But even as everyone turned to look, the cloaked figure was gone.

Chapter Fourteen

Secrets in the Library
of Records and Antiquities

All the party guests had left by the time the first lightning flashed and thunder boomed.

The boys didn't sleep a wink that night as the raindrops drummed down on the windowpanes. In less than twenty-four hours, not only had they received a mysterious box and an odd prediction from an odd candle, but they also had so many questions about both:

Who had sent them the box?

What did the markings say?

What did the prediction mean?

The wood was old and crackled, and there were embossed letters along the top of the box. Blake actually thought it was just a piece of old wood with pictures and carvings. That changed when Morgan put the box up to his ear and shook it. Whatever was in the box made a rattling noise.

Now that they had their mysterious box with pictures on it, along with Silvestri's prediction with the reference to 'an unexpected mystery' that involved pictures, it looked like the two were related.

JD saw Morgan was in deep thought. He asked, "There's something else, isn't there?"

Morgan looked like he was a thousand miles away, and he looked right through JD when he said, "I was just thinking about what Master Jindrake said." Morgan refocused. "He thinks we've been chosen for something. We are 'the brothers three.' It is our mystery to solve."

"And what about Brianna hearing us through the bottle and finally coming here? Do you think that's part of it, too?" JD continued. He couldn't help but look at Morgan, and the two of them traded fretful stares.

"No—not between Brianna and the box," Morgan said hesitantly.

"But you do think that man was here because of the box, right?" JD said.

"It certainly is creepy that someone was watching us at our party," Morgan explained cautiously. "Someone wants the box, and that takes us back to what Silvestri said."

Blake listened closely to his brothers, and he really wanted to find out who had sent the box to them. They could be jumping to all the wrong conclusions.

Although JD still had doubts about a connection among the recent events, his sense of adventure was beginning to kick in. After a few minutes, he flashed a sly smile.

"It *is* kind of exciting, isn't it?"

Blake puckered his lips at the same time he sucked in his cheeks. He looked like a fish. The more they talked about the series of events, the less he wanted to find a way to open the box. He didn't agree with JD at all and didn't find it fun anymore. Thank goodness it was their bedtime, so he wouldn't have to think about any of it.

The following morning, the smell of breadfruit pancakes spread through the bottle.

After they had eaten two stacks of pancakes, JD asked, "Dad, are we still going to Jinwiddie?"

Aristede nodded. He took a sip from his cup. Jindrake would be expecting them at the library at ten o'clock, although Cassidy wondered if the rain would postpone their trip. Aristede assured her it wouldn't. In fact, *The Orbular Times* indicated the rain was moving east. It already had passed through Jinwiddie.

"Can Brianna come with us? There still is so much of the city to show her," Morgan said.

"I don't see why not," Aristede said. "It's nice that you want to include her. Where is she, anyway? I haven't seen her all morning."

Morgan took a quick bite of his toast covered with kiwi jelly before he went to find Brianna, who had spent the morning alone next to the fountain, writing in her new journal. The splashing water had a soothing effect and allowed her to think about what she wanted to include. She scribbled on the blank parchment paper, filling three pages. It reminded her of Granddad when he wrote in his notebook.

She began with the voices she had heard and quickly shifted her story to life inside the genie bottle. She wrote about how different it was from what she had believed it would be like based on the stories she had read about genies. There were so many more things, like Jinwiddie and the people she had met. She eagerly wrote about it all.

When Morgan joined her, he sat on the square cushion and wrapped his arms around a scarlet pillow. He was excited about going to Jinwiddie again, and he longed to begin the trip. He wished that they would leave immediately after they were done with the morning meal.

"I hope you find what you're looking for," Brianna said softly.

"We may not learn too much until we find out who sent it to us. If only there was a name on the card," Morgan said. "Dad said you could come with us. Will you?"

"No. I don't think so. I think I'll just stay here," she said. She then hunched over her journal to write a few more thoughts. There was so much to include about life in the genie world.

Brianna then lowered her journal and peered around the edge of the window frame, gazing blankly through the glass. There was a reason she chose to write at the window that looked out on the Carrutherses' home, and Morgan knew exactly what that reason was. He wanted to be sensitive to her feelings while at the same time provide her with encouragement.

"It will be okay. We will find a way to get you back home."

"You don't know that. It's been weeks now, and the opening to this bottle is still closed. Your dad even checked at work about another way back home."

"That does not mean you will be here forever. The tops of bottles get uncorked all the time. I remember when Maximilian, one of our instructors at the academy—"

He didn't have a chance to finish his story.

"I haven't seen them since I've been here," she whispered to herself. The yearning to see her granddad and gramma was overwhelming.

"I am sorry, Brianna. I did not mean to upset you," Morgan said.

When he saw her reaction, Morgan didn't need to be asked to leave her alone right now, and he knew right away that it was best to give her some privacy. He rejoined the rest of the family in the eating area.

"Mom, Brianna wants to stay here," he announced.

Cassidy turned to him. "Anything the matter?"

"She misses home," Morgan said. "She thinks she will never get back to her world. I tried to tell her it would happen, but she does not believe me."

"Poor thing. The party yesterday must have made her homesick. Maybe spending some alone time, just the two of us girls, will help," Cassidy said.

After the morning meal was finished, it took only a few minutes for Aristede, JD, Morgan, and Blake to leave for their meeting with Jindrake in Jinwiddie. JD, with the box under one arm, joined his free hand with Blake's, and Blake grabbed Morgan's arm. A few seconds later, they were gone.

Cassidy went over to Brianna and sat down close to her.

"Have you seen anyone yet?" she asked.

Brianna shook her head.

Cassidy brought some of the boys' chocolate-covered grasshoppers, but Brianna refused to take one. Cassidy gave her a nudge, telling her they really tasted like chocolate-covered raisins.

Reluctantly, Brianna picked up a piece of chocolate and took a few bites.

Her eyes widened to the size of a dobler, showing the whites around the pupils. Someone had appeared at the window. The face was lost in thought, looking for a book on the shelf. That face belonged to Christian.

"Granddad!" she shouted. She frantically waved her arms about her head. "I see Granddad. There he is. Granddad! Granddad!"

The view of the large tree had given way to the human world again. The change took place so quickly, Brianna blinked to make sure it had actually happened.

Christian went to the side of his desk and pulled open the drawer, from which he retrieved a brown leather-bound photo album. He just sat there in his chair, turned the pages, and looked from photograph to photograph. Brianna hopped up on her knees to get a better view of the pictures.

The black-and-white photographs in the family album showed the first Carrutherses, who had come to the United States in the early 1900s. There were pictures of her great-grandfather Robert and his wife, Margrit, in front of a Victorian house and standing next to their first automobile. There were pictures of other members of their family—Robert and Margrit's three sons (one of whom was a young Christian) and two daughters.

Brianna thought her granddad looked sad sitting there.

Cassidy went pale watching the Outsider. She had a faraway look on her face.

"Is he a good grandfather, Brianna?" she asked.

"The best. I love him and Gramma, and I know they love me."

"I think he's worried about you."

Cassidy's unbroken stare continued, even as she pushed aside a tear from her face, her hand shaking. Christian flipped several album pages. When he came to photos with Casey, Carson, and Kyle, the corners of his mouth turned up and grew into a wide grin.

"Miss Cassidy, are you okay? You're . . . you're trembling," Brianna said. "What's the matter?"

But before she could get an answer to her question, Brianna bounded to her feet. Someone else had just joined Christian.

"That's my grandmother. Her name is Isabelle, but Granddad calls her Belle."

Brianna and Cassidy became eavesdroppers and listened in.

"There you are. I thought you were going to the workshop to play with your trains."

"I was," Christian said. "And I don't *play* with my trains, dear."

"I was hoping to get a smile out of you."

Isabelle sat next to him on the armrest, wrapped her arms around her husband, and settled her head on his.

Christian closed the photo album and let it rest on the desk.

"I was just looking at pictures of the family," he said solemnly.

"Kyle is down with the police investigators again," Isabelle told him.

Brianna was surprised to hear that her mother and father were there, too. They were on their way home when she had left. It was one of the wishes she had made.

"Allison is in her room. She's so upset," Isabelle said, sighing.

"And what about us, Belle?" Christian asked, coming close to losing his calm demeanor.

"They still blame us for Bree's disappearance," Isabelle said. "One minute she's here; the next minute she's gone. No trace of her whatsoever. Just like—"

The back door slammed.

"There's Kyle. He's back from the police station."

Christian clutched Isabelle's hand and patted it before they made their way into the other room. The support they got from each other felt reassuring.

And just as quickly as the outside world appeared, it vanished before Brianna and Cassidy's eyes. The last remnants of the wet storm replaced the view of the human world. Brianna crept close to the window and cleared away some of the fog off the glass pane.

"I'm still here!" Brianna cried out. "Granddad! Gramma!"

Cassidy tried her best, but she just couldn't take it any longer. She took Brianna into her arms and held her tightly, rocking the girl for a few moments.

"The rain has stopped," Cassidy said. "Let's take Sherbet, Tango, and Tangerine outside for a while and play with them. Then we can make a wonderful midday meal for Aristede and the boys."

Brianna could only raise a flimsy smile and nod. Cassidy tenderly released Brianna from her hold before patting her lap with her hand. The three tigers, who had been resting by the fireplace, came to her.

As they went outside, Brianna said, "Do you really expect they have information about the box in the library?"

"Like Jindrake said, they'll be able to make out what the markings say. It's a start."

"I hope they find out a lot about it."

The Library of Records and Antiquities was a separate building on the other side of the shopping mall, facing the obelisk in the center of Jinwiddie. Aristede, JD, Morgan, and Blake materialized in front of the building near the only public entrance to the grand hall.

One of the two eight-foot-tall guards held one side of the double doors open and welcomed them inside.

Many more guards were scattered throughout the first floor. There they stood like statues, protecting their culture's most revered icons. These guards had devoted themselves to a lifetime of service.

The library was a magnificent place, and the triplets' eyes darted around to absorb it all—the intricate mosaic floors in the entrance chamber between the outer door and the inside of the building, and the floor-to-ceiling bookcases on either side of the vast room. In the glass display cases were a long, narrow carpet made of dried hemp (a floor mat that the information plate said was one of the first flying carpets) and genie containers from through the ages (bottles, lamps, rings, and even small hand mirrors).

A variety of smaller items filled other cases. There were clay jars, pewter medallions, hairbrushes, goblets, cutlery, and early, yet crude, kaleido-bubbles. A tall case stood at the very end of the row. It looked like a glass closet, since it contained a colorful gown and a pair of silk slippers belonging to one of the human princesses who had become one of the first jinn.

Halfway down the massive hall was a grand staircase. A set of polished stone steps rose to a single platform. Branching off either side of the landing were more steps, making the staircase look more like a bird in flight than a set of stairs. However, these stairs were rarely used, since genies usually vaporized to the second level. Iron railings circled the upper balcony space. Along the walls were rows of diamond-shaped compartments that were divided into four holding shelves, with each compartment containing rolled-up parchments.

Many attendants stood on hovering carpets. Some were pulling out the parchment rolls, while others were returning them to their proper slots on the library's many shelves.

Below the narrow walkways, others busily scribbled out information. They were so engrossed in their personal research that none of them looked up as Aristede and his sons walked under the staircase and straight to the far end of the building, where they met Jindrake at the reception desk.

Behind the desk, sitting on a large carpet, was a lone elderly genie. He held a parchment page close to his face and adjusted his glasses so he could examine the writings closely. Every once in a while, he made a notation on another sheet to his right.

"Good morning," Jindrake said respectfully. "Very good to see you, Mr. Vincent."

The old genie's expression, eyes widened and mouth opened, made it apparent that Jindrake was the last person he had expected to see.

"Master Jindrake!" he exclaimed. "It is good to see you again. What can I do for you on this fine day?"

"We need to access the ancient scrolls."

"The *ancient* scrolls? The ones in the Hall of Scrolls?" Mr. Vincent asked. "Certainly, for you, Master Jindrake—anything. But I'm not sure about your friends. Do they have security clearance?"

"I can vouch for them. This is Mr. Aristede. He works for the DFC. And these are his sons. I am their godfather."

Mr. Vincent thought for a moment. But this was Master Jindrake's request, and he still had a lot of authority in the genie community.

"Of course, Master Jindrake. I'm sure you have a strong reason for them to go with you."

The carpet floated up with the stern-looking, beady-eyed man and flew to the door leading to the next room. He moved his hand, and he bowed as the visitors to the library passed him through the open door.

Jindrake led Aristede, JD, Morgan, and Blake into the Hall of Scrolls. It was home to the genies' most precious and sacred writings.

Jindrake pressed on the brass latch of the door handle. The door teetered open, and they proceeded to tread into the shadowy corridor and onto the steps of a narrow spiral stairwell, up two curved flights.

Six guards lined the long vaulted passageway. These guards faced each other with their legs crossed as they sat on four-foot-tall granite pedestals.

At the far end of the hallway stood a massive door. Flames from the torches, bracketed to the walls, reflected light from the bronze door handle, which he pulled open.

"These carvings on top go back several thousand years, but the scrolls here will be able to help us," Jindrake said. "They are difficult to read. Let's see what we can find."

He hopped on a carpet, and it took him slowly upward. Then it went sideways a few feet before stopping. Jindrake looked at a few scrolls, pulling them from their places and then returning them, before finding one that might have what they needed.

"Here we are," he said.

Jindrake then unrolled the parchment slightly to read the introduction to make sure.

"Yes, this is it."

The carpet descended, and Jindrake climbed off. He spread the scroll out on a table and carefully smoothed the brittle parchment paper. He snapped his fingers, and four small paperweights shaped like small brass lamps appeared, one on each corner, to keep the paper from rolling back.

"That scroll tells about this box?" JD asked.

"Not the box, but it does have what we need to read the markings," Jindrake said.

He moved in close to look at the symbols. Starting with the ones at the top corner of the box, Jindrake translated the portion of the page. It had been written in the language of the original jinn. He had to look closely at the directions of the lines and the sequence of the shapes.

He pointed to one sign when he found a match. It was *jinn* in their ancient language.

Jindrake then went to the next piece of writing. He constricted his eyes to be sure he had made the right connection between the carved markings and the design on the paper. His eyes moved back and forth between the box and the parchment, looking carefully at each wavy line, every detail.

"What we have here is a riddle box. It says, 'The Riddle Box of the First Jinn.'"

"What's a riddle box? What does—" Blake began.

Jindrake held up his hand and stopped him from asking any more questions.

"There's more," he said.

He now focused his attention on the carved symbols along two sides of the box. They were the only other places that had any markings. The translations came much more quickly than they had before.

Jindrake raised his right hand and waved it, and a parchment appeared. He picked up a black-feathered quill from the table and proceeded to scratch down what all the words from the box meant.

"Treasure . . . awaits . . . the . . . ones . . . who . . . answer . . . the riddles."

"Does it say what the treasure is?" Aristede asked.

Jindrake shook his head and continued interpreting the ancient writings.

"Beware . . . the one . . . who pursues . . . the power."

When Jindrake completed his task, he repeated the inscription in its entirety:

"The Riddle Box of the First Jinn.
Treasure awaits the ones who answer the riddles.
Beware the one who pursues the power."

"That's all it says, I'm afraid," Jindrake said, clicking his tongue.

"I don't understand," JD said. He scratched the side of his head and made a face similar to the one Silvestri had made when the seer candle was unsettled. "What riddles, and how do they open the box?"

"That it doesn't say," Jindrake said.

He looked again at the top of the box, to make sure one final time that he hadn't missed anything during his examination. No, he had translated all of the writings.

"It goes back to the twelve original jinn who created our world. They were the sultan's children—mortals in the human world. Have you heard about them?"

"I knew that there were twelve of them, but I never knew they were mortal children of a sultan," Morgan said.

"Surprise, surprise!" JD said mockingly. "There's something you *didn't* know—eh, brother?"

The look on Morgan's face soured.

Jindrake walked to a table with a large wooden box on it. He took a key from a small pocket vest and put it into the lock, turning it carefully. Jindrake took out a scroll and unrolled the parchment.

It was their four-thousand-year-old Creation Scroll.

"Since it is the Riddle Box of the First Jinn, the sultan's children, let them tell us," Jindrake said.

Chapter Fifteen

The Sultan's Children

"Our history begins in the outside world," Jindrake said before beginning to read what was in the scroll.

> There once was a sultan of a faraway land who was kind and charitable, concerned with the welfare of his subjects. His queen was an exceptionally beautiful woman, and together they ruled their kingdom. They loved each other very much, and their wedded union produced twelve children—seven sons and five daughters.
>
> In the forests beyond the mud-bricked walled city, the sultan hunted wild game with his sons. Their names were Sundhar, Casimir, Caleb, Bahktiar, Kareem, and twins Rahmani and Amarr. While the sultan spent time with them, the royal daughters—Reena, Mikayla, Tamerisa, Zoli, and Fatima—helped their mother plan garden parties.
>
> It was while entertaining guests in the gardens on the far side of the enclosed walls that the queen announced she was expecting

another child. But the happiness faded when, after a difficult childbirth, the queen became very ill. She removed the headband that stretched across her caramel-colored forehead and gave it to the new princess, whom they named Karyna.

With the last moments of life remaining, the queen made a final request. She asked her husband to watch over their newborn daughter and protect the other children.

To heal his heart, shattered at the loss of his beloved wife, the sultan devoted his life to raising his children, and ruling all those living inside the city and on the fruitful lands of the plains.

Jindrake stopped reading, and before they knew what was happening, a fog erupted from the paper. JD, Morgan, and Blake watched their surroundings change into the gardens of the long-ago sultan's palace. When the fog cleared, four people (three men and a young girl) stood before them. The man with the thick white-streaked beard was fastening the chains to his gold-and-purple silk robe. It was the sultan. The others were his advisers and his youngest daughter.

Jindrake, Aristede, and the boys weren't part of the unfolding scene, but they stood close to the people in it. Blake reached out to touch the sultan, but his hand passed through the figment. He tried a second time with Karyna, and the same thing happened. They were spectators at Princess Karyna's fourth birthday. The sultan had declared a national holiday and invited all the children in the land to a party. He had presented his daughter with an all-white pony with a curly ivory mane; it looked just like a unicorn.

Karyna had been used to getting what she wanted from her brothers and sisters, and none of them could resist her. If Karyna wanted to be carried, all she had to do was push out her bottom lip and bat her eyelashes at Sundhar. She shrieked as he lifted her up on his shoulders and galloped in and around the palace, her giggles echoing in the corridors.

"What else would you like, my darling?" the sultan asked.

Princess Karyna looked around and pointed to two parrots that had been sitting on a tree branch. As she ran down the pathway, the birds flew off to take asylum in the tall palm trees. Karyna started to cry, and the sultan ordered his servants to retrieve them. It took two hours before they finally caught the birds.

"Your Highness, you spoil the child," one of the loyal advisers, Tarik, said.

"No more than any of my other children," the sultan replied. He added that Karyna deserved the incredible gifts he had given her.

"Giving in to her every whim is not good," Karziz, the other, shorter adviser added.

"For my child? What do you mean 'not good,' Karziz?" the sultan asked. There was a scowl on his face.

"Well . . . you see . . ." Karziz said.

He stumbled over his words as he quickly searched his mind for a response.

"Your Highness, what I meant to say is that it is not healthy for your other children. They will become jealous and eventually resent their tiny sister."

"Nonsense, Karziz. All my sons and daughters know that I love them equally," the sultan said proudly.

"I beg your pardon, Your Highness," Tarik said.

"Yes, Tarik," the sultan replied. He was wary of what his adviser was about to tell him.

Tarik folded his hands. "Giving gifts and giving love are not the same."

"I know that!" the sultan said.

"You do give more of both to Karyna than you do the other children," Karziz said.

The sultan became outraged at the mere suggestion.

"Would you have given a pony to any of the other princesses when they were four years old?" Tarik asked.

The sultan kept himself from saying anything.

"And would you have sent servants after those parrots for anyone else?" Karziz asked as he raised one of his dark eyebrows.

The sultan started huffing and mumbling that he would indeed do the same things for all his children and not just for Karyna. Moreover, Karyna was still a baby.

"She is a four-year-old child. She is not a baby," Tarik said, whispering under his breath.

The sultan grew impatient with his advisers and marched away from them, ending his conversation with them.

The people dissolved to their home in the written words on the parchment.

JD, Morgan, and Blake wanted to see more of the sultan and his family, and they got the chance when another set of vapors emerged from the scroll. They were thrilled as they watched one of the servants pull out the sultan's chair so he could take his position at the table. The children joined their father for the morning meal, with the princes sitting to the sultan's left along one side of the long table, and the sisters facing opposite them to the sultan's right. One chair, however, was empty. It was Karyna's.

The food servers began setting plates in front of the members of the royal family.

"I see Karyna is not here," the sultan said. "Has anyone seen her this morning?"

"She had trouble getting to sleep last night, Father," one of the daughters said. Aristede whispered to his sons that this was Mikayla, the purple jinn, and they were her descendants.

"She was sleeping when I looked in on her. I thought it was best to let her sleep this morning. Shall I go and—"

Another servant whisked into the hall, waving her arms above her head. The frantic look on her face announced to everyone that there was something dreadfully wrong.

"The Princess Karyna has fallen ill! She has a fever and refuses to get out of bed."

The sultan stood up and exited the dining hall, making his way up the stairs. His other children followed, talking among themselves, until they all turned the corner leading to the bedchambers.

They knew it was serious, since the little princess was usually the first one up and ready to play.

"What do you suppose is wrong with her?" Bahktiar asked.

It had taken only a few minutes to find out. Everyone had walked quietly to Karyna's bedside. The small child had been restless and moved around all night, and now she lay in her bed, oozing sweat across her face and down along her cheeks. The sultan gently sat next to her and pushed the damp wavy golden strands back across the top of Karyna's head to feel her forehead.

Princess Karyna closed her eyes, and the sultan and his family dissolved back into the parchment page.

"Will she be all right?" a concerned Blake asked. "Karyna will be okay, won't she?"

"Let's see," Jindrake said softly. He continued reading.

Word had spread throughout the kingdom about the seriousness of the young princess's illness. Healers came to nurse the young princess back to health, but she struggled to swallow even a sip down her dry throat. Many subjects also arrived at the palace with broths for Karyna to drink and salves for her body. The remedies were useless, and Karyna's fever persisted.

Before they knew it, a new set of vapors flew out from the scroll. Karyna was still in bed, with one of her sisters at her bedside, reading a story about three dragons that lived in a cave.

"One day, the mama dragon cooked some oats for her family. While they waited for the oats to cool, Papa Dragon, Mama Dragon, and Baby Dragon took a flight around the mountains. Meanwhile, a little girl wandered through the forest, smelled the oats, and entered the dragons' cave."

Standing nearby for several minutes, eyeing his sisters closely, was Casimir, and he was snickering.

"Zoli, are you boring her with that story again? 'Who has been eating my oats?'" he mocked, walking toward them. "Tell her a real story."

"What story do you want to tell, little brother?" Zoli asked with a wistful sneer.

For the first time in several days, Karyna perked up and chuckled. She found her siblings amusing.

Casimir sat on the edge of Karyna's bed and pulled colorful scarves from his pocket. He folded the pieces of fabric until one looked like an elephant and the other a tiger.

"Are you ready for a show, Karyna?" he asked.

Princess Karyna, with her eyes half-closed, forced a smile. The sweat on her head had dried and matted her hair down the sides of her face. She listened intently as Casimir wove a rousing tale.

The puppet animals captivated Karyna, especially when Casimir changed the tone of his voice to create different sounds for the puppets.

When the scene changed, many weeks had passed. They watched as Karyna lay listless in bed. She had refused to eat the meals the cook had prepared for her, and Karyna grew weaker. Her father spent each night with his sickly little girl, holding her hand.

"I love you, Father," she said. Her voice was raspy.

She then smiled and closed her eyes. Her body was lifeless, and the sultan knew she had left them forever.

He rushed from her bedchamber and eventually found himself down by the pools. He dropped to his knees and hid his face in his hands. He sobbed.

Reena, his oldest daughter, joined him. She took his arm and pushed it in hers. As swans swam nearby, Reena shared memories about when Karyna was learning to walk. The cook had made a delicious midday meal for them.

The sultan grinned as he remembered how Karyna had wandered into the water and fallen on her bottom. She had not cried, but she immediately enjoyed splashing in the water. Reena laughed.

As she gave her father's hand a tight squeeze, she and the sultan whisked back into the parchment paper. Jindrake read on when the last vapors vanished.

Following the little princess's death, the sultan's advisers made burial arrangements. They chose the temple in the center of the city as the resting place for Karyna's stone coffin.

Day after day, the sultan quietly strolled through the gardens and ended his walks at his daughter's resting place, never spending much time in the temple. He stayed just long enough to feel closer to his baby girl again.

But then he came to a troubling realization! If he could lose one child so quickly and unexpectedly, what would keep this tragedy from happening to any of his other beloved children? It was all the sultan could think about. When his fears became overwhelming, he had a secret meeting with a trusted ally in the third level of the ziggurat.

A foul, strong odor, like that of rotten eggs and stinky cheese, filled the air. JD, Morgan, and Blake pinched their nostrils on their crinkly faces to keep from smelling the scent of rancid food. The unpleasant odor was coming from the parchment.

Out of the vapory smoke, denser than the others had been, a wooden door appeared and slowly opened. There was the sultan again. He set his candleholder down on a table, and the flame quivered in the drafty tower. Cobwebs draped the walls, and a stubby figure crept out from a dark corner. It looked as though he appeared out of thin air. The sultan immediately recognized the bald, portly man.

"Ah, Frassrand. Good of you to meet me here at this time of the night," the sultan said.

"Good evening, Your Highness," Frassrand said. He peeled the hood back from his head.

His dark eyebrows were pointed at the outer tips, giving a glaring look to him. The green-lined black robes had sleeves with extra-long openings, tailored for a much taller man, and that only made him look physically smaller. Metal bands were wrapped around his wrists, and these manacles caught the light from the candle flames. A gecko looked quite at home perched on the man's shoulder.

"Tell me, magician, what does the future hold for my children?" the sultan asked.

Frassrand bowed.

"Absolutely, Your Highness. May my power allow me to see nothing but good fortune."

Reaching up to remove the gecko, which was now crawling down the overly long sleeve, Frassrand placed the creature in the palm of his hand, and he stroked the reptile's scaly back before putting the lizard down on the floor to stalk after spiders.

Frassrand paused, closed his eyes, and after several grueling seconds for the sultan, started again.

"I see death! Your sons and daughters will fall ill and die. You will find yourself very much alone, brokenhearted indeed."

"No!" the sultan cried. "It cannot be! So you may see no more suffering, I should have your eyes ripped from your head."

"Alas, what I have foreseen is true, Your Highness," Frassrand said. He lowered his head and clasped his hands together. "For the next two hundred full moons, they will be in danger."

The poor sultan turned away and looked out over the flat roof, his hands resting on the window opening. It appeared as though he were about to collapse.

How can this be true? How unfair it all is, the sultan thought. He gave a desperate plea: "There must be something you can do. You must have a spell so that I will not have my children taken from me! I implore you, magician!"

"Your Highness, I can help you. I have brought my enchantment sands with me."

In the shadowy area, the sorcerer picked up a leather pouch, untied the bindings, and dumped the contents on the table. The sultan turned and watched closely as Frassrand ran his finger through the sands. The granules slowly shimmied along the outline of the squiggles Frassrand had made. The squiggles shifted around into symbols that only the magician could read.

"They can be kept alive and well, but for a price. You must send your children far from any danger that threatens them here. Your Highness, I know of a place far, far away. Such a marvelous place indeed." Frassrand smiled, eyes closed, picturing the peacefulness. "After two hundred full moons have come to pass, they may return, and everything shall be well."

The sultan furrowed his silver eyebrows. He did not want to send his children to some far-off place. He wanted to ensure that he not lose his children.

"Could there be another way?" he asked hopefully. "It is such a drastic measure to take."

"I understand, Your Highness. We do not need to proceed. You may hope my prophecy is inaccurate and that nothing happens. You may continue to live out your life with your children, and perhaps they will all have long lives. Yet have any of my past predictions been wrong?"

The sultan's mouth pinched to one side. He paced and paused at the window again, looking out across the night sky. From experience, he knew what Frassrand said was true.

To add to the sultan's pain, the more they delayed, the more the children would settle back into their lives in the kingdom. Frassrand did have a special potion that would ensure their safe passage.

"But if your potion can ensure their safety on their journey, why can it not protect them here?" the sultan asked.

"There are limits to its power. They must be far away where death cannot find them."

But would he live long enough to see them all safely return to the kingdom? Knowing that, the sultan thought, would make his children's absence somewhat bearable.

Closing his black eyes and placing his fingertips to his temples, gently rubbing them, Frassrand added, "I see you with many, many great-grandchildren. You are playing with them in the palace gardens."

Frassrand produced a silver drinking chalice from within an oversized sleeve. He handed the drink to the sultan to help him decide what to do. The strong scent of mint in the liquid was inviting.

The sultan sipped the magician's soothing beverage. Within seconds, a serene look on his face replaced the painful expression that had been there before.

"Then let it be, Frassrand. I am confident your plan is the only solution. I made a promise to their mother that I would protect our children. That is all that matters. I will obey your every command. Make all the arrangements, and see that they are safe and well cared for, even the older children. They may think they have grown and should be treated like adults, but they are still children to me. I will provide the gold for their care."

The sultan retrieved the candle from the table and moved toward the door. Frassrand bent down and stretched out his arm. He said something the sultan could not understand, and the gecko scrambled into his hand. The reptile returned to its place on Frassrand's shoulder.

The two men left the room, and their figures evaporated into nothingness. Jindrake read more:

In the temple the children sat on the floor, all eyes on their father, wondering why he had gathered them together.

The sultan explained how Karyna's death had been very difficult for him and how he feared for them. The children saw how depressed and grief-stricken he had been.

He couldn't bring himself to reveal what Frassrand had foretold. He simply told them that the next several years would be dangerous if they stayed.

The sons and daughters of the sultan expressed their outrage, even questioning their father's extreme action. They attempted to persuade him to change his mind. But he had to remind them all that they all would be making sacrifices, including himself.

He asked that they trust his decision. It was his final word on the subject. He hoped that someday they would understand when he could send for them when it was safe for them in the kingdom.

A smoky mist of Frassrand on his way to the temple now flowed out of the yellowed paper. A smile grew slowly on the magician's face. He looked like he was up to something.

At a small table, Frassrand picked up a tin tray embossed with leaf shapes along the edges. There were twelve chalices on it. He poured a minty-smelling liquid into each. When the potion began bubbling, Frassrand sprinkled in pinches of crushed herbs.

Sundhar gave a penetrating leer before he picked up the chalice with the red steam flowing from it.

Amarr made a toad-like face and gave out a belching noise that sounded like a croaking frog.

"What is in here?" he asked.

Frassrand hid his displeasure with the twelve-year-old child's question by assuring the boy that the harmless liquid contained rare plant sap and spices.

Sundhar set the example for his siblings by being the first to drink the brew. The others followed Sundhar's lead. It tasted even sweeter than it smelled, like a blend of chocolate, peppermint, and oranges.

Mikayla took a heavy breath, clutched Zoli's trembling hand, and together they drank the magic potion.

Tamerisa pressed on her burning chest and let go of her chalice.

"I-I feel s-strange!" she cried as she felt her insides twisting.

Tamerisa was not alone. Her brothers and sisters also reacted violently to the brew and doubled over in great pain.

"Wh-what have y-you done t-to u-us?" Caleb screamed as he jumped out at Frassrand in a full rage.

The young prince succumbed to the potion's full effect and fell to the floor. Frassrand enjoyed watching the misery on their faces. One by one, the young highnesses had the same prickly feeling over their bodies and began to experience physical changes. They each transformed into a different color of smoke. These colored vapors moved liked charmed snakes in a well-choreographed dance. It was hypnotic.

Frassrand motioned with his finger, and the colored smoke streaked toward various containers he had hidden behind the draping curtains. Within seconds, each vapor found its way into a clay jar. By closing off the openings with stone stoppers, the magician sealed all twelve of them inside their prisons.

The robes Frassrand wore muffled the clanging of his manacles against the containers as he slinked out of the royal compound. Like a shadow, he slipped through a gap in the outer wall and down the long flight of stone steps. The swift-moving water drowned out the sounds of Frassrand's footsteps.

He dumped all twelve containers into the icy water, and they drifted off to their final destination—the ocean.

"The sultan will be so happy to hear that his sons and daughters are aboard the sailing vessels and safely on their way. It is an ingenious way to do away with all the heirs, if I do say so myself. Simple. Clean. No mess at all. No questions asked," Frassrand said to himself as he stood on the riverbank.

The gecko on his shoulder shot out its tongue. Frassrand reached up to stroke the small reptile's head. Before Jindrake, Aristede, JD, Morgan, and Blake knew it, Frassrand arched his head back and laughed before evaporating into the scroll. The echo of his cruel laugh followed right after him.

.

Chapter Sixteen

The Three Spiders

"What a story!" JD exclaimed.

"Not a story. That was the history of our beginnings," Jindrake reminded them. "Those events actually happened and have been preserved in the scrolls."

Blake, who normally would shy away from sharing his opinion, openly expressed how he felt about the parchment figures. "I didn't like that magician."

"Frassrand put the sultan under his spell, did he not?" Morgan asked. "It was the drink he gave the sultan when they met in the tower."

Jindrake nodded and told them, "You learned a great deal today."

"Maybe so, but not about the riddle box. It had to be after they became genies," JD said. "When did that happen?"

"When the sultan's children escaped their bottles, they used their magic powers and created the world we now live in."

"There's something else I don't understand. How did they get their genie powers?" a confused JD said. "Is there anything else in the scroll that tells how that happened? Or is that in another scroll?"

"Let us see what else we have here," Jindrake said.

158

He stretched his arm straight out in front of him. Another scroll of papyrus parchment lifted from its place among the ancient documents.

While hovering in midair, the two wooden rollers pulled apart. Jindrake's eyes moved rapidly down the page as he read. As he got to the bottom, he stopped short, and his face went a deathlike white.

Aristede and the boys knew at once that there was something more, but before anyone could ask, Jindrake tapped his bony finger on the bottom of the page so only Aristede could read. He recognized immediately that his boys must leave the room.

"They can wait in the small chamber down the hall," Jindrake said.

The uproar was immediate. They had been able to see the events in the other scroll, so what was different with this one? What was it the adults didn't want them to see?

Jindrake stepped closer, arms down and palms toward them. He herded them out and watched as they made their way to a small waiting area near the stairs. Blake looked around the stale-smelling room. He took a sniff or two as he looked at all the dusty cobwebs, which had netted small bugs. Blake sat down in one of the chairs in the room, which was filled with more cobwebs than chairs.

"What do you think it says—in the scroll, I mean?" Blake asked.

"It must be something important. They obviously did not think we could handle it," Morgan said.

"You're probably right. But aren't you curious about what it is?" JD told him.

"Certainly, I am," Morgan said. "But the only way we will find out is to wait for Dad to tell us when he comes back after he and Master Jindrake see what comes out of the scroll."

"That's *if* he tells us," Blake said. "If they didn't want us to know now, what makes you think they'll tell us anything after what they see?"

What Blake had just said made them stop and think. Both JD and Morgan knew he was right, but JD had another idea. The only way for them to really know was if they saw everything for themselves. The question remained: how could they sneak back into the Hall of Scrolls?

"Sneak? Into that chamber! Past those guards?" Blake said. He started to get nervous, and his twitching ear showed it. He even flicked his finger at this ear as a way to calm himself down. He felt as though someone was about to push him into a den of bears that hadn't eaten in months. "Look at their muscles! Look at the veins bulging out of their arms!"

"It is obvious that we cannot wait until the guards are not looking, and we cannot just vaporize," Morgan said.

"Why not?" Blake asked.

"We would be seen. The only way to be undetected is if we are invisible," Morgan said.

"What if we blend?" JD asked.

"Possible, but there is still the door. The best way to get past that obstacle is if we could be small enough to go under it," Morgan added. "We would have to be small, like the size of bugs."

All this talk only led them back to the original question: how?

JD felt a tickle on a tender spot on his skin, like eight tiny legs scurrying on his hand. He raised his other hand and slowly brought it down over the spider. But Morgan saved the little arachnid's life by stopping JD from swatting it.

"Spiders! That is the answer. If we changed into spiders, we would be small enough to creep under the door without anyone seeing us," Morgan said.

"I-I don't want to be a spider! I-I hate spiders!" Blake exclaimed.

His concern about being an arachnid only increased as he watched one of the spiders eat a fly.

"Get over it. It's the only way," JD said.

"What if the guards step on us?" Blake said.

"Do not be such a gleeb," Morgan said. "They are not allowed to move. We are wasting time. We must hurry."

JD and Morgan raised their hands into the air. Blake knew it was fruitless to argue once he was outnumbered, and he raised his hands, too.

The transmogrification darkened their light hair, and as they shrank to the floor, the triplets found they had four sets of jointed limbs, long and spindly. There was a heavy feeling inside them as they crept under the heavy, three-inch-thick door and moved close to the wall, down the long corridor. In step together, the spiders had to be oh so careful every inch of the way. One misstep by the sentry, and they could be crushed.

After making it to the heavy chamber door without getting swatted, captured, or eaten by a larger insect, the spiders crawled into the Hall of Scrolls just as a vapor rolled from the parchment.

A single hooded man stood before twelve shadowy figures that were placed comfortably into chairs at a high half-round table. It looked as if a trial was in progress.

The man standing before the others pulled his hood back. Aristede gasped. There was no doubt in their minds as to who it was.

"Frassrand! You are here before this High Council so that we may hear your testimony," the man in the middle said. Aristede and Jindrake recognized him as Prince Sundhar.

Sundhar's face had matured with high cheekbones and steely blue eyes that were not about to show any mercy. Aristede and Jindrake recognized the others, too—all grown—the sultan's children.

"Who are you to judge me?" the magician asked.

"Silence!" Casimir shouted.

"You are in our world now. That gives us the right!" Tamerisa said. She now looked very much like her late mother.

"She is right. You invaded our world!" Mikayla said firmly. "You made Sundhar your slave and made him bring you here."

"You planned to use our power to rule the human world!" Amarr added sternly.

"You must have been surprised to learn what happened to us when Sundhar returned home," Tamerisa said.

Frassrand stared blankly at them and did not respond. Sundhar rested his hand on a black object. It was the riddle box.

"Obviously you never expected to see any of us again," Caleb said. He turned to his other brother. "Sundhar, tell us what you found when you returned to our beautiful palace!"

Sundhar gazed without so much of an eye blink. His stare was icy. Finally he spoke.

"No one there even recognized me. Nor did they remember any of you. Frassrand had cast a spell erasing us from their memories. His aim was to rule our country, and to do that he had to get rid of Father. That he did. He seized control after Father's body was discovered with a dagger in his back in the temple near Karyna's coffin. Father's subjects fled under Frassrand's barbaric rule."

Murmurs of "scoundrel," "traitor," and "murderer" made their way through the chamber.

"What do you have to say for yourself?" Bahktiar asked.

Frassrand raised his arm. He was blatant about how he pointed his fleshy finger in their direction.

"Yes. I was truly surprised at your survival," he said. "You were never meant to return. Drinking my unique potion—"

Rahmani interrupted the magician's tale. "In reality, a sham. That drink was only intended to confine us in the containers."

Sundhar raised his hand to his siblings to stop any further interruption of the proceedings. He wanted Frassrand to finish and said, "Tell us, Frassrand, why we became what we are now."

"You want to know? You actually want to know? All right, I will tell you. Apparently when I prepared the elixir, I pricked my finger and some of my blood mixed in with the other ingredients. As a result, some of my own powers transferred to you."

"And when you put us in those containers, we had changed into jinn," Amarr said. Amarr had grown into a confident adult, very different from the boy he was back in his father's kingdom.

"You learned of this place my sisters and brothers had created. You were curious about it, and once you gained possession of my bottle, you became my new master. Your first wish was to bring you here. Not only did you want control over our father's kingdom, you decided you also wanted to control the entire world. You were consumed with the desire for power, and you developed this evil plan to use us as your slaves," Sundhar added.

A grin grew across Frassrand's face.

"You are not as stupid as I always thought you to be."

Zoli gave a hateful look at the evil man.

"Then you admit to your crimes?" she said.

"But of course. What can you do about it?" Frassrand said. "You are ill-equipped to stop me."

"You do not understand," Sundhar said, continuing his fearless gaze. "There is a great deal we can do."

He surveyed his brothers and sisters, who were self-controlled as they sat around the table.

"I believe we are all in agreement. Casimir will announce our judgment," Sundhar said without raising his voice.

Casimir folded his hands on the table. It looked as though he was still formulating how he would hand down the verdict.

After a few seconds, he said, "For your ruthless actions, Frassrand, this High Council finds you guilty. We will take your powers away from you. This will ensure that all jinn and all of humanity will be protected from you!"

"Do you really think you can keep my powers from me?" Frassrand asked. "What makes you think this is possible?"

"Let me be more clear. We will take the source of your power from you," Sundhar said.

Fatima leaned forward from her place and said, "We know that your power source cannot be destroyed. However, we have a way to make sure you will never find where we hide it."

"You underestimate my abilities. Your lame attempts to stop me will fail," Frassrand said.

The mockery Frassrand was making of the court angered Kareem. He forcefully kicked at the table without realizing what he had done.

"So you think our plan is flawed?" Kareem asked.

"I do," Frassrand said. He looked at them with cold indifference.

"Your power source will be placed in this box," Kareem continued. "In addition to us, only six identical pupils of the jinn will be able to open it. And to make this even more interesting, the box will select these heirs. You will never know who they are."

Frassrand scowled.

"You are all fooling yourselves if you think you can stop me. This conversation is futile anyway."

"We will take the source from you!" Mikayla said. "Then we will send you back to the human world from which you came. You are not welcomed here."

"You have no right!" Frassrand said firmly. He then spat at the base of the table.

"We have *every* right!" Mikayla shouted back. "And when this High Council combines its powers—a power greater than yours—we will banish you!"

Frassrand turned to Sundhar and with a look of disdain, said, "I control you. Remember, as your master, I give the commands, and I command you to make your brothers and sisters *my* jinn, too!"

Everyone looked to Sundhar to see what he would do next. Quietly and calmly, they were prepared to follow his example. Frassrand could clearly see something was about to happen, although he couldn't imagine what that might be. For the first time, the evil magician felt vulnerable.

"Your mistake was wishing for me to bring you here," Sundhar said. "When you did that, your role as my master ended."

"*No!* You tricked me! How dare you!"

His booming voice forced Aristede and Jindrake to step backward. A cold chill moved down their backs.

"Beware. You will not achieve your goal. I will not let you or these heirs you speak of take my powers!" Frassrand said.

He held up his left arm, displaying a gold manacle wrapped around his wrist. As the light clipped the cold metal, its reflection was almost blinding. Jindrake squinted as Aristede turned his head downward.

"Behold! You will never take what is mine!" Frassrand declared.

"Watch us!" Reena said.

"No. You watch this," Frassrand boasted. He slowly ran his finger across the silky hairs on his brow.

For a still moment, everyone waited as Frassrand raised both arms and mumbled a few words, phrases that sounded like an incantation. His sleeves folded over as they fell from his wrists, bunching around his elbows and exposing two shiny metal bands. Each manacle had a reddish-orange glow. His body became feathery, and his arms became wings. All eyes were on an eagle that squawked loudly and flapped its wings frantically.

"Stop him!" Caleb cried.

"He must not escape!" Tamerisa shouted.

All the members of the High Council sprang to their feet, but they were too late to take hold of Frassrand, since he was no longer a man. The eagle's crimson red eyes fixed on Kareem as he, Kareem, pulled out a sword and sliced downward with his muscular arms.

In an instant, the sounds of the shrieking eagle faded, and streams of smoke returned to the scroll.

As soon as the figures were gone, the three spiders began their return journey to the small chamber before anything happened. They inched backward, crept under the door, and moved quickly.

Even as they were near the door to the small chamber, a shadow loomed over them, larger and hairier and the same shape as the three spiders. It closed in on them. The spiders ambled across the marble-floored hallway as fast as their eight legs could carry them, one step ahead of the stalking tarantula, until they could slide under the door. As luck would have it, one of the guards snatched the tarantula and placed the hairy creature on his arm, petting it affectionately.

Once they were back behind closed doors, the triplets began to undergo changes to their bodies. The extra skinny legs slowly receded at the same time that the spider bodies grew back into their normal selves.

Blake took a quick whiff at his underarms and said, "We still smell like spider!"

"It will go away," JD said. "We just tell Dad it's because of this musty room."

"Speaking of Dad, where is he?" Blake asked. "He and Master Jindrake should have been back here by now."

"You are right, Blake," Morgan said.

They turned to the door and waited a moment or two for it to fling open. When that didn't happen, Morgan crouched and put his eye to the keyhole. He could see Aristede and Jindrake standing in the corridor. They both looked serious as they talked softly to each other. Every once in a while they took a step past the guards.

"I'm glad we didn't let them see this. It would have frightened them, and I wouldn't want that. So thank you, Jindrake, for alerting me to what was in the scroll," Aristede said.

"But you will tell them something? They will ask, won't they?" Jindrake said.

"I'm sure of that. I know my sons," Aristede said. "Couldn't you confiscate it and tell them that since the box belonged to the original jinn that it belongs here in the library's antiquity collection?"

"Won't that make them even more curious?" Jindrake asked. "They'd want to know why it hasn't been here with all the other artifacts."

"We didn't know about its existence, and it has been lost until now," Aristede said.

"That does make sense. After all, Kareem said it would be hidden and appear only to the heirs so that Frassrand would never know when that would be."

Jindrake saw there was still something bothering his friend.

Aristede hesitated. Why did his sons get this box? Kareem had said the six pupils of the jinn were the only ones who could open it.

"All part of the mystery," Jindrake said. "The box may be on its journey to those six pupils. It may be in their possession only for a short period of time, at least until it changes hands."

"But we don't know when—or if—that will happen," Aristede said.

"Since they don't have the riddles to open the box, I believe it is safe for the boys to have it," Jindrake said.

Aristede agreed to abide by what Jindrake had said.

"But to be vigilant, I do have one request to make: if you do notice anything happening to the box, or if it does vanish, let me know immediately."

"I will," Aristede said.

Inside the chamber, the boys watched the doorknob start to turn. Before they could safely move away from the doorway without making a noise, Aristede swung the door open. It almost looked as though Aristede and Jindrake were not going to tell them anything, leaving them in the dark. It might have remained that way if Blake hadn't asked about what they had seen.

"We saw the original jinn again. But this time they were all grown up. There was a heated argument between them and Frassrand," Aristede said.

"What about?" Blake asked.

"For imprisoning them," Jindrake added. "What we saw was not appropriate for you to see."

JD and Morgan became a little jumpy. Although they were eager to hear the details, they were almost wishing Blake hadn't asked, because if they asked any more questions, they might let it slip about what they already knew.

"And *the box*?" JD asked innocently.

Aristede exchanged another concerned glance with Jindrake, who said, "Nothing more was said about it other than that it's opened by answering riddles. I am afraid we will never know what those are. You have a decorative box . . . a replica, I believe. It is a wonderful connection to our ancestors."

They had all the information they could get from this visit. It was time for them to return home.

Jindrake escorted his friends to the front lobby of the library, and because of the small talk, none of them noticed a hooded figure in the far corner, peering over a sheet of wrinkled parchment. He observed their every move. It wasn't the first time he had done that, either.

This library visitor was the same hooded figure that had watched the triplets at their birthday party.

Chapter Seventeen

The Little Man Speaks

Cassidy was hectically moving around the food preparation area, cooking the midday meal. She made patties from dragon meat by flattening them between her palms and piling them on a platter. Brianna was at her side, trying to keep up with the genie mom as best she could.

Next, Brianna watched Cassidy stuff dumplings with spinach and cheese, and then finely chop roasted nuts before mixing them in with dragon whiskers. The delicious smells filled the eating area.

Then it dawned on Brianna that Cassidy was preparing the meal from scratch. She wondered why she hadn't used magic (except for waving her hand to send patties into the frying pan and arranging the assorted food), so she decided to ask.

Cassidy thought about it for a few seconds and then replied, "Yes, I could have done it that way. It would have been much easier, but I must admit that I enjoy cooking. You could call it a hobby."

The conversation was interrupted when, in the archway, smoky purple mists cleared, and there were Aristede, JD, Morgan, and Blake.

Cassidy put the ladle down and flicked her fingers at the pot. The cooking flame died down so the bird's nest soup would simmer slowly.

"Why this wonderful feast?" Aristede asked as the wide-eyed children ogled all the tasty treats.

"It's to celebrate what you found at the library and," she whispered, "to help Brianna feel better."

Aristede made his way to the low table.

"So—tell us what you found," Cassidy said.

"The sultan's children created the box. It's a riddle box. We still don't know how it works," Aristede told her. With help from JD, Morgan, and Blake, he went on to explain the markings on the box itself.

Hearing what the translations said made Cassidy a bit uneasy, and to her it sounded as if the box was cursed. Perhaps they should have left it at the library.

"We talked about that, but since we don't have the riddles to open the box, Jindrake believes everything should be okay. And he says it could be just a copy of the original riddle box," Aristede said. "Now let's enjoy this wonderful feast."

The boys took their forks, skewered some meat, and placed it between two bread buns, adding a spicy dressing containing a mustard and ketchup relish with basil and oregano. When they finished eating their burgers, Cassidy brought out a cold parfait dessert with rice, a bit of orange, syrup, ice cream, and whipped cream.

The mealtime conversation, as expected, was about the visit to the library. The boys became animated as they acted out everything that happened when the people appeared. Every once in a while they paused, in part for dramatic effect, but also to catch their breath. It looked as though Cassidy and Brianna couldn't hear enough about the parchment and the people appearing right out of the paper.

"I didn't know there was royalty here," Brianna said.

"Not anymore. They were human princes and princesses who had become the original jinn," Cassidy explained to her before turning to Aristede. "Why did they make this box?"

"No one knows," Aristede replied, which was a white lie. He justified the lie with the same reason he hadn't let the boys witness

Frassrand's trial. And so long as nothing happened with the box, what harm was it? This decision would soon prove to be a mistake.

As night fell, JD, Morgan, and Blake changed into their nightclothes and dropped on their beds, tired from the day's events. Of the three, JD was the only one who wasn't ready to turn in.

He looked at the carvings on the riddle box, which now sat on the table next to his bed. All the paintings on the box showed a life long since passed. He was eager to solve the mystery of the box and was about to put his ear to it to see if he could hear anything rattle inside when he heard a voice suddenly say, "Psst!"

He turned to see if one of his brothers had tried to get his attention, but they were fast asleep. JD wasn't sure if the sound he heard had been his imagination or if, perhaps, he was just tired.

JD pulled the covers over himself, and after a while, he, too, fell asleep, dreaming about the riddle box. In his dream, the little man was playing a flute. Next to him were snakes dancing to the music. Then the still pictures were still no more. The same strange man in all the pictures smiled and winked at him. One by one, the little men started to jabber. They were talking slowly at first, but when they were all speaking, it sounded more like braying donkeys than actual talking. The noise got louder and came faster, and JD had to cover his pounding ears.

He bolted up. He was confused at first, and it seemed like he had been sleeping for hours when, in reality, a mere few seconds had passed. Once JD regained his bearings, he looked across the moonlit bedchamber where he saw Morgan and Blake in blissful slumber. Although JD's dream had been vivid, he was straining to recall what the little men had said. He tried sorting out the meaning of it all.

Then it occurred to him that perhaps the whisper came from—
"Psst. Psst."
—the box.
"Psst!"
The voice, a little louder this time, had come from the picture showing a young man sitting on a chestnut Arabian horse in tall meadow grasses. His arms were outstretched through his long-sleeved robes, and he had just released a flock of small bluebirds. The birds were flying toward a palace in the foothills overlooking an ancient city.

JD almost wet his pajama bottoms when the figure in the painting turned his head and faced him. It was the only part of the little man that moved. Everything else in the picture—his body, the horse, and the trees behind him—looked frozen in time.

"Listen closely, young jinn." The man paused for a moment. "Your journey begins now."

He swallowed a couple of times, jiggling the skin covering his larynx, and gave a little hack.

"Taking flight in the sky or feeding on worms in the ground, you can find these. What are they?"

The little man had expected a quick response from the boy, and when he didn't get it, he said, "Come, come. You know the answer." It was a tease, a way of encouraging him.

JD was stunned. It took a while for everything to sink in, and of course he knew the answer.

"Birds. They fly and eat worms."

The little man loudly and happily exclaimed, "Correct, young jinn!"

He bowed and returned to his original pose.

JD jumped off his bed, dashed over to Morgan and Blake, and, without being gentle, shook them both. One question down.

"You mean he talked to you?" a shocked Blake asked.

"Yes! I told you before that the man moved," JD said. "This is how we get the riddles—the little man gives them to us, and they have something to do with the pictures."

"Then if we deduce this correctly," Morgan began, "there are five pictures, so we should get five riddles!"

He picked up the riddle box and turned it in many different directions, looking at every side. When he got to the painting from which the little man had given JD the first riddle, he frowned, one eye narrowed more than the other. There was something unexpected that had happened to the picture.

Morgan scraped his finger across the dried paint. The colors were fresh, clear, and vibrant. Gone were the layers of dirt that had concealed the brushstroked textures. It was as if someone had scrubbed the painting clean.

That was enough for Blake, who by now had lost all interest in the riddle box. In fact, he found the whole thing was too creepy. Even though JD found it fun, Blake had been scared by what they had seen in the library, and he still wondered why Aristede hadn't told them everything.

"Mom and Dad still think of us as little boys," JD said.

"I-I don't think we have any choice but to tell them, especially now that the man in the paintings is talking to us," Blake said.

JD put his hands together and rubbed them. His face showed the same excitement, with the same impish grin, that it had when he first made his griffin fly to him at the age of five.

"And spoil our fun? Not me! I want to solve all the riddles and open this thing. That's what the inscription said. 'Treasure awaits the ones who answer the riddles.'"

"There was a warning, too," Blake reminded him.

"I have been pondering about that all afternoon," Morgan said. "We must keep all this to ourselves until we see what happens with the other riddles . . . that is, if we get more."

"What about Brianna? We can tell her, can't we?" Blake asked.

"No. She has a lot on her mind, thinking about home and everything. Let's not tell her about this yet," JD said.

Blake took a breath. He had been dreaming about the Jinn Cup Derby and wanted to see who won. But before he could climb back under the bedcovers and go back to sleep, JD jumped up. There was one more thing they had to do.

"We have to make a pact to keep this to ourselves," he said. "Agreed?"

Before they went back to their beds, JD stuck out his arm with his fist facing them. Morgan closed his hand over and put his fist against JD's. Both boys looked at Blake, who reluctantly joined his hand with theirs in a knuckle pact.

"One . . . two . . . three!" they chorused before pulling away their hands.

Exhausted from all the excitement, Morgan and Blake fell back to sleep. JD's eyes keenly focused on the box as he laid his head on the pillow. He heard another "Psst."

It was the same voice he had heard before, only this time it came from the side panel of the painting in the same meadow as in the first painting. Clouds of gray moved across the skyline. A steady hand had painted the dainty feathers of a bird on the little man's leather glove, which protected him from the powerful claws. Behind him were more birds all crammed together, swooshing and soaring upward. JD could almost hear the high sound of their screeches.

And just like before, the little man turned his head to face him.

"Get ready for the next riddle, young jinn," the little man said.

JD didn't say anything, only nodding his head. He just looked at Blake, who had let out a sudden grunt.

The man bowed his head before he gave the next riddle. This one also had something to do with birds.

"A hawk, a falcon, and an eagle! What kinds of birds are these?"

JD scratched his head and frowned. The little man rolled his eyes when he saw that the riddle stumped the boy. He coughed once before speaking again.

"I don't have all night, you know."

JD screwed his face to clearly show how bothered he was when the little man smacked his lips, showing his yellowed teeth. A loud snort from the bed across from JD grabbed his attention. He looked up and saw Morgan staring at him through his droopy eyes, his pillow tucked under his arms.

"Why are you still up?" Morgan asked.

JD climbed out from under the blanket. The moon's light guided him to his brother's bedside. Morgan by now had put the pillow on his lap.

"Morgan! Tell me what a hawk, a falcon, and an eagle have in common!"

"What?" Morgan yawned. "Why do you need to know that *now?*"

"That little man spoke to me again. It's the second riddle."

"He sure must like you better than us," Morgan said.

"That's not funny. Now can you think of the answer?"

Morgan rubbed his eye with a fist.

"A hawk, a falcon, and an eagle?" Another yawn. "They all have wings and beaks."

JD knew that was too easy. *Why would he mention those three birds,* he wondered.

"It is elementary. They are all predators. You know, they prey on other animals. That is why they are called 'birds of prey.'"

JD got up slowly and moved back to the other side of the bedchamber, setting his eyes on the riddle box. Did the second painting change as the first one had? He lifted the riddle box to eye level and turned it so that Morgan could see the painting. Yes, it had changed!

"That's correct, young jinn," the little man said.

JD couldn't hide his satisfaction that two riddles now had been solved. He looked to his brother. Morgan knew that JD's smile and silence were his way to say thank you.

Across the room, Blake flailed his arms among the bedcovers, gave a sudden snort, and yelled out phrases:

"That's it. Go higher!"

"You're too close! Get away from me!"

JD began to make his way over to Blake, but Morgan stopped him.

"Shouldn't we tell him about the second riddle?" JD asked.

Morgan shook his head.

"Let him sleep. We can tell him tomorrow."

JD fluffed his pillow and pulled the blanket almost over his head again. Morgan lay there briefly when he heard, "Flap your wings harder!" He looked over and found Blake sitting up in his bed flapping his arms. Now they had something else to look forward to: the Jinn Cup Derby.

Morgan rolled over and went back to sleep, too.

Chapter Eighteen

Camels, Dream Chasers, and the Jinn Cup Derby

At dawn on the day of the biggest race of the season, the Jinn Cup Derby, Blake said to Brianna, "Wait until you see the camels," just before their flying carpet lifted off the ground.

When they were close to Jinwiddie, the carpet turned, as the Jinnetti Downs Racetrack was still about another hour away to the east. They could enjoy the views of the lakes and land below as the early morning air grazed their faces.

Time seemed to slip by quickly, and before they knew it, they arrived at a clump of trees overlooking Jinnetti Downs, where a tint of pastel yellow shadowed the dome-topped circular towers.

Blake explained to Brianna how a former camel racer, Roman, had won the Jinn Cup Derby seven times, five in a row, and Miss Omarosa was the first woman cameleer to ever win. She now trained camels in the north.

"*Cameleer*? That's what you call a camel flyer?" Brianna asked.

Blake nodded.

"The best cameleer now is Nicolas," he said. "You'll get to see him when he races."

Aristede strolled with his family through the racers' sleeping quarters until they reached the endless rows of animal enclosures. Many trainers talked to the well-brushed, tawny-colored animals, a few of which had patterns shaved on their hides. Some camels were flittering their wings; others made bellowing noises.

The triplets didn't have any problem finding Uncle Jasper among all the people. He was feeding his racing camel, Native Flyer, just like many of the other camel keepers were doing with their own valuable racing animals. Jasper was a short, small-framed man with a firm jaw similar to Aristede's.

"Uncle Jasper!" Morgan called out, waving his hand to get his attention.

"There you are, my boys. Here at last," Jasper said. Among all the camel owners and cameleers, his baritone voice carried over those of everyone around them.

The boys' eyes were gleaming.

Jasper opened his hand, palm up, and pressed his outstretched hand against theirs.

"And who is your friend?" Jasper asked.

"This is Brianna," Morgan said.

"It's very good to meet you, my dear. Have you ever been to a camel race?"

"No, not really." Brianna crimped her nose and took one whiff. "What's that smell?"

One of the keepers was shoveling camel dung out of the tarp-covered stables, and the stench was overpowering. The more Brianna breathed, the more she nearly gagged. It was definitely not a desirable place to be. She held her nose as she moved away.

"Oh, don't worry. In time, you'll get used to the odor." Uncle Jasper smiled.

"So this is the camel destined to win the Jinn Cup this year, eh?" Aristede said. "He looks strong. Wings are firm."

Native Flyer stood motionless with his two wings furled along his sides. Aristede went over to the racing camel and untethered the bridle. Twigs crunched under Native Flyer's hooves as Aristede and Jasper walked him. When they stopped by a thick growth of trees, Jasper reached into his robe pocket, pulled out an apple, and held it under the camel's mouth. It didn't take any sweet-talking for Native Flyer to snap at the red fruit.

"I'm confident he will do well. He finished in the top three every time during the qualifying races," Jasper whispered. "Come. Let us leave him with the trainer."

As Jasper rubbed along the side of the camel and took hold of Native Flyer's wing, Native Flyer hopped. The two men turned and trooped back to the enclosures.

Jasper introduced a man in a white shirt. His name was Mandeville, and the dark eyebrows and long eyelashes almost concealed his light blue eyes.

"My family came to the races to be our cheering section," Jasper said enthusiastically.

Mandeville frowned. It was one of those frowns that showed he knew something that the others didn't.

"Did you say cheering section, sir? I thought one of them was here to take young Roger's place."

"No one's here to race for Roger," Jasper said.

"Mr. Jasper, Roger has taken ill," Mandeville said. "I doubt he will be well enough before the race begins. He is resting in his tent."

Jasper looked worried.

"What will you do now?" Aristede asked.

"I'm not sure," Jasper said.

As Jasper and Mandeville talked about possibilities as to who could fly his camel if Roger couldn't, Native Flyer seemed to have ideas of his own. He was enjoying Blake's gentle touch as the boy rubbed the camel's head and nose. He seemed to enjoy this even more than the apple Jasper had fed him a few minutes earlier. When no one was watching, Blake untied the bindings that tethered the camel, and to his surprise, Native Flyer remained sitting on the ground.

Blake lifted himself onto the camel's back. He squirmed on the hump, trying to find a way to stay on and not slip off. It took a bit of adjusting until he felt secure. As Native Flyer got to his feet, the sudden movement startled Blake.

With a light kick from Blake's heels, Native Flyer took a few skittish hops. Camel flying wasn't natural for Blake, as he had been on a camel only once before, on a trip to Jasper's camel farm.

Once both wings fanned out on either side of him, Native Flyer's hooves brushed across the green blades before he took off. Blake closed his eyes and felt the camel's muscles at the wing joints.

Before anybody knew it, Blake was high above the ground. He took command of Native Flyer by pulling on the reins, and he circled the enclosures. Native Flyer flapped faster and faster.

"What's he doing?" Cassidy said. She pressed her hand on her belly to control the butterflies she felt.

"What do you know!" Jasper cried. "Just look at him up there. Another cameleer in the family."

Blake leaned keenly to the left, over some palm trees. With a few final flaps of the wings, Native Flyer glided gracefully back to his tent.

Jasper hurried over to him and put his hands on his nephew's shoulders. Staring into his eyes, he said, "Good job, Blake. Good job, indeed."

Everyone cheered—everyone except for Cassidy, that is.

"Native Flyer doesn't take to strangers this easily. Roger has been the only cameleer who can keep Native Flyer calm—that is, until now," Mandeville said. "He must like you."

Native Flyer nudged at Blake's back, forcing the boy to take a step. If Blake hadn't known any better, he would have thought Native Flyer was volunteering him for flying duty. Nonetheless, the surprising prod built up the courage for him to announce, "I'll take Roger's place!"

All eyes turned to Blake. Jasper couldn't be more excited, slapping his knee with vigor.

"That's my boy. We're still going to be in this race and show them all," Jasper said. "We still have time to alert the racing officials of the change."

Cassidy thought it was a joke.

"No . . . no . . . I don't think so," she said. She brushed aside the very thought of her son racing a camel. "He has no business flying in a race. It's too dangerous."

Blake shot a glance to Aristede and Jasper, hoping they would convince his mother that he was quite serious about flying in the race.

"Actually, he can," Jasper said, picking up on Blake's hint. Native Flyer would be scratched from the race, and the only way to keep that from happening was if they found another flyer. "Without a rider, we're out of the race."

"Even experienced riders can get hurt," Cassidy said.

Cassidy was right. Injuries happened all the time when riders tangled with others flying around them. Camels were very unpredictable, and just about anything could happen. Like their land cousins, winged camels had been known to stop and nap during races. Sometimes they would just fly off in different directions. Most accidents occurred when one camel tried to fly under or above another and wings became tangled among the hooves.

"Seriously! You really think I would let Blake fly? When I said *no*, I wasn't joking!" she said.

"Flying is in his blood," Jasper said. "Blake is like his father. Aristede could have been a professional cameleer. That's why I know Blake will be good, too."

Cassidy thought she knew everything about the genie she had married.

"You—Aristede—flew camels?" Cassidy asked.

Although JD, Morgan, and Blake were impressed with this tidbit about their father, Aristede just brushed off his camel flying as something he had participated in during his youth.

"So . . . can I?" Blake asked hopefully.

"I'm sorry, Blake. I know you only want to help your uncle Jasper, but not at the risk of injury," Cassidy told him.

"But, Mother . . ."

But she wasn't answering him. She was more upset at Aristede, since he hadn't said anything to put an end to this nonsense. In fact, he remained disturbingly quiet.

With no concern about being rude, Jasper said, "You're not giving Blake any credit."

"I'm looking out for his safety. He flies once—halfway decently, I must admit—so you think he's ready to fly in a race against professionals. He's not a professional cameleer."

"But he can ride," Jasper said back to her.

"He has no training."

"But he can ride."

"He has no experience."

"But he can ride."

Cassidy was getting more unsettled by the minute. If Jasper said "but he can ride" one more time, she was going to seal his mouth closed with a snap of her fingers.

"I will say it one more time. My son *will not* be in this race!" she said before storming away from them.

"Dad. Do something," Blake pleaded.

Aristede went after his wife so they could talk . . . rather in this case, argue. As Aristede looked down and shook his head, it became quite obvious to Blake that his mother wouldn't allow him to fly. Jasper went with Mandeville as he walked Native Flyer around the animal yards.

Suddenly they heard a cackle behind them. Each triplet felt a lump in his throat, like a cat about to cough up a hair ball.

"Who would have believed it? Triplet Three—a cameleer?"

The triplets recognized that voice immediately, and when they turned around at the same time, there she was: Indra-Jindra. In his usual role as sidekick, Ian stood at his sister's side.

"Oh, peacock feathers!" JD said.

"Triplet Three looked like a scared monkey holding on for dear life," Indra-Jindra said. She imitated how a monkey would fumble around on a moving camel. "The High Council must have changed the rules to let monkeys fly."

"Watch what you're saying!" JD said. "That's our brother!"

"Yeah, I can see the resemblance. A protruding mouth and hairy arms."

"You stop, Indra-Jindra, or I'll send you to a far-off cave with a boulder blocking the opening to it. It will take your parents two weeks to find you!" JD said. His arms were raised up.

Morgan seized JD by the back of his shirt collar. He couldn't pull his brother away from her fast enough.

"Why are you here anyway?" she asked loudly. "Are you cleaning up all the dung after the race?"

JD's arms went up again. She was getting closer to that cave where he had threatened to send her. To everyone's surprise, Blake stepped forward and boldly announced, "If our uncle's cameleer can't race, then I'll be his replacement."

JD and Morgan were quite surprised, and it showed on their faces, their mouths gaping wide.

"If you do fly, I'll bet you'll fall off that old camel of yours on the last turn," Indra-Jindra said, snickering.

"He can fly better than you any day," Morgan said.

"I doubt that. My father owns Blushing Wildly, and I've been riding camels since I was three. I can prove I'm a better rider," Indra-Jindra said with a sneering grin. "I'll race you anytime you want."

"Fine. Just tell us when," JD said.

"How about after the race tomorrow?" Indra-Jindra snarled.

Ian, who had just been watching and hadn't said anything (which was not unusual where his sister was concerned), burst out laughing.

"Shall we make a bet, too?" Ian asked.

"Sure. What will the bet be?" JD asked.

Indra-Jindra snapped her fingers and said, "The loser has to ride through the animal enclosures in his underwear."

Ian turned to her. "You'd do that if you lost?"

"Not me! You, little brother. Remember, I'm a lady," she said as she tossed her hair back.

"Me!" Ian cried. He licked a couple of fingers with his tongue and brushed up his hair on his forehead.

"All right then, it's a deal!" JD said.

"We'll meet you guys behind the tents after the race," Indra-Jindra said as she ran past them, laughing girlishly.

Ian, on the other hand, didn't like this wager. He did manage to stick out his tongue at them as he chased after his sister. Morgan had to cross over in front of JD and Blake to stop them from going after the two.

JD gritted his teeth because of Indra-Jindra's bragging. She was right, though; she did have more experience flying camels than Blake did.

The corner of Morgan's mouth tweaked, and he looked as though he had just bitten his tongue. "What did we get ourselves into? Blake—why did you go and tell her you are replacing Roger? You know Mom will never let you be in the race."

"Well . . . you never know, so it wasn't really a lie."

"You'd better not count on that happening. The only race you'll be in is the one *after* the Jinn Cup is over," JD reminded him.

The confidence on Blake's face was really false. He didn't really enjoy the takeoffs, or even the landings. But other than that, once they were in flight, Native Flyer would do all the work. Blake knew he just had to hold on to the rope and not fall off. But he wasn't about to let his brothers know how easy he thought it would be.

The following morning was fairly clear, with only a few clouds sprinkled on a blue sky, and there was a light breeze in the air. Blake lay on his cot with thoughts only about the upcoming race.

"Psst!"

Blake looked around.

"What was that?" he asked. Across the tent he saw JD and Morgan staring at the riddle box.

"Quiet. It is the little man," Morgan said.

"He's about to give us the next riddle," JD said as he quickly picked up the box.

This time it was the little man with his hands on the rim of a marble railing, staring out across an overgrown garden.

"Young jinn," the little man said. "Here is riddle number three. It makes no sound whether moving or still and goes away in darkness, but always returns the following day."

Each of them had the same look of confusion. Morgan got up, moved toward JD, and without asking whether he could, took the box out of his hands. The little man rolled his eyes, waiting for an answer. The riddles were getting more difficult to solve.

However, there were more important things to worry about, and they didn't care if they didn't have an answer for him. The little man would just have to wait. They had a race to watch.

The little man just turned his head away from them. There was a faint whistling sigh from the painting.

"I don't think it is difficult to answer, young jinn, but . . ." the little man said to them.

JD and Morgan weren't listening. The little man was put out by this, and he turned his head back into its original position. If he had his way, he wouldn't give any more riddles to these three ungrateful youngsters.

By nine o'clock in the morning, hundreds of genies were filling the stadium towers that outlined the racetrack. Colorful bunting and banners hung below the gold-domed balconies. Cassidy and Brianna heard sounds of rowdy whoops and roars as they gave their tickets to the attendants and made their way to their special balcony seats, which were reserved for important dignitaries and guests.

The rows of silk carpet seats moved up and down, which allowed for quick movement. This feature was essential in order to avoid stray flying camels, which actually happened at the Jinn Cup Derby of 1957. The camel favored to win that year was Dragon Fever, flown by Miss Omarosa. But as the camels stood up, Dragon Fever bumped its head against one of the many flagpoles and became so disoriented that it flew toward the crowds, dropping dung on spectators sitting in rows three, eight, and nine.

Behind the south part of the track, by the racers' holding pens, Aristede and the triplets were with Jasper. Native Flyer waited for his rider to come and climb on to the saddle on his hump.

But when Mandeville arrived, the look on his face was not good. Blake kept his eyes on his uncle, who had had his heart set on Native Flyer being in the race. The thought of him now just watching the race, disappointed, made Blake think how he could help at this crucial moment. Aristede knew that Jasper needed some time alone and steered his boys toward the fourth stadium.

Aristede, JD, and Morgan moved quickly past a group of giddy teenage genies discussing the bets they had placed on Blushing Wildly. Before they started up the stairs, JD and Morgan saw that they were missing Blake, so Morgan and JD hurried back to the racers' area.

They pushed their way against a crowd of owners, handlers, and even camels going across the backside of the racetrack just in time to see Blake, who had been listening behind a stack of hay bales, step out and talk to Jasper.

"What's he up to?" JD asked.

Morgan knew that the answer to his question would become clear if they waited and watched long enough. The wait was not very long. As soon as Blake climbed onto Native Flyer, they knew. Neither JD nor Morgan had given him credit for being so brave. He was going to fly.

Morgan began pushing JD back so they wouldn't be seen. It would only make Blake more nervous.

Morgan and JD crouched low to slip away unseen. They managed to get to the spectators' towers and join their family just as the race was about to begin. They were quiet so they wouldn't bring any attention to themselves. Once the race began, there wouldn't be a second thought about Blake. By the time he was airborne, there would be nothing anyone could do, as it was against the rules to interfere with the race once it had begun.

Like all the other cameleers, Blake pushed his feet in just behind the wing and settled firmly in his seat. Mandeville led Native Flyer to the racetrack.

"I know your mother isn't sure about this, and she'll be furious with me, but I believe you can fly a camel in a race. Show everyone you can do this," Jasper told him. He looked around and then whispered, "I've seen you with Native Flyer, and he likes you. Trust him to do his job, and just keep a tight grip throughout the race."

"But what about Nicolas?"

Jasper's satisfied smile filled his face.

"You're going to beat him, too! No other cameleer has what you have! You fly because you like it, not because it's your job."

In the center of the racetrack, hovering fifty feet high, was the skybox for Jinn Cup Derby commentators Tony and Conrad, who had a 360-degree view of the flying camels. The lineup of camels included Moonbats, Sheba's Dainty Wings, Mad Rush, Passion Delight, Blushing Wildly, Miss Charisma, Flamingo Lady, Native Flyer, Bottlecaps, Market Place, and Fire Ball Rider.

Some of the camels grew tired of waiting, flapping their wings as they tried to get loose.

"Uh-oh! There's some restlessness among the camels," Tony said.

The camel trainers moved swiftly to grab hold of the ropes to keep the animals in line. The riders, too, worked hard to keep the camels calm and keep them from bumping into each other.

Brianna giggled at the ruckus. She thought they looked like big hummingbirds. Morgan gave her a dirty look.

"Hummingbirds!" he exclaimed. He was very put off by the thought. "They are magnificent creatures."

Brianna tried to restrain herself, but she failed miserably and finally burst out laughing.

"They look so dopey!"

"Mom. Did you hear her?" Morgan asked.

Cassidy looked out on the field and tried hard not to laugh as well.

"I have to admit, it is a funny sight to watch, isn't it?"

Over the speaker, Tony said in a clear voice, "All the camels are just about in line. The story for these finals is that there are three beginners. They are Miss Charisma, Moonbats, and Native Flyer."

Miss Charisma let out a deafening bellow. The jumpy camel then lurched forward suddenly and flexed her wings as the trainers struggled to rein in the animal.

Now with a delay in the race, Conrad ran his hand over his slicked-back hair and continued with his report.

"The favorite for the Jinn Cup final today is Sheba's Dainty Wings."

"She may be the favorite, but I like Fire Ball Rider," Tony said. "I pick him for his speed and because he has the most experienced cameleer. That's my prediction. This is the camel to beat."

Cassidy watched as both Jasper and Mandeville gave what appeared to be last-minute coaching to their rider. She couldn't take her eyes off the cameleer sitting atop Native Flyer. She wasn't quite sure why, but there was something familiar about him under the traditional racing clothes he wore. Maybe it was the light hair peeking out from under the headgear; maybe it was the jittery way he tried to stay perched on the camel. Perhaps it was . . .

"You know, Roger looks very much like Blake."

Then, as Cassidy looked around for her son, it hit her: it *was* Blake. She jumped to her feet and aimed a slender finger toward her son. She was about to take her son out of the race when Aristede pushed her arm down so that her finger pointed to the ground.

"No," Aristede said. "Jasper was certain Blake could fly with the best of them. Furthermore, our son is determined to fly. Let's respect his decision."

Cassidy brought her hands together and nervously rubbed them so hard that the pain numbed the uneasy feeling she felt in her stomach.

Back on the racetrack, Blake pressed his kneecaps at Native Flyer's hump.

Mandeville then whispered to Blake, "Just steer him gently, and let Native Flyer do the rest. Don't worry about the other riders. Does no good worrying at all."

There were a few of seconds of silence before a bell rang, signaling the start of the race. The camels froze as Flamingo Lady took a pee. The camels then darted off jogging, and Blake felt as though his throat was dropping down to his stomach, sticking at the base of his abdomen. What would people think if he fell off? He shuddered at the possibility.

Then, with wings expanded, all the camels moved quickly, to the crowd's wild cheers. Blake hunched over, holding tightly to the bridle as Native Flyer pumped his supple, outspread wings. With the other cameleers bunched together as they gained altitude early in the race, he almost forgot to look down until he heard the cheers below. The crowds looked like tiny ants.

Uncle Jasper's words echoed in Blake's head: *Trust in your camel to do his job!*

"It's a decent, even start. Passion Delight comes out to lead on the extreme outside. Blushing Wildly and Bottlecaps are right on Passion Delight's heels," Conrad said. "No bumps early on."

He spoke too soon. Without any warning, Moonbats made off in the opposite direction. The crowds gasped in loud oooohs and aaaahs.

"Oh, there goes Moonbats toward the grandstands. I hope it's not a repeat of 1957. What a mess that was!" Conrad continued.

Moonbats climbed higher and higher before veering back to the track, while the other flyers were already in the first turn. JD and Morgan watched with alarm as Moonbats flew directly in Blake's way. It looked as though a nasty collision was about to occur, and Blake knew he had to do something to avoid such a disaster.

Back in the stands, Cassidy jumped up from her seat.

"He's going to get killed!"

So it seemed until, at the last possible second, Blake pulled sharply on the reins so Native Flyer soared upward above the others. However, Blake's uneven flying startled Fire Ball Rider, nearly clipping him and setting the camel awry. Nicolas was forced to fly an agitated Fire Ball Rider to the ground, landing in front of the third set of towers.

Blake felt a twinge of guilt in his stomach, knowing that Nicolas's misfortune was his fault. He pulled the reins sideways and followed a circular course, corkscrewing down. Native Flyer spread his wings to glide to a gentle landing, a touchdown with a soft bounce. Blake was glad he was no longer airborne and dismounted. His only thought was to go to Nicolas as fast as he could.

"Are you all right? I-I'm sorry about what happened up there," Blake said.

Nicolas looked very much as he did on Blake's poster back home. He was much taller, and his brown hair, streaked with red, was longer and wavier in person.

Nicolas soothed his camel by stroking Fire Ball Rider's head and rubbing the underside of his neck.

"I couldn't help it," Blake said.

"That is what makes you a very good cameleer. It is your ability to fly the way you did," Nicolas said. He looked intently at Blake through his almond-shaped eyes.

A feeling of disappointment came over Blake. He had so wanted to be in the race for Uncle Jasper, and now not only was he out of it, but so was a great racer like Nicolas. Blake glanced up to the azure skies at the remaining flying camels.

"If you're game to try something, I think I have a way we can still be a part of this race."

To the surprise of all who were watching, Blake *and* Nicolas mounted Native Flyer. Nicolas wrapped his arms around Blake's waist and pressed his knees above the wings.

Then within a few moments, Tony announced, "An interesting development in the race. They're resuming the race together. This is fantastic! These two riders are demonstrating true camel racing sportsmanship."

Racing fans exploded again in resounding applause as Native Flyer picked up speed, even though it would take a brave effort for Blake and Nicolas to catch up with the others on the back turn of the track.

"Passion Delight still has a slight advantage going into the turn, followed by Mad Rush. Flamingo Lady is chasing on the inside," Tony said. "Moonbats is still behind. He'll need to pick it up. Market Place is weaving his way through the pack and giving everything he has."

"Native Flyer is showing a lot of heart," Conrad said. "Here they come and—uh-oh! Passion Delight has decided to take a nap in midflight. Now Sheba's Dainty Wings makes a move into the lead.

All flyers are coming to get her. Native Flyer is not wasting any time getting back in the race. Look at that camel go!"

Although Native Flyer had moved past several camels, he still had a lot of catching up to do. Miss Charisma tried to fly above the others, and Moonbats couldn't maintain her pace. Blake and Nicolas continued to move Native Flyer along the inside of the track and through the field of camels in front of him. Blushing Wildly moved into the lead.

To get a better view of the race, JD and Morgan floated their carpets up and hovered above their family. They heard hoots and hollers directed at Blake coming from behind them.

"Triplet Three sure looks stupid," Indra-Jindra said to Ian. She spoke loud enough to make sure JD and Morgan heard her.

JD turned to Morgan and said, "Have you ever seen a squashed dung beetle, Morgan?" There was a pause as he shot a look at Indra-Jindra. "All its insides oozing out between the top shell and its underbelly. Not a pretty sight."

It took Indra-Jindra several seconds before it sank in that the question was meant for her, and she didn't find the comment funny at all. As the self-centered look withdrew from her face, JD knew he had hit a nerve. Resuming her usual leer, she turned her attention back to the race.

"Here they come to the final turn. Blushing Wildly is starting to fade. Perhaps he pushed a little too hard. Now Sheba's Dainty Wings is moving in to take it away from him. Either of the two camels could still win."

"They're in the last stretch, and that new rider, Blake, with Nicolas, is letting the camel just take off. It's Blushing Wildly and Sheba's Dainty Wings in front. Blushing Wildly and Sheba's Dainty Wings are neck and neck. It's Blushing Wildly and Sheba's Dainty Wings! Blushing Wildly and Sheba's Dainty Wings! It looks like it's nose to nose at the finish!"

To the sounds of great cheers and the waving of thousands of flags, Sheba's Dainty Wings blew past the finish line first.

JD and Morgan smugly looked back at Indra-Jindra and Ian.

"If Dad had let me fly him, I would have won. Don't forget to meet us. I'll show you who is the best," Indra-Jindra said before scuttling out of the stadium tower. Her giggles dissolved among the noise of the streaming crowds.

As the other camels crossed the finish line, the message board flashed the order of finish in green lights: Sheba's Dainty Wings, Blushing Wildly, Moonbats, Bottlecaps, Miss Charisma, Native Flyer, Market Place, Flamingo Lady, and Mad Rush.

"Passion Delight is still sound asleep on the back stretch," Tony announced, sighing.

Blake and Nicolas flew to the ground and dismounted a second time to thundering cheers drifting from all directions. Blake threw off his headgear, as many admirers had flooded the racetrack, catching him off guard with the pats on the back. It was as though he had just won the Jinn Cup. His cheeks went from a rosy pink to a full-flushed tomato red.

Cassidy also made her way down from the tower. When Blake saw her, he was sure he was in deep trouble.

"I'm sorry, but I had to fly. I just had to. You can punish me—"

Before Blake could even finish explaining his reason for disobeying her, Cassidy pulled him in for a tight hug.

"I am soooo proud of you," she said.

Relief that a son wasn't seriously injured in a camel racing accident was one way for a mother to show that everything would be all right. His face was turning purple, and he barely managed to utter a short cry. "Mom." He tried his best to release himself from his mother's firm grip.

By now Jasper had made his way through the crowds, smiling all the way.

"Blake! Blake, my boy! The ride was magnificent. You were as good as your dad ever was," Jasper said.

"But we didn't win."

"As a true champion, you didn't give up when you encountered a little setback," Jasper said to him. "Look. One of the viziers is coming to join us."

This vizier, rather rotund with a round belly, had been a prominent camel trainer before he was tapped for a position on the Supreme High Council of the Jinn. He had a full head of red hair and bushy sideburns in the same deep orange color. He invited the racers, camel owners, and their families to his tent for the festivities.

"If you don't mind, Uncle Jasper, we'll take care of Native Flyer," Blake said, reaching for the bridle eagerly.

"Don't be long," Cassidy said. "We'll be in the vizier's tent."

The triplets ran at full speed across the grass toward the training grounds, fully expecting to find Indra-Jindra waiting for them. The grounds were vacant. Besides the occasional bellow of the camel, the only sounds came from the tarp tents flapping back and forth when the winds kicked up.

The boys were pacing quickly, passing each other several times.

"I don't think the coward's even coming," JD said angrily.

After a few more minutes had passed, two hazy figures moved slowly behind the tent. Finally, Indra-Jindra led Blushing Wildly out, with Ian sitting atop the camel.

The three brothers stepped forward and arranged themselves opposite Indra-Jindra and Ian.

"Are we ready to get this thing started?" JD asked, brushing past Morgan and Blake. "The racetrack is empty, so—"

Indra-Jindra erupted in pompous laughter.

"Did you seriously think my brother would race any one of you? Our father would have a fit."

"We most definitely are going to have a race. We had a bet, *remember?*" Morgan said.

"We never shook on it."

"Why, you stinking weasel!" JD yelled. "You never intended to have a race, did you?"

Indra-Jindra took hold of the camel's right wing above the joint and pulled herself up onto Blushing Wildly. Their camel took off, and Indra-Jindra and Ian circled above the triplets. She called down, "Catch you later!"

One truth to come out of all this was that Indra-Jindra could fly a camel extremely well, even if she lied about other things.

The mighty flapping helped Indra-Jindra turn the camel in midair. Blushing Wildly came closer and closer and then swooped low overhead. A massive shadow crossed over and stunned them before Indra-Jindra and Ian flew away.

"I can't believe she tricked us," Blake said.

"Forget that!" Morgan shouted. "I know the answer to the third riddle. Come with me."

Morgan hustled away from the racing area. JD and Blake did their best to keep up with him.

When he got to their tent, Morgan stopped to take a breath before entering the sleeping quarters. He was panting heavily from running and waited for JD and Blake, using the time for his breathing to slow down. Seconds later, the two arrived, also panting.

Morgan lifted his pillow and looked at the painting in the third panel. He repeated the riddle:

"It makes no sound whether moving or still and goes away in darkness, but always returns the following day."

"I know the answer," Morgan said. "It is a shadow. I am sure that is it!"

Just as JD and Blake pushed the tent flap back, the little man tilted his head and said, "Correct, young jinn."

A few tents away, celebratory singing reminded them that they had to join everyone for the Jinn Cup after-party. They hurried past many people jubilantly celebrating the cache of doblers from their racing bets.

Chapter Nineteen

The Arrival of Aunt Majo and Aunt Saffire

Blake spent hours watching the orbular of the race over and over. He was amazed that JD and Morgan didn't share his enthusiasm and find the whole experience as thrilling as he still did. Everyone had lost interest in the race, thanks to Blake's nonstop chattering—he talked about it every chance he got, to the point that he was unbearable to be around. Blake ignored everyone and went about viewing the events, from his decision to ride for Uncle Jasper to his dismount of Native Flyer at the end of the race. That was, until JD hid the milky sphere.

"Where is it? I want my orbular back!" Blake demanded.

It wasn't until Aristede and Cassidy stepped in that the orbular was returned to Blake.

Within a few days, everything was back to normal. Brianna had become adept at playing JinJi, winning more games now (she had picked up on the differing strategies the triplets used). She was tickled when the boys involved her with their magic practice, particularly judging who made the best (and most creative) transmogrifications. She eagerly added entries in her journal about the magic and genie life in general.

But the uneventful life wasn't about to last.

One day, a rolled-up parchment appeared inside the gold-tinted genie mail jar. Unlike the whistling orbulars, which broadcast their arrivals, there was no such announcement with this parchment.

There was nothing out of the ordinary about the letter until Aristede pulled out the crisp paper and read it.

"Aunt Majo and Aunt Saffire are coming," he said cheerfully.

Aristede's joy was countered by Cassidy's disdain. She knew the upcoming visit was going to be an ordeal, and it made her stomach sink.

Majo and Saffire were Aristede's two unmarried aunts, who prided themselves on being able to trace their family line directly back to the blue jinn Bahktiar. They were his mother's sisters, and they seldom spent time at their own home due to all the traveling they did. Every few years they would come for a visit. Cassidy had seen them on only a few occasions, but Aunt Majo and Aunt Saffire always managed to disrupt the family whenever they came.

Cassidy had first met them on her wedding day thirteen years earlier. They had many questions about where she had come from, and they made just as many rude remarks about her family, none of whom attended the wedding ceremony.

Another time, right after the birth of the triplets, the two aunts had made it quite clear that the only reason the boys were so handsome was that they looked like Aristede.

During a visit nearly five years ago, Aunt Majo had brought her pampered pet monkey, Malcolm. After three days of torn cushions and scratched curtains (not to mention the monkey droppings throughout the house), the aunts had packed their belongings and left. Malcolm had never been back since.

The only blissful time when there were no communications, let alone visits, was when both aunts had to serve an Outsider who had gained possession of their bottle. It took him a long time before deciding on his wishes.

"And how long will they be here *this* time?" Cassidy asked. She made their visit sound as though it were a prison sentence.

"It doesn't say," Aristede said.

"When will they be arriving? I need to get ready for their visit," Cassidy said.

Aristede scanned over the rest of the letter.

"Today!" he said in a panic. "They should be here by one o'clock!"

"Naturally." Cassidy sighed as she rolled her eyes.

Brianna whispered to the triplets, "I don't think your mom likes your dad's aunts very much, does she?"

"They are not her favorite relatives. We are not too fond of them, either," Morgan said.

As it got closer to one o'clock, Aristede paced through the center chamber. When it was half past two, Aristede began to worry. He quickly moved beyond utter panic, and by four o'clock in the afternoon he was ready to organize a search party to find them. He had already imagined their bodies mangled, broken, and bloodied at the bottom of a ravine.

"Relax, Ari. I'm sure everything is fine," Cassidy said with halfhearted reassurance.

She waved her hand, and a tall glass appeared, and she ever so calmly began stirring her plum wine with a celery stalk.

"They're never punctual for anything," she said. She took a swig of her wine.

Aristede had begun his pacing again when, quite suddenly, he heard a pitchy woman's voice.

When the door opened, three people were sitting on a large rug made of red-and-purple threads with gold fringe on the edges. Traveling trunks were piled on the rear part of the hovering carpet.

"Hello there," Aunt Majo said, waving over to them as she knelt on the hovering carpet.

Aunt Majo was a petite lady who wore a tweed hat with a feather sandwiched between pink and blue ribbons rather than a thin scarf around her head. She had short, curly brown hair with honey-blonde highlights, and she had the same green eyes as her nephews.

Clutching tightly to the edge of the rug was a much larger woman, Majo's sister, Saffire. The royal blue sash around her waist rippled over the rolls of her frumpy midsection. Her frizzy black hair was streaked with gray. Her chubby cheeks had a pinkish tinge to them.

The two aunts weren't alone. There, sitting with Majo, was a white-haired man—a person neither Aristede nor Cassidy had ever seen before.

The carpet descended gently until it was low enough for Aunt Saffire, Aunt Majo, and Majo's male companion to step off. With a quick motion of Saffire's pudgy fingers, the traveling trunks flew off the carpet. JD and Blake leaped out of the doorway to avoid being knocked over.

"Aristede, my favorite nephew!" Aunt Saffire cried. Her arms were extended, and she obviously anticipated a hug from him.

The stout woman threw her arms around his thin body, pulling him in tight and even lifting him off the ground; her hugs were brutal. Once she finally put Aristede down, she kissed each of his cheeks.

Aristede exhaled silently as he regained his breath.

"Cassidy," Aunt Majo said. She extended a hand to greet her with a polite hand press.

The two well-dressed women took hold of Aristede's arms and ignored Cassidy altogether, treating her like a servant as they tossed their handbags to her to carry for them. They both appeared to relish every bit of it, too.

"Aunt Majo," Aristede whispered as he turned sideways to look at his aunt's male companion. "Who is that man?"

"This is Sigmund," she said fondly. She took his arm with her free hand. "Sigmund and I are very close friends. Siggy, this is my nephew, Aristede, and his wife."

The six-foot-tall, skinny-faced man bowed and said, "Pleased to meet you."

The pointed turban on Sigmund's head made his ears look smaller than they really were. Aristede just stared at him. There was something curiously familiar about the man, and he racked his memory to recall from where he had seen him.

"Sigmund," Aristede began. "You look familiar. Have you ever worked for the Jinn High Council?"

"No. I have not."

"If I could just remember. How about last year's dricketts championships?" Aristede said politely. "I keep having this feeling we've met before."

"You do?" Sigmund asked. "I have never been to a dricketts match in my life."

"I usually don't forget a face," Aristede said.

"Perhaps I just have one of those commonly ordinary ones."

"That's probably it," Aristede said with a half smile.

Brianna glanced at the others and saw how uneasy they were, just like how she was feeling. The aunts went on about all the traveling they had been doing recently. Brianna didn't know what to make of them. She wasn't even sure if she liked Majo and Saffire.

When Majo found out Brianna was an Outsider, she was aghast.

"Oh, dear! Outsiders are such dreadful creatures. I remember that horrid man who kept Saffire and me in his power so long. He just couldn't make up his mind about what he wanted. I got even once we were finally released. I turned him into an octopus."

Brianna was now certain that she detested these two women as much as the triplets did.

"Aunt Majo, that's an awful thing to do!" Cassidy exclaimed. She looked utterly horrified.

Pretending not to hear Cassidy, Majo said, "I think he's in a tank in some restaurant, waiting to be served as someone's dinner."

Majo then covered her mouth with her dainty fingers in an attempt to suppress a high-pitched giggle. She had no regard for what her family thought about what she had done.

The aunts sank down to sit on the plush pillows near the bubbling fountain in the sitting retreat. Sigmund followed but remained standing. He had something for each of the children.

"Your aunts told me you recently celebrated your birthday, so I knew I just could not come empty-handed," Sigmund said.

Sigmund raised his arms straight above his head and gently brought them down until they crossed lightly over each other. The boys stepped forward at the same time. They had the excited look that they had had at their birthday party.

"What is it?" Blake asked.

"Watch and see," the man said.

In an instant, each of the triplets held a tiny wooden animal. The animals were sculpted from teak, a hard yellowish-brown wood. JD was holding a giraffe, Morgan had a rhinoceros, and Blake received an elephant that happened to match the elephant on his talisman.

"Look!" Blake shrieked. "I don't believe what I'm seeing!"

The carved animals were different from their other toys in that they moved as if they were alive. Like windup mechanical toys, these moved at a snail's pace up their arms. It was difficult to hold on to them, so JD, Morgan, and Blake placed their animals on the floor. The animals plodded along in different directions. Halfway to the step leading up to the center chamber, the elephant trumpeted with its trunk.

Sigmund turned to Brianna, who smiled at him weakly. But it appeared that he wasn't finished. She wasn't going to be left out.

Sigmund tapped a long finger three times to his split, stubbly chin.

"I have a gift that I believe you will enjoy."

Again, he raised his arms and waved them. The children were standing very still with carved animals in hand and looking at Mr. Sigmund. Brianna could have sworn she saw something twinkle. A carved animal just like ones the boys had appeared in her hand. Sigmund had expected Brianna to be as excited as JD, Morgan, or Blake (probably more so, since she was an Outsider).

A long hush of several seconds passed as the wooden animal crept up her sleeve, braying all the way.

"It's a donkey," Brianna said.

She stared at it . . . not because she found it delightful, but because she was disappointed in the kind of animal it was.

"You do not like it. I can tell," Sigmund said mildly as he sat down next to her.

Brianna didn't want to offend him. Before she could say anything, Sigmund added, "This one is different from the others. Watch this—"

He looked over his shoulder to Saffire and then to Majo. He winked at Aristede and Cassidy. When Sigmund stroked the back of the donkey with his forefinger, the animal let out a squeaky sound, and suddenly a fantastic thing began to happen that amazed the children. After a string of brays, the little donkey changed into a little lion.

Another stroke on its back, and the lion became a hippopotamus.

Blake gently stroked his elephant's back, hoping his would change, too. He quickly came to realize that the elephant would remain an elephant.

"Only Brianna's pet changes," Sigmund explained. "It is my way to say that things will change, and I believe she will go home soon."

Brianna thanked him. Majo got up from her place and strolled over to Sigmund, where she wrapped her arms around him.

"That was so considerate of you, Siggy, to give such a wonderful gift to an Outsider." Then Majo strode toward the bedchamber hallway and stopped about halfway. She turned to the others. "Are we in the same room as before?"

Cassidy nodded.

"The boys will be sleeping down here, so you'll sleep in their bedchamber," Aristede said, pointing to the hallway at the top of the stairs.

"Splendid," Aunt Saffire said, clapping her hands together.

She aimed her hand at the trunks again and, with a quick swish of her finger, used her magic to steer her trunks to the bedchamber.

But there was a problem. Cassidy awkwardly said, "Aunt Majo, we weren't expecting anyone else. We don't have any room for your friend." She turned to Sigmund. "I'm so sorry."

"Oh, yes. You *do* have such a humble place. You and Aristede with the triplets *and* this Outsider girl," Majo said. Her left eyebrow rose while the other narrowed down. This was her "snooty attitude" look.

It was shameless of Majo to remind Aristede that she and Saffire had a more spacious bottle, where they lived in the northern region. As she pompously moved around the reflecting pool, she made sure that everyone observed her tart face.

Aristede offered Sigmund the small pantry off the eating area. All it needed was a bed.

But Aunt Majo had another idea. If they gave the Outsider the pantry, then Brianna's bedchamber could be given to Sigmund.

"After all, he's practically family," Majo said as she stepped in between them, batting her eyelids.

The pushiness of Aristede's relatives did not sit well with Cassidy. As far as she was concerned, Brianna was part of the family.

Objecting to her nastiness and looking angrier than ever, Cassidy said, "Furthermore—"

Brianna didn't want to be the cause of any family problems, even though just the thought of sleeping in a closet-sized room, no larger than the storage shed in Brianna's grandparents' backyard, was an unpleasant one. She would have to make the best of her new sleeping arrangements.

She was taken aback when Aunt Majo patted her on the head, the way she would for a dog. Blake whispered to Brianna that it was nothing personal and that they treated everyone badly.

Brianna agreed with almost everything he had said, with one exception—they didn't treat Aristede as if he were some kind of bug.

Majo picked up a blue pillow, patting it first and then pulling it from the center as if she were playing an accordion. The fringes vibrated as she fluffed it. Finally she clutched her arms tightly around it.

Aristede offered to get her some coffee.

"That would be lovely!" Majo smiled. "You always know just the perfect way to make it."

Aristede snapped his fingers, and cups and saucers flew out from the eating area. When one of the cups reached Saffire, she sniffed at the steaming brew, and the spicy scent brought a thin smile to her face. After her first swallow, she told him how sweet it tasted. However, when Aristede told her that Cassidy had made it, Saffire made a sour face. She was quick to tell Aristede how to improve the coffee blend a great deal by adding some beans from the winkle plant.

At ten o'clock the following morning, two blue vapors drifted down the hall corridor and around the fireplace. Majo and Saffire didn't come into a room in an ordinary way. Why should they when they could vaporize? They were genies, and it was for that reason genie magic was used.

Looking around, Majo asked, "What do you have for our morning meal?"

"We ate two hours ago," Cassidy said sharply.

"So are you saying that you're not preparing anything for *us*?" Saffire asked, pushing her front bangs neatly into place. "We're famished. We haven't eaten since yesterday."

"You don't say," Cassidy said. She wasn't very sympathetic.

"She certainly isn't saying that, are you, Cassidy, dear?" Majo said hopefully, trying to be helpful in her own selfish way. "We're simple folks. We don't expect anything fancy."

Saffire snapped her tongue in her mouth. "We must remember how busy she is, Majo. She has no time for us," she snipped.

"I'm certain Aristede will prepare a meal for us that would be much more suitable than anything Cassidy could prepare," Majo said. Her forced grin broadened to a wide smile as she turned to face Aristede.

Cassidy closed her eyes, brought her teeth together, and clenched down hard. She took a deep breath before waving her hand to send the last of the tableware back into the drawer.

Before making an expedient exit, Cassidy said, "If you'll excuse me."

Aristede wanted nothing more than to please his relatives. With a snap of his fingers, a beautiful table setting appeared on which was an assortment of tasty foods. Saffire stuffed herself with large helpings, especially of the fried potatoes and bacon. Watching her chew was like watching a stray cat eating after not having any food in a long time. Majo helped herself to the melon, but she just nibbled at her portions.

Frowning just a little bit, Aristede was still thinking about Sigmund.

"Anything wrong, dear?" Saffire asked.

"Well—" He stopped short.

"Go on. Tell us," Majo said.

"Aunt Majo, I still can't get over this feeling that I've met Sigmund before. It's still nagging at me. Tell me, how long have you known him?" Aristede asked.

Rather than respond right away, Majo shoved a large portion of sausage links into her mouth and chewed slowly.

"About a month or so," she eventually replied. "Isn't that right, sister?"

Saffire nodded. Her bulging cheeks made her look like a chipmunk.

They proceeded to explain how they had met him in a quaint specialty shop. He was looking for a gift for his daughter. It was the same shop where they had bought the triplets' birthday present.

Majo twisted her mouth and added, "I'm surprised the boys didn't thank us for that rare box."

"The riddle box! You're the ones who sent the riddle box to JD, Morgan, and Blake?" Aristede uttered.

"Is that what you call it? We liked it because of the peculiar pictures. The card told them the box was from us," Majo said bluntly.

"There was no card, Aunt Majo," Aristede said.

"No card! Nonsense," Majo exclaimed. "Sister, you did put the card in with the boys' present, didn't you?"

Saffire stopped eating, which was unusual, since once she started her meals she kept on eating until there was virtually nothing left on her plate.

"Card? Yes, of course I did."

The looks on their pasty faces were ones of wild surprise, which lasted for only a brief second or two.

"Dear me," Majo said. "I wonder what could have happened to it?"

Excitement bubbled inside JD, Morgan, and Blake when they finally learned who had sent them the box. After Majo and Saffire finished eating, they made their way to the seating area and plunked themselves down in the pillows. That was where the trio found them.

"Do you know how to open it?" JD asked.

"Oh, heavens, no!" Saffire exclaimed. "We thought you would enjoy figuring out how to open it. Boys are much more curious than girls when it comes to those sorts of things."

"I liked the paintings on it. I thought they were quite interesting," Majo added. "According to the shopkeeper, the box is quite old, and there's something valuable hidden inside it."

Saffire shook her head and pushed her bottom lip out. "I think he just said that so he could make a sale."

And that it did. Majo and Sigmund got into a bidding war over the fascinating little object. Sigmund finally gave in when he found out that Majo had been looking for something special for their eleven-year-old nephews.

"We never dreamed the riddle box came from you," Blake stated.

Majo frowned, as if she were angry. "Why on earth do you call it *that*?"

"Because we did not know who sent it," Morgan added. "It was a complete mystery. A riddle."

"Precisely," Saffire said, without batting her long eyelashes.

"It means a great deal to us that you like our gift," Majo said.

"If you thought it was so unique, why did you not keep it for yourselves?" Morgan asked.

"Oh, my! We have so many treasures of our own," Saffire explained. "One more wouldn't have meant very much to us."

"All this talk about the box has tired me," Majo said, sighing. "Sister and I will return to our bedchamber for some rest. Come, Saffire."

The triplets watched as blue smoke replaced the solid shapes and drifted to the other end of the bottle house.

It was at this time they became aware that Sigmund had been watching them from the top step leading to his bedchamber. How long he had been standing there, the triplets couldn't say for sure. They moved to the reflecting pool and sat on the polished marbled edge.

Sigmund took a few steps to the center chamber and cheerfully said, "I was there when your aunts bought that box for you and your brothers."

JD nodded. "Yes—I know." Maybe it was his imagination, but the riddle box seemed to be the primary focus of his gaze.

Sigmund moved in closer to the boy and sat on his right. JD became stiff, and as he tightened up, a prickling feeling ran down his neck.

"May I?" Sigmund asked.

JD shed a look at him from the corner of his eye. Though he really didn't want to give Sigmund the box, he respectfully (albeit reluctantly) handed it over to him nonetheless. Sigmund seized it from him without a thought and carefully brushed his dried-up and shriveled finger along the worn corners and along the painted portions.

"Beautiful paintings. All different," Sigmund said. The grin on his face was eerie. "But they're not how I remember them. I see you've cleaned some of them. You have taken good care of the box. I wanted it for my daughter, you know."

JD politely said, "Mm-hmm."

Sigmund then stood up, and before he started to leave, he said, "If you do open it, please let me know right away. I am curious to learn what you discover."

All six eyes were fixed on Mr. Sigmund until the fastening for the door closed behind him.

"What was that about?" Blake asked.

"I think he still wants the box," JD said suspiciously.

"Not the box. What is inside of it," Morgan said. "We have to be careful."

Chapter Twenty

Cassidy's Headaches

Cassidy couldn't remember the last time she had a week like the one that had just passed. The mood was overly gloomy, and she wisely decided that it was best to stay out of Majo and Saffire's way. For Aristede's sake, she cooked the aunts' favorite meals. She prepared rack of dragon ribs with a creamy alfalfa sauce, deep-fried elephant ears, and roasted termites and crickets. One afternoon, Cassidy spent many hours preparing a tasty dessert: mocha almond—flavored octopus tentacle sticks. Instead of giving accolades, Majo and Saffire voiced nothing but complaints:

"The cream sauce has *lumps*."

"The tentacles are *too rubbery*."

"You *overfried* the ears."

The one houseguest who seemed to appreciate his meals was Sigmund.

"I think everything has been wonderful. It all tasted very good," he said. "The giraffe tonsils were sautéed to perfection."

Sigmund's lovely compliments about Cassidy's cooking surprised Majo. He was such a diplomat, and Majo thought he should be working for the Jinn High Council.

"Thank you for those kind words, Sigmund," Cassidy said. She ignored Majo's comment.

But Cassidy's cooking wasn't all the aunts found that, in their opinions, wasn't up to their standards. Majo listed all the things that her niece did wrong, from cleaning ("The house needs deeper cleaning") to child rearing ("My nephews turned out as well as they did surely because of the job Aristede did with the boys"). Unsolicited advice was given on just about everything.

Cassidy was at her wits' end with her snooty houseguests.

Early one evening at the beginning of the second week of the aunts' visit, Majo requested that the family join her and Saffire in the sunken retreat. From a leather satchel, Saffire pulled a mahogany box, inlaid with bamboo strips. She placed it on a flat, firm cushion, and when she lifted the lid, there were twenty small orbulars, each in its own distinct compartment. The flames from the chamber's urns softened the surface of the spheres.

"We don't go anywhere without these," Saffire said happily. She was like a child opening a beautifully wrapped gift.

She touched the orbular in the first compartment and released it into the air. There it floated as though it were a small helium-filled balloon. Saffire relished telling marvelous stories about the time when she and Majo had attended Jinn University.

Majo had lured a three-headed viper out of a round woven basket by playing her flute. The control she had over the viper as its heads shot toward her was impressive.

Saffire had displayed her talent for dancing. Although she was a plump child, the image showed her moving gracefully, tapping her thumb cymbals together to the crescendo of the music.

The orbulars were amusing and, as was evident by the belly laughs that filled the room, it was the most relaxed time since Majo and Saffire had arrived. Here they were laughing at themselves rather than criticizing Cassidy.

In one orbular the sisters' parents, Jonathan and Charisse, were playing with three little girls. They were youthful Majo and Saffire, with Aristede's mother, Melissa, flying around on a carpet. Jonathan, whose thinning black hair revealed his peach-colored scalp, taught enchantment law at Jinn University. His attractive wife, Charisse, displayed her porcelain-white teeth every time she smiled.

Saffire let out a soft sigh when, in one orbular, a dragon rodeo came into view, and for a few fleeting seconds she remembered her first dragon rodeo with all the pageantry and ferocious dragons. She especially recalled meeting the handsome dragon wranglers who were friends of her grandfather Bruno. Bruno appeared in an orbular, and for a husky man he was an excellent competitor, especially with dragon broncos. His hefty arms and mighty hands were just what one would expect from a dragon wrangler.

Lying among the soft pillows, the boys were caught up watching the dragon rodeo as their ancestor lassoed the fire breather, throwing a rope around the dragon's neck. At one point in the orbular, Grandfather Bruno fought to stay on a dragon that mightily tried to knock him off its coarse back, snapping its razor-sharp teeth.

"Grandpapa always got us front-row seats," Saffire said.

"We have all his awards at home," Majo added.

Aristede remembered how scared he had been of his great-grandfather, who, with the strength of ten yaks, had once pressed a genie down to his knees with his strong hands.

"Now, Jasper was never afraid of toddling after Grandpapa into the dragon pens," Majo said. "His behind got singed more than once, I tell you."

"It seems like only yesterday, doesn't it, sister?" Majo said. "Hard to believe that it was one hundred fifty years ago." Then a burst of color exploded inside another orbular. "Oh, look. Here's one with you, Aristede."

Crowing whoops filled the sunken retreat. Aristede almost didn't recognize his six-year-old self on his first winged camel. The flush on his face, and the memories flashing before him, were not very flattering.

Adult Aristede covered his eyes, although he did move his fingers apart so he could see. The laughing quickly died down when young Aristede took the reins and kicked his heels into the sides of the animal. He fought to stay on, but on an unanticipated soar upward and around a palm tree, Aristede slipped off the hump, and the camel bucked him off completely. For a quick moment, he sat on the hard ground, stunned. When he finally got up, he briskly brushed the gravel off his arms.

The last orbular was of a more recent event. Majo and Sigmund's smiling faces appeared. Sigmund put his bony arm around the small woman, and she gave him a dreamy-eyed gaze.

"We were traveling in the eastern region before we came here," Majo said, sighing. "It was a dreadful trip. The elephant train was so crowded that time. I swore I would never travel that way again."

"We had to push our way through the crowds," Sigmund said, smiling. "It was not the best way to get to know each other."

"We got to go on the elephant train once, when we went to visit Uncle Jasper," Blake told her.

"That is sweet, dear," Majo said. She was not a bit interested in what he had to say. She turned to Sigmund and said, "You did get travel sick, didn't you, Siggy?"

"I certainly did not feel my normal self," Sigmund said.

To show everyone just how sickly he looked, Sigmund made a face. When Aristede's eyes met Sigmund's, there was, finally, a look of recognition of their guest—he remembered the man in *The Orbular Times* crying out in anguish: *Get him out! Help! Please! Help me!*

Aristede pointed his finger directly at Sigmund in an almost accusatory way. "You're *him*!"

All eyes were on Sigmund. The well-groomed man who sat before them was the same unkempt man in *The Orbular Times* whose daughter had been eager to get him to the healers.

"It's true. It was such an unfortunate time in my life. I was not well," he said. He lowered his head, ashamed.

Majo sidled up to Sigmund and said, "Aristede, Sigmund told me all about that time in his life."

"You appear in better health than you did. You must have gotten the help you needed," Cassidy said.

"Help?" It was a question. "Of course! Yes, I have been cured," he told them.

"Why didn't you just tell us?" Aristede asked.

"I was embarrassed by it all," he said. "I know that I owe you an apology and must explain myself. There I was, ranting and raving like some lunatic, imagining that all sorts of people were after me. I truly believed they were going to take me away to Jingrey Healers for the Mentally Unbalanced, where I believed I would be forever. I did not want to risk my new life. You understand that, don't you?"

"Of course he does, Siggy," Majo said. She clutched his hand and held tightly. "It's getting late, and we can look at some more orbulars tomorrow."

Saffire waved her hand in a circular motion, and the orbulars stopped spinning. A second later the hanging spherical objects returned to their snug places in the mahogany box.

Brianna's new sleeping quarters had barely enough room for a narrow mattress, a nightstand, and a clothes rack. Without any windows and only a candle to keep the darkness from totally surrounding her, Brianna lay on her stomach, crossed her arms on the mattress, and rested her head on the back of her flattened hand, writing in her journal. When a feeling of the walls closing in started to take over, she pulled off the blanket and even tried to change her sleeping position. Perhaps if the door was opened, even just a little, that would help her deal with her fear.

She gently pushed the door, opening it just a sliver. At first look, the eating area appeared to be empty, but that wasn't the case. Someone was there.

What's Mr. Sigmund doing? she asked herself.

She was going to say something, but she quickly realized that he was definitely thinking of something else and was clearly unhappy. She didn't mean to eavesdrop, but because he was talking to himself, she didn't have much of a choice but to listen.

With his hands clasped behind his back, Sigmund paced. His eyes narrowed, furrowed deeply across his forehead.

"The box has not been opened yet! This time the box is changing, and it didn't do that before. It wasn't until Majo said she had triplet great-nephews that I thought they might be the ones to open the box. I guess three heads are better than one."

Sigmund chuckled to himself, since he alone understood the joke.

"Three heads . . ." He chuckled again, this time a little louder. "This will work out quite well for me. I will now be able to accomplish so much more than I had thought." He tapped his finger on his left cheek. "They will never know what happened to them."

Brianna returned to her small bed and climbed under the covers. She tried to go to sleep, but she couldn't get Mr. Sigmund's voice out of her head, and she knew she had to tell someone. When she peeked out again, Sigmund had left. She pushed the door open and crept softly into the center room.

The flames in the brass urns had been put out much earlier, and now the warm glow of the fireplace embers kept the room from total blackness.

JD, Morgan, and Blake slept spread out across the floor. Brianna tiptoed to the sunken area and squatted down by Morgan. A feather had freed itself from Morgan's pillow, which she used to swish across his ear.

"Morgan. Morgan," she whispered. "Wake up. I have something serious to tell you."

He brushed the side of his head as though shooing a fly.

"Morgan," Brianna said louder.

When there was no response, she grabbed him by his shoulders and shook him robustly. Morgan sat up, but he wasn't too happy about being awakened.

"What?" he groaned. With the slightest push, he could easily have been tipped over.

Brianna moved next to him and put her mouth near his ear. "Morgan. I have something to tell you, so listen to every word I have to say."

"Can it not wait until morning?" he asked, eyelids drooping.

"No," she said, and she continued, "Mr. Sigmund was just in the eating area."

"So what?" Morgan yawned. "Maybe he was hungry. Maybe he was sleepwalking."

"He was talking to himself," she added. "It was about that box of yours."

"Really?"

She now had his undivided attention.

"Mr. Sigmund wants what's inside it. He sounded so very different than when he first got here."

Morgan was silent for several seconds.

"You know, Mr. Sigmund took an interest in the riddle box earlier and even wanted to know when we opened it," Morgan said. "Come to think of it, what do we really know about him?"

"I know he's been very nice to us. He even brought us presents."

"But you heard what Aunt Majo said—they have not known each other very long. I think we need to watch him. We can see if he does something peculiar. Can I get some sleep now?"

Brianna nodded and returned to her tiny room. Morgan lay back down.

He lay on his back with closed eyes. Then there was a noise. It couldn't be JD or Blake. JD lay there with his arms wrapped around his pillow. As for Blake, his mouth gaped open occasionally, and he gave a piglike snort.

"Psst!"

Although Morgan really wanted to get some sleep, there were only two riddles left to solve, and the box was too important to ignore. Likewise, the little man wouldn't give up trying to get Morgan's attention.

When Morgan heard the second "Psst!" he rolled onto his stomach, pushed at Blake's head, and tugged at JD's arm. His brothers were groggy, so for a few seconds they weren't quite sure where they were.

"What is it? It's two in the morning," Blake moaned before rolling over on his side.

"The little man's ready to give us the next riddle," Morgan said.

At that moment, making the same whistling sound as it had when it first arrived, the riddle box rose and rotated until Morgan was looking at the panel where the little man moved.

"It's about time," JD said. "What took so long?"

"All in the right time, young jinn. Are you ready?"

The triplets bobbed their heads, but only JD managed to say, "Yes. We've been waiting for this."

Clearing his throat with a cough, the little man said, "Death or severe illness is serious indeed, and so is being without sight or hearing. What other loss to one could there be?"

"Oh, peacock feathers!" JD snarled. "What kind of riddle is that?"

"I don't get it. That's a real tough one," Blake whined, shrugging his shoulders. "How can we figure out this riddle? We're only eleven."

"Tsk, tsk, young jinn. If it were easy, then the prize would be meaningless," the little man said as he shook his head. "And you cannot go on without solving this riddle. I will be waiting right here."

He bowed his head.

Things were about to get worse. If the evening drama was the lead-in, then they were about to enter the main event.

Aristede was the last person up the next day. He didn't talk to anyone during the morning meal.

The low table was laid out with plentiful portions of breadfruit pancakes, scrambled eggs, fresh fruit, sweet strawberry bread, and pitchers of yak milk and pomaberry juice. Cassidy floated a plate of breadfruit pancakes and poached peacock eggs to him.

Aristede gave a piercing look at the meal and in a low voice asked, "What is this?"

"I know you have a lot to do at the department this morning. I just wanted to make you something special," she said.

"And you thought *this* would do it?" Aristede snapped. "I will have you know that I'm not going to work today."

The way he spoke to her was not at all like him. Stunned silence fell as the family waited breathlessly to see Cassidy's response.

"Ari, you were up very late last night and tossed and turned in your bed," Cassidy said sincerely. "I think you're overly tired and need more rest."

Aristede jumped up. He was not amused.

"Do not patronize me!" he replied harshly. He hammered his closed hand on the table.

Brianna coiled her body tightly. If Aristede had struck the table two inches to his right, his clamped fist would have broken all the fingers on her left hand.

There was a collective gasp. That is, everyone gasped except for Saffire, who only made matters worse when she added that Aristede was right, and the meal didn't look very appetizing.

"And you shouldn't have said anything about Aristede's lack of sleep. There is so much on his mind with his job and his family," Majo said.

"Thank you, Aunt Majo and Aunt Saffire . . ." Aristede said politely.

The two women grinned proudly.

". . . but I do not need two old women jumping to my defense."

"Aristede!" Cassidy cried.

"Well, I never!" Majo said as she placed the palm of her hand on her chest to steady her fast-beating heart.

Saffire's chin dropped open, and bits of food dribbled out the left corner of her mouth.

Cassidy was noticeably shaken, her hands trembling. The others half-expected her to leave the room. It was soon evident that this wasn't going to happen. It took a great deal of self-control for her to stay calm, even though Cassidy really wanted to take hold of him and squeeze his neck. She took a deep breath and asked the children to feed Sherbet, Tango, and Tangerine.

JD led the way. Even though the foursome made their way under the arched doorway, they couldn't help but feel awkward listening to Aristede's continued tirade about the morning meal, and Cassidy made it well known that his behavior was unacceptable.

But that wasn't all. A labored wheezing came from the stair step landing near the fireplace. There, holding his chest, was Sigmund leaning against the wall. It was apparent by his gasping for breath that Sigmund was weak. He struggled to take a few steps toward them.

"Wh-where a-am I?" he asked in a strangled voice. Up close he did not look well at all. "Please h-help me."

JD, Morgan, and Blake rushed over to Sigmund before he collapsed. The ill man put his arms around them for support until they could get him to the cushions nearby. His drawn-out groans were loud. Within moments, Cassidy and Aristede, with Majo and Saffire right behind them, joined the children.

"Oh, dear!" Saffire exclaimed.

"Siggy! What's the matter?" Majo asked. She reached out to her sister for comfort.

His blood-drained and colorless face was even sallower than it had been before. Sigmund looked very much like a corpse.

"I-I d-do not u-u-understand. Wh-who are y-you? Wh-where i-is m-my d-daughter? I do not know this place." He could only stare at her. "The memories I have . . . they . . . they're scrambled."

Majo's eyes misted before she burst into tears. In between sobs, she lamented how her Siggy couldn't remember her.

"It looks as though the poor man has had a relapse. Most likely he will need to return to Jingrey Healers for the Mentally Unbalanced," Aristede said. There was no emotion in his voice.

Cassidy swept past her indifferent husband to make a broth for Sigmund. The chilly look she gave Aristede showed mistrust of him in her normally gentle eyes.

Aristede held out his arm to stop her.

"I didn't mean what I said before. I didn't mean any harm," Aristede said. "You're right. I'm tired from lack of sleep. I apologize for my outbursts. I don't know what got into me."

For the moment, he appeared to be his old self, his compassion intact. Although he sounded remorseful, Cassidy still had her doubts.

The children moved away from the adults. Blake fell back against one of the larger pillows and brushed his fingers through his sandy-blond hair. JD passed the time by slinging grapes above his head and catching them in his mouth. Within a few minutes, his handful of fruit had been eaten.

"Don't you think it's peculiar that your dad acted the way he did, and that Mr. Sigmund is ill again?" Brianna asked the triplets.

"I think it is more than just a coincidence," Morgan said.

Chapter Twenty-One

Impostor Unmasked

"What?" Brianna asked softly, cracking the awkward silence at the morning meal the next day.

It didn't help that Aristede was sitting next to her, which made it hard to talk to Morgan. Aristede was in another one of his moods about the children's eating habits. It was so bad that JD and Blake had gobbled their food and had decided to avoid Aristede as much as possible. It had developed to the point where they began looking for excuses not to be in the same room with him.

Saffire didn't help the situation when she said that the children's poor habits must have come from Cassidy's side of the family, since they had never existed on her side. Cassidy became so upset that she rubbed her temples with her fingertips, trying to comfort a developing headache. More than anything else, Brianna wished she could just disappear, or at least move away from Aristede.

Morgan couldn't wait any more, and he leaned over, whispering again to Brianna.

"I have an idea about how we can find out what is happening around here."

When she opened her mouth to respond, Aristede looked directly at her with sharp, narrow eyes.

"What's the matter with you?" Aristede said gruffly. "What are you two whispering about anyway?"

A hush fell throughout the room again. Cassidy slapped her silver fork down on the table before returning to the food preparation area. When she did make eye contact with Aristede, she showed how she felt by the frown on her face.

"It was nothing, Dad," Morgan said, smiling weakly. "I just told Brianna a joke."

Morgan looked sideways at Brianna, and she knew that was her cue to giggle. She did so promptly.

Morgan quickly ate his food, and when he finished, he gently turned his head and gave Brianna a quick nod before he left the room. She, too, hurried to finish and then met up with him by the mantel.

The only sound they heard was the snoring of the porcelain people on the picture frames and of the seer candle. Morgan looked at Silvestri, then Brianna, and back at Silvestri. Morgan took hold of the sleeping candle, and the two children rushed out of the bottle house.

Brianna and Morgan lounged on the hill. Brianna pulled her knees up and wrapped her arms around her legs. Morgan, on the other hand, was more relaxed. He gently set Silvestri down. He used his arms, bent at the elbow, to prop himself up. He could speak more honestly with her now that they were away from everyone else.

"Why did you bring Silvestri?" Brianna asked.

"He is a *seer candle*. Maybe he can tell us what is going on. You saw how suspicious Dad was. He has never been like that before."

Morgan moved in closer until he was an inch from Silvestri's face. A quick snort in between wheezing snores startled him so much that he jumped back with the sudden movement, awakening the sleeping candle.

"What are you doing to me *now?*" Silvestri demanded.

"Silvestri," Morgan said. "W-we th-thought you c-could help u-us by telling us wh-what has h-happened t-to Dad."

"If I must," Silvestri said. He disdainfully rolled his eyes.

With his lids closed, he slowly began to sway. This time, he wasn't sleeping. Rather, he entered his *seer* trance. After a few moans, he gave the following premonition:

The box and its contents
Are the problems of it all.
The impostor's desire is intense.
Never into his hands must it fall.

Silvestri's eyes fell on Morgan and Brianna before he slumped forward, exhaling a drawn-out wheeze. His eyelids drooped, and a long, slow yawn matched the sway of his head. He was asleep once more. Morgan realized that it was too late to ask Silvestri any questions.

"That was cryptic," Brianna said. "Who do you think the impostor is?"

"Mr. Sigmund? I cannot think who else it could be."

But Brianna had her doubts. After all, he was sick, barely able to stand up on his own. Morgan gently reminded her that she was the one who had seen him pacing in the eating area the other night.

"It only makes sense that it is Mr. Sigmund, because of his interest in the box," Morgan said.

"Silvestri said the box is where all the problems come from," Brianna began. "And it changes. The pictures, I mean. Don't you think that's pretty weird?"

Morgan turned away. He stared at his feet and avoided eye contact with her, but he could still feel her stare on the back of his head.

Brianna reached over and tugged on his sleeve. When he did glance at her, for a quick second, all he could say was, "Why are you looking at me like that?"

Judging by his reaction, she knew that something huge must be going on. Since JD, Morgan, and Blake had come back from the Library of Records and Antiquities, they were more protective of the box. There must be something he wasn't telling her. She demanded to know what it was.

Morgan sat there for a while and said nothing. He started looking nervous as the long seconds ticked away. There was still the pact he had made with his brothers, but he was beginning to feel bad that they hadn't told her about the box before. Deep down, he knew he could trust her, and he finally decided not to keep it from her any longer.

It took Morgan some time to tell her everything he, JD, and Blake had found out in the library's private chamber. Brianna fell back limply against the tree trunk.

"Unbelievable!" she finally said. "And the man in each painting comes to life?"

"When he is ready, and just his head moves."

"And once you answer all the riddles, the box will open?" Brianna asked. She wanted to make sure she understood the workings clearly.

"JD, Blake, and I decided not to say anything, because we did not want to scare you."

"That was thoughtful, but after being here in your world, I don't think anything could do that. Like Silvestri here . . . I'm not scared of him. It's just a little freaky. Look at him. How can a candle be alive? It's just a head made of wax. It has no body, no arms, no legs. There's not even a real neck."

She waited for him to say something more about the orange candle. What she got instead was raised eyebrows and a set of twinkling eyes staring at her.

Morgan sat up on his knees and said, "That is also the answer to the riddle the little man gave us last night."

He told her about the *serious loss* beyond death, illness, sight, or hearing. When he finished, she was fascinated by the mystery, too, and could understand why the boys were so attracted to the riddle box.

"Do you not see? We have to tell JD and Blake right away!" Morgan continued sitting on his knees on the same spot on the grass.

Brianna had more questions and hoped that Morgan would be able to answer them.

"Tell them what? What's the answer?" she asked.

"You will see. I will tell you at the same time I tell JD and Blake. Come on."

Helping each other up, Morgan and Brianna hurried down the hill and quietly slipped into the house, where Morgan put the sleeping Silvestri back in his usual place on the mantel.

"*JD! Blake!* It is the loss of limbs. That is the—"

A voice startled them.

"Good. You're just in time," Aristede called. He waved with his hand for them to join him. "I want to talk to you about that box of yours."

Morgan and Brianna took places next to JD and Blake. The children were sitting on the floor while stone-faced Aristede stood over them. He reached down and took the riddle box from JD.

Morgan didn't like the way his father held the box. It was the same uncanny way Mr. Sigmund had handled it. From the fourth panel, which was now facing them, the little man bowed and smiled before returning to his pose in the painting. JD and Blake seemed lost, but Morgan knew he had solved the latest riddle successfully.

"The box has changed since we came back from the library," Aristede began. "It used to be dull and dirty, every panel. Now some of the paintings are crisp."

"It just needed a little cleaning," JD said.

The fake smile on Aristede's face faded, and his eyes lacked any warmth. He gave a hard stare and began pacing as he held the box with both hands.

"Jindrake told me that if anything happens with this box that I was to let him know. That I have done, and now I've received a letter from the Jinn High Council," he told them.

Aristede reached into his vest pocket for a small parchment square. He read it aloud:

Dear Mr. Aristede,

The Supreme High Council of the Jinn has received information that your children have a valuable artifact. We have reason to believe someone is after the box that is now in your sons' possession. Please return this treasure to the Council within the next three days.

Sincerely,

Miss Circe
Senior Administrative Assistant
to the Supreme High Council of the Jinn

"As your father, I am responsible for everyone's safety in this house. I will take custody of the box and make sure the proper authorities get it!" Aristede declared.

There was little doubt how much he wanted the box or his determination to get his hands on it.

No sooner had he finished making his declaration than the floor started to rumble. Unlike the time when Brianna's grandfather had picked up the bottle, this time it didn't tip over. Suddenly the riddle box rattled, popped like a firecracker, and instantly disappeared.

Aristede wheeled around the room and began searching every corner and behind every curtain with a fine-toothed comb. He frantically sent the pillows and cushions flying in all directions, but the box was nowhere to be found.

When Aristede turned, he said, "I suggest the four of you begin looking elsewhere. We must find the box immediately. Bring it to me when you find it!"

At half past midnight, Brianna joined the triplets, who were sitting together with blankets over their crossed legs. JD slid over to make room for her.

Morgan had arranged for this meeting so he could tell them about Silvestri's prophecy without anyone else hearing him. He paused briefly and then told them there was another reason he wanted to talk to them in secret.

"I made the riddle box disappear!"

"What?" Blake exclaimed. He was up before he knew it.

"You're full of surprises!" JD said.

Morgan motioned his brothers to shush.

They were eager to know where it was. Morgan smiled broadly. Out of the corner of his eye, he locked onto the reflecting pool. Among brightly colored pebbles, on a decorative rock, sat an unfamiliar clam.

He pulled himself out from the under the blanket, took a few steps, and reached his hand into the bubbling water. Curious to see what Morgan was reaching for, JD hopped to his feet and saw the clam coddled in his brother's palms.

It was a wise, yet handy, hiding place. Everyone passed the reflecting pool a hundred times a day. Rarely did any one of them notice the stones and ceramic animals that spruced up the pool. If they had known it was right there the entire time, they would have been so surprised.

"That's it? You transmogrified the box into a clam?" JD said. "Brilliant thinking."

Morgan waved his hand over it, thus changing it back into the riddle box. A croaky cough announced that the little man was about to talk to them.

"It is about time," the little man said in a very unpleasant tone. "I have been waiting! Here is your final riddle: Power cut loose from the renegade, now resting within the box. What is it?"

He winked at them before becoming a part of the painted scene again. Unlike the other times, he didn't wait around for their answer. They didn't know why. Perhaps he knew it would take them some time to solve it.

A muffled growling noise came from the other end of the bottle house, where Sherbet, Tango, and Tangerine had retreated to their beds; it appeared that they were in restless dreams. Brianna crossed the cold floor and rubbed their heads.

"Why do you have them in the house?" she asked. The three tigers purred with delight and flicked the tips of their long tails.

"They are here to guard the riddle box. Jindrake said that they would make superb protectors, so I brought them inside," Morgan answered. "I do not think we should keep the box out too long. I'd better put it back in its hiding place."

But it was too late!

"Not before I take possession of the box," a cold voice said.

Someone had vaporized out of thin air and was creeping behind them.

Blake winced, and his arms became goose-pimply when he saw a man-sized figure step out from the black shadows. JD, Morgan, and Brianna froze as he straightened the collar on his neatly pressed shirt. Aristede was that someone!

Morgan wondered whether his father knew it was he who had hidden the box in the first place. If this was indeed the case, he didn't want to get caught off guard and suffer Aristede's wrath.

"I knew you would eventually bring the riddle box back. I just had to be patient and wait. And here you are with it," Aristede said.

But as Aristede opened his mouth to say something more, the three tigers let out bold growls.

Aristede looked at them crossly and said, "Be sure those overgrown cats keep their distance. I don't like those felines."

Sherbet, Tango, and Tangerine had grown so large that they were too bulky to be held in anyone's arms. They stared steadily at the man just as Aristede fixed his eyes on them. There was a gleam in the tigers' eyes that seemed to indicate they didn't trust the man.

JD directed the cats to the far side of the center chamber. Tangerine grudgingly followed JD's order to get out of Aristede's way. She offered one loud growl before settling down on a thick blanket. Within a few minutes, the tigers were in deep slumber. Every once in a while, all anyone could see were whiskers and tiger stripes.

"Give me the box!" Aristede said.

He stuck out his hand. The light darkened one side of his face, making him look more menacing. The four children watched as Aristede stepped toward them.

"D-D-Dad, you're scaring us," Blake said.

"You're afraid? Of me? You needn't be afraid of your—"

Another voice cut Aristede off. "That is not your father!"

Sigmund stood there; his withered face sadly fit the fragile shape of his body. The hunched man sat down on the reflecting pool rim and steadied his shaking hand. He could barely breathe.

"The spirit that . . . had possessed me . . . is now in him, and . . . he wants what . . . is in the box."

Aristede dismissed the man with a simple flick of his hand. The laugh that followed added insult to the elderly man standing before them.

"Mr. Sigmund is mentally ill, and now he's just trying to confuse you," Aristede said.

Morgan stared unblinkingly at him. Although it was hard to comprehend it, and as much as he didn't want it to be true, their father's change in behavior suddenly made sense. Lifting his chin in defiance, he wasn't about to turn the box over to him.

"Mr. Sigmund is right. You are not our father!" Morgan said firmly.

Morgan waved Brianna and his brothers over to him, and they huddled around him. His arms tightened around the box, and he drew it close against his chest.

As Aristede took another step, it was plain to see by his smoldering gaze that he would stop at nothing to get the box again. JD stepped out from behind them so he was between Aristede and the riddle box.

"Of course. I have to get it to the Jinn High Council. I told you that."

Morgan looked over JD's shoulder directly at Aristede. He knew what Aristede had said was not true.

"You did not get a letter at all. You just said that so we would hand the box over to you," Morgan said.

Aristede stopped cold. "What makes you think that?"

"Because there was no official seal of the Jinn High Council on the page you had. That is how I knew it was a fake," Morgan explained.

Aristede stared for only a second. The deadpan look gave way immediately to admiration.

"How clever of you, noticing that small detail," Aristede said. "You are absolutely right about that. I want the box."

"But why?" Blake asked.

The sly look on Aristede's face meant they were about to find out.

"Because what is inside belongs to me!"

"What!" JD exclaimed. "How could you know what's inside? Only the twelve original jinn were the ones who knew, since they were the ones who made the riddle box."

"No. That is not entirely correct. There was one other," Aristede told them. There was a hint of hatred in his voice. "I remember the trial as if it were yesterday."

"You *remember?*" Blake asked. "H-h-how could you? I don't understand."

Morgan had a heavy feeling in his gut, as though he had swallowed a giant boulder. His eyes broadened, and he slapped his left palm to his forehead. "That is the only thing that *does* make sense!"

As unbelievable as it seemed to him, Morgan knew who the impostor in Silvestri's warning was.

"Mr. Sigmund was telling the truth. The spirit was in his body, but now he is in Dad," Morgan said.

"That's why Dad has been acting so strangely," JD added.

"Not a spirit. A soul," Aristede corrected. "Your father is still deep inside."

He paced in front of them. JD, Morgan, and Blake kept quiet and watched him. His walk, fingertips touching, was not Aristede's swagger. It was not Aristede.

"Let the proper introductions begin," the stranger in Aristede's body said. "I am—"

"Frassrand!" Morgan gasped. It was the only explanation.

Chapter Twenty-Two

The Sandwalker

"The Magician?" JD said. "That's who's in Dad's body?"

"B-b-but how?" Blake asked. He was still trying to make sense of it all.

Morgan knew it was foolish to ask a lot of questions. It was smarter to listen to what Aristede had to say.

A few evenings earlier, Sigmund had put his finger on Aristede's forehead when they were alone in the bedchamber corridor. Aristede's strength had eased, and his breathing strained. The world had swirled around him, and he promptly collapsed to his knees. Although he had tried to fight it, it was a useless effort. Sigmund, whose body had been inhabited by Frassrand, was just too powerful.

"Let me help you, Aristede. You do not look well," Frassrand's spirit said through Sigmund's body.

"Wh-what a-are y-you d-doing t-to me?" Aristede asked.

"Weakening your mind so that your body will be mine. I will possess it, just as I have possessed others over the centuries to evade discovery, but my spirit will have a new body in you, Aristede, a young, active man. You will make a perfect host. I will not only get back what belongs to me, but I will have the opportunity to fulfill my destiny. And with me will be three skillful and intelligent *sons* to influence and guide!"

Aristede had doubled over sideways and collapsed, hitting the floor as pain shot through his body and caused his eyes to roll back in his head. He lay helpless, and the world around him dissolved into a sea of white light.

"Good night Aristede," Frassrand said to himself.

Frassrand's soul was in full control of Aristede's body and mind.

"Do not worry. You will not have any memory of the possession. It will be as though you are in a deep sleep."

Frassrand was blatant about how he was feeling now that he had shared how he possessed Aristede's body. He turned to the children.

"Now you know how it happened," Frassrand told them.

"Why are you telling us all this? Why now?" Blake asked.

With his hand outstretched in a demanding way, he said, "Because I want what is rightfully mine!"

"I still don't understand how the box can be yours when it was the Jinn High Council who made it," JD asked. He was more curious than before.

Frassrand pulled back a sleeve, revealing a frightening sight. He ran his fingertips around the one manacle he still owned. He took a deep breath, remembering what had happened to him so long ago.

"You are indeed very intelligent youngsters. Those twelve jinn wanted to take my power away. I became an eagle to escape, but the sultan's third son, Kareem, tried to stop me," Frassrand said as he rubbed his wrist. "My poor hand. I learned how your ancestors had placed the source of my power in that box. Now that I have found it, I want it back!"

Without thinking, JD boldly said, "But you couldn't open it even if you did have it, because of the riddles."

Frassrand squinted at JD for the daring statement he had made.

"Unfortunately you are correct," Frassrand replied. "I had found the box several times, and I learned quickly that only the heirs would be able to open it.

"I had believed that one person would answer one question and then another pupil would answer the next until all the riddles were solved. That was not the case. In fact, the little man hadn't given the riddles to anyone who had the box before."

"So that's why you watched us, to see if anything happened to the riddle box while we had it," JD said. "You were the one at our birthday party, too. You were the person Brianna saw at the window."

"Exactly," Frassrand said. "Based on the prophecy, I thought six pupils meant six jinn."

But the question remained how the triplets could be the heirs about whom the Jinn High Council prophesied.

"Pupils are students, but there is more to it than just that," Morgan said as he closed his eyes. He then began mumbling to himself, "Think. Think. Six pupils."

He said it over and again until his eyes held a glimmer of understanding. He spun around to his brothers, hoping they had the same realization about what Casimir had meant.

"The sultan's children did not know about us, but they charmed the box to give the riddles to *six identical pupils*. Pupils do mean students, but not in this case. Pupils also mean eyes. Six eyes! Get it? Six eyes."

Blake shook his head and said, "Now I'm lost."

"Six eyes. How many people is that?" Morgan repeated, pointing to his right eye.

JD's expression changed.

"Six eyes mean three people. And identical pupils mean three people who look exactly alike, like us—triplets. Together we have six eyes. It must mean the three of us! That is why the little man on the box chose to give the riddles to us."

That was where Frassrand had made his mistake. He had befriended Aunt Majo after learning she had identical triplet nephews.

"I found she wanted the box for the three of you. That is how I knew you must be the heirs," Frassrand added. "The sultan's offspring believed they were so shrewd."

"Now that we have only one more riddle and are close to opening the box, you are making your move," Morgan added.

Morgan slowly moved his eyes to look at the riddle box. He examined the different paintings and thought over the riddle solutions. Under his breath he repeated them.

"Bird . . . birds of prey . . . a shadow . . . missing limbs."

All the clues and what they saw as spiders added up to the final answer, and Morgan blurted out, "I got it! An eagle is a bird of prey, and that's what Frassrand became. When the eagle flew away, there was a shadow. Kareem swung a sword at him that chopped off the eagle's talon, and it lost a limb. That is what the riddle means. That is what is in the box."

The little man, for the final time, bowed and said, "Correct, young jinn."

Everyone in the room watched as they realized the box had begun to change. Morgan braced the box with both hands. Slowly, the sides slid under the box's platform and unfolded before them. The room glowed in a reddish tint. Sigmund and the children covered their eyes against the blinding beam. Within seconds, the light dimmed, and the riddle box finally disclosed its contents: the eagle's talon (with the other gold manacle around it), resting on a base of green fabric. Brianna covered her mouth.

Morgan's hands were trembling so much that the talon vibrated on the pedestal. A second later it toppled to the floor.

Frassrand and Morgan eyeballed each other. Each anticipated what the other would do and reached for the talon at precisely the same time. As Morgan dove, Frassrand grabbed hold of his arm roughly, flinging him aside. He spun a half turn before his feet tangled together, and he fell back against the metal railing separating the center chamber from the sunken retreat. He slumped to the floor.

Frassrand finally had what he had been seeking.

"Armed with the pair of manacles, I will now be able to use my full powers and control all the genies." Then, turning to the triplets, Frassrand said, "I admire your courage. I have decided that you will join me."

The boys looked at him in disbelief.

JD's face cringed at the repugnant offer. "You're crazy if you think that'll ever happen," he said.

"You will change your mind," Frassrand said.

For some reason of which they were unsure, the three of them heard the same thing echoing in their heads. It was Master Jindrake's voice: *The three of you together can make anything happen!* Perhaps it was because they were triplets, and just like many twins, triplets showed a special connection where one or two of them could sense what the others were feeling.

The boys squeezed their fingers around their talismans. Within seconds they felt the charms begin to vibrate and the cold metal heat up, warming their palms and fingers. When their grip on the talismans lessened, red sparkling beams escaped through their fingers. A focused beam of energy hit Frassrand, and as it pounded him flat against the chest, he let out a harsh, piercing shriek.

Frassrand thrust his hand in front of himself to block the red energy. It did no good. His fingers and the sides of his hand basked in a ring of blinding light. The center of his palm seared in pain, which quickly spread through him.

"*No!*" he shouted.

Although it was Aristede's voice, it was Frassrand who felt the agony. Unless he did something quickly, he would be forced out of Aristede and have to find a new host body. The nearest adult was Sigmund, and the spirit latched onto him.

Sigmund, who had been watching everything that had occurred, clutched hold of his shirtfront. Frassrand's soul shot into Sigmund's body once more.

When that happened, Aristede collapsed to the floor.

Letting out a horrific scream before falling, Sigmund also collapsed.

Quickly JD and Blake put Aristede's arms around their shoulders to support their father as he fought to get back on his feet. His breathing was shallow but steady. Aristede began to slowly recover from his ordeal.

"I-I'll be a-all right," he told his sons. "My head feels like it's inside a bass drum with someone banging on it."

Sigmund staggered to his feet as well. Hunched over, holding his head in pain, he was breathing heavily. His red eyes were the same crimson eyes the boys had seen on the eagle back in the Hall of Scrolls.

With a hoarse, raspy voice, he said, "Your victory will be short-lived."

Suddenly the floor began to tremble, and Sigmund's body tightened up. Aristede spread out his arms across the children to protect them from the coming danger.

The curtains began to ripple like flags waving on a blustery autumn's eve. The woven cloth swayed along the bedchamber corridor, pounding the walls and awakening the sleeping bottle dwellers.

Blue vapors meandered toward them from the bedchamber hallway. Within minutes, there they stood, Majo and Saffire, dressed in their flowery nightgowns.

Cassidy soon followed, charging down the stairs while tying the belt to her robe around her waist.

"You interrupted our sleep with all the noise," Saffire complained loudly.

"Siggy! What are you doing out here at this time of night?" Majo muttered. "You should be resting in bed!"

Instead of giving her a response, Sigmund's face contorted, and he let out a hissing noise. Majo backed away, her sister cowering behind her.

"Omigosh!" Brianna shrieked. "He's turning into a giant scorpion!"

Brianna was partially right. It was a huge crab-like creature with the beak of a bird.

That wasn't all. Four boulder-sized pincers, two on each side of the horse-sized body, thrashed and struck the fireplace, knocking the porcelain man and woman off their perches and causing the picture frames to plunge to the floor. Both curled scorpion tails served as deadly weapons, stingers dripping with venom, ready to fight the creature's enemies when the time came.

"Not a scorpion—a *sandwalker*!" Aristede cried over the snapping pincers.

With the little strength he had, Aristede pushed the children behind the reflecting pool.

The sandwalker began scuttling across the floor, snapping three pincers almost without end while using the fourth one to reach over the reflecting pool, seize Brianna, and throw her onto its wide hardback shell. Her fearful scream sent the sandwalker into a violent rage.

As the danger persisted, the two people who knew how to deal with the sandwalker hid on the other end of the fireplace. JD bent at the knees and then hurtled himself to Majo. A long, thin tongue shot out of the sandwalker's open beak, brushing JD's arm and slashing his nightshirt's white sleeve.

"You've been around a long time, Aunt Majo," JD said.

"Not as long as you think, young man," she said.

JD went on.

"Your grandfather was a dragon wrangler. You must know how to stop a beast like that." He had to shout over the loud hisses of the animal.

"There is one way," Majo told him. "Three pinches of dragon dust that has been simmering in a silver bowl until it boils."

"Dragon dust? Where are we going to get dragon dust?" he asked.

"Scrape the cave wall of a dragon's nesting ground. Mix the dust with dragon blood. The potion is guaranteed to stun a sandwalker," Majo explained. "It will last for only a short time, however."

"Oh, peacock feathers! We don't have time to get dragon dust," JD replied angrily. "There's got to be another way."

Since Aunt Majo wasn't helpful at all, JD turned to Aunt Saffire for another idea. She was trembling uncontrollably, still clinging to her sister.

Saffire looked at the sandwalker and stammered, "Th-the a-a-aroma of a r-red b-bell p-p-pepper. It will stun him for a minute or t-two."

After another loud hiss and Brianna's scream, Cassidy wanted nothing more than to subdue the creature. Someone had to take charge, and since she had been listening to Saffire, she made the decision as to whom that would be.

"Let me try," she announced.

"It's too dangerous, Mom," JD said.

But Cassidy shook her head. She brought her hands together and, in a flash, red peppers filled them.

With a watchful aim, she began striking the creature until one or two peppers wedged in its beak. The sandwalker's movements became very erratic as its heavy body hobbled sideways, pincers and tails flailing in all directions. Its breathing was difficult.

JD patted his hand on his leg, signaling Sherbet, Tango, and Tangerine to come to him. He would need them as he formulated a rescue plan. Their power, speed, and agility would prove to be quite helpful.

He whispered to the tigers. He didn't want anyone else to know what he was up to. Sherbet, Tango, and Tangerine growled as if to say they understood, and they leaped over the boy.

The sandwalker flicked its tails, narrowly missing Tango's head when the tigers got closer to it. The scratchy hisses and the snapping pincers frightened Brianna, and she pushed with her feet to keep from sliding backward. Her foot slipped into a joint in the shell.

She pulled on the calf muscle in her leg as she strained to free herself, but it wasn't until the sandwalker extended the pincer that Brianna was able to pull her foot out of the narrow opening between the hard shell joints.

"Brianna!" JD called.

She looked sideways without moving her head. When she saw JD, he put his hands around his mouth and cried, "Climb onto Tangerine!"

But she didn't move, and JD could see the terrified look on her face.

"Brianna, I know you can do it!" he called to her. "On the count of three, okay?"

She nodded nervously and closed her eyes as she gathered enough strength to do what he had asked.

"One . . . two . . ."

Before his count was done, Sherbet and Tango distracted the sandwalker as Tangerine sprang to the sandwalker's back. She sank her claws into the soft fleshy folds between the hard shells.

"Three!"

Brianna threw her arms around Tangerine and pulled herself onto the tiger's back.

But they weren't out of danger yet. The sandwalker flicked its sharp-pointed tails. With a deadly aim, one of the stingers struck Tangerine. The blunt wallop was so forceful that it sent the tiger to the floor. Brianna's hands held on to Tangerine's furry neck, grappling to stay on as they slid into the base of the fireplace hearth.

Brianna let out a dull groan as the lump on the back of her head throbbed with pain.

"That was close, wasn't it?" She winced.

Tangerine lay still on the shiny floor. Brianna rested her head against Tangerine's belly and saw that her brave-hearted rescuer's breathing was shallow. As she wrapped her arms across the orange fur and rubbed the large tiger's side, her hand was soaked in blood. Brianna was aghast at the dark red fur. The stinger had broken off and lodged deep in Tangerine's rear left side.

The poison moved through her bloodstream swiftly, and its action was deadly. Tangerine picked up her head one last time and wobbled weakly before slumping without so much as a whimper.

Brianna got to her feet, her head still pulsing in pain. She, as well as the others, watched as within a few quick seconds Tangerine's body vanished, leaving behind only her whiskers and black stripes. After a few more seconds, even those were gone.

Tango and Sherbet moved swiftly to avenge their sister's death. They both plunged their razor-sharp teeth into the hard outer shell on the sandwalker's leg. The creature let out a shrieking hiss and pounded its pincers on the floor. The force of the slams dislodged Sherbet and Tango's teeth. The sandwalker treated them like unwanted scavengers and threw the pests off. Then, with a burst of brute strength, the sandwalker butted its pincers against the window. The glass shattered; cracks throughout the panes held together for only a second before the hundred pieces dropped from the frame. The sandwalker's underbelly scraped against broken shards as it made its way out, scrambling toward Jinwiddie, blood flowing from its wounds.

Chapter Twenty-Three

The Garden of Wegelius

Aristede cleared away the jagged pieces of glass in the window frame and saw the eagle's talon sandwiched between two cushions. When no one was looking, he crouched down to retrieve it and then laid the talon back in the box. He had contacted the Jinn High Council about the riddle box, which had returned to its original shape with a hinged lid.

The viziers were in a special meeting to discuss the disposal of the talon, and until a decision was made, they placed a charm on their home. It was a precautionary measure should Frassrand decide to come back, although the viziers believed that was most unlikely. Frassrand would expect the Jinn High Council to do whatever they could keep the manacle from falling into his hands. The best course of action for now was for Aristede to keep the eagle's talon with the family at the house.

Blake held on to a pillow tightly. He wanted it to be Frassrand so much that he rolled his fist into a ball and struck the pillow as hard as he could. The blow made a dull, muffled sound. Then he punched the pillow again and again and again, each time with more anger than before. When he was finally done, he flung the pillow across the center chamber with all his might.

"Frassrand could come back in another body, and we would not even know it," Morgan said. He could still hear Frassrand's terrible words, unable to pry them out of his head.

Cassidy sat down next to Brianna, who was dabbing ointment on the cuts on her arms. She cradled the girl with both arms. It had been such a painful experience for everyone.

"I was so scared," Brianna managed to say. She was desperately trying to keep the tears from flowing. "I never meant for anything to happen to Tangerine."

JD rubbed Tango's warm belly and declared, "Tangerine saved you. She did her job as a protector."

But that didn't seem to help very much. All Brianna knew was that Tangerine, a beautiful and powerful animal, was no longer with them. Tangerine probably could have survived the physical attack, but her body couldn't fight off the poison. Brianna didn't care whether she was acting like a baby in front of them or not, and she finally let her emotions go.

Cassidy pushed the lock of brown hair to the opposite side of Brianna's forehead. Brianna found this comforting. She remembered her grandmother's touch, her gentle voice. A smile replaced the look of sadness.

"You're a lot like Gramma. She did that, too," Brianna said. "You'd like her and Granddad."

"Would I?"

"Gramma's always taking care of everybody, just like you. She says the most important thing in life is family," Brianna said in a hushed voice. "Maybe when I finally get to go home, you can come with me and meet them for yourself."

Cassidy stiffened as she closed her eyes, shook her head, and waved her hand.

"Oh, no! I couldn't leave the bottle."

"Yes, you can. You've been out there before, haven't you?" Brianna asked.

"Well, yes, but—"

Brianna lowered her head and sighed. "You're right. I'm getting ahead of myself. I'm sorry."

Cassidy continued brushing Brianna's hair back a couple more times. Her hand was soft as she pressed the girl's head, running her hand down Brianna's fine hair.

"Brianna. There's something I need to tell you," Cassidy began.

Before she could say anything else, a loud cry, loud enough to raise the dead, echoed throughout the bottle house.

"Oh, my Siggy!" Majo cried loudly. "He used me. Sigmund used me to get that box. I'm such a foolish old genie."

Saffire tried calming her sister as Majo then twisted her raised hand, and a lacey handkerchief appeared. She dabbed the corners of her eyes with it and then started weeping endlessly, all her work to dry her eyes undone. Saffire had had enough and grabbed her sister by the shoulders and started shaking her.

"Come to your senses, woman! It *wasn't* Sigmund. It was Frassrand. He was evil. Don't forget that. You were living in a dream world with him," Saffire told her.

Majo looked at Saffire through soggy eyeballs. "I just miss my Siggy."

The tears had left streaks down her cheeks. She needed her rest and wanted nothing more than to go back to bed. Without making a sound, Majo and Saffire streamed to their bedchamber.

When the last bit of vapor drifted down the hallway, Aristede stared at the misty trail his aunts had left.

"I think what we need now is some lemongrass tea. That would help settle everyone's nerves," he said.

He brought his fingers together and snapped them once. A tray that contained a pitcher and several chalices hung in the air within their reach. The pitcher moved along, filling each chalice without assistance from anyone. An endless supply of the brew made sure no one would have to wait for refills. Cinnamon sticks were in each drink to help everyone relax.

Blake and Morgan sipped their tea slowly, enjoying the taste, while JD drank his in one big gulp, smacking his lips after downing the last drop. Meanwhile, Brianna's unsteady hands kept her from holding the chalice for more than a few seconds and, before she knew it, the chalice slipped, spilling tea over the floor. Her face went red with embarrassment.

Cassidy gave a quick hand wave, and the mess was no more. She gave an unforgiving stare at the box and wished they hadn't let the boys keep it. "I shudder to think what could have happened," she said.

"You were right. I should have listened to you," Aristede said.

"Too bad we didn't figure it out when we saw the trial of—" Blake broke off when JD hit him in the chest with the back of his hand.

JD and Blake were stone still. Morgan was the only one who lowered his head and tried hard not to look at his father, but the boys all knew that it was time to tell him everything.

"We saw it," Morgan admitted.

"What do you mean, 'We saw it'? How?" Aristede asked. He was now very, very curious.

Once the boys explained everything, instead of being angry at what they had done, Aristede slowly began to grin. A sense of pride swelled through him.

"My boys! Spiders!" he muttered. "I couldn't do spider transmogrifications until I was fifteen."

After thinking about what his three boys had already accomplished, he stared in astonishment at them.

Majo and Saffire reconsidered staying another week and decided to leave as quickly as they could, cutting their visit short. Cassidy thought that it would be a long time before they would visit again.

So, by eight o'clock the next morning, Majo and Saffire's bedchamber was empty. It was the first time in their lives that the two aunts had gotten up that early. Their traveling trunks were piled on the flying carpet, with the orbular satchel securely stowed between the trunks.

The boys made faces when their aunts showered them with hugs and kisses, but they remained kind to the older ladies by not saying anything about the mushy affection. The ladies even hugged Brianna.

"Good-bye, dear. We hope you get to go back to the outside world soon to be with your family," Majo said.

Majo shifted her bag from one hand to the other so she could get hold of Aristede's hand. He assisted his aunts as they stepped onto their hovering carpet. They complimented Cassidy on a wonderful job with the sandwalker.

They waved for several minutes, and Saffire shouted, "We'll send genie mail and orbulars!"

The carpet bobbed in a strong breeze. Majo held her hat in place to keep it from being blown away. The carpet turned in place and took off, becoming a small speck in the distance.

"If only I had the power to go home as easily as they can fly," Brianna said.

That gave JD an idea. Could the manacle's power be used to open the portal? He was surprised that he hadn't thought of it before.

"Do you think it would work?" Brianna asked hopefully.

Aristede sighed. "I'm afraid not. You see, the stopper has to be removed by an Outsider before any of us can leave. Besides that, we need to remain cautious and alert while we wait to hear about how the Jinn High Council plans to dispose of the manacle."

As everyone slept that night, Aristede sat alone on the fireplace hearth with the riddle box resting on his knee. Every once in a while the low flames crackled. The wrinkles deepening across his forehead showed that the look on Aristede's face was serious. The viziers were certainly taking their time, discussing the situation long into the night. He put his hand to the back of his neck and massaged the tense muscles. He couldn't wait for their lives to return to normal.

Then it came—a soft voice from the reflecting pool: "Aristede."

Aristede sat up straight. Closing the box quickly, he waved his hand, and the box transmogrified back into a clam. After placing it gently on the rim of the reflecting pool, he looked into the water.

As if a storm was brewing, the water's surface rippled and bubbles emerged. Once the innermost section of the pool cleared, one of the vice viziers peered at him.

"Your Excellency," Aristede said respectfully as he bowed.

"All the members of the Jinn High Council finally agreed that the riddle box needs to be returned to the Garden of Wegelius," the vice vizier said.

"The Garden of Wegelius?" Aristede asked, opening his eyes wide.

This was the place where the original jinn had come together once they were freed from their bottles. It was the most hallowed place for genies.

The water bubbled again, distorting the vice vizier's face and making is look as if boils were breaking out. Once all the boils popped, the image in the water changed from the vice vizier to that of a floating oasis in the middle of the southern desert, and the temple, surrounded by trees and mature vegetation, now appeared.

"We will be sending two highly regarded genies to take the riddle box as soon as our conversation ends."

The image of the garden and temple faded into nothingness. The water became still, and Aristede could again see the bottom of the pool.

"Your Excellency, wait! Before you leave, I have to ask one thing." He paused. "I want my family to be the ones to return the box."

There was no response. Sediments from the bottom of the pool made the water murky. Aristede continued to stare into the dark waters. Were the viziers considering his request?

Aristede tried to be patient. The wait seemed more like hours than the mere minutes that passed. When he felt he could wait no longer, he asked, "Did you hear me? You must understand, my wife and sons would feel safer if they could actually see the riddle box in a place where Frassrand couldn't enter."

Slowly the activity in the pool increased; Aristede was about to get his answer.

"The viziers grant your request," the vice vizier said. "But you must all go at once. We will be watching, and, if there is any sign of danger, we will intervene immediately."

Now that he had permission from the Jinn High Council to take the riddle box to the Garden of Wegelius, Aristede woke everyone. There was a cold nip in the air as they departed.

They vaporized to the gateway leading to the temple. Statues of lions sat atop the pillars, one on either side of the locked gates.

"I don't see the temple in there," Blake said. He tried pushing open the gates.

Blake and JD started rubbing their hands on the pillar surfaces, looking for some kind of lever to gain entry to the garden—even a way to climb over.

Then Blake climbed on JD's shoulders and reached upward, grasping hold of the lion's raised paw. *Snap!* The lion's paw broke into two pieces. Blake fumbled to maintain his balance and fell, bringing JD down on top of him. There was no lever.

"Ouch!" JD exclaimed. "That hurt."

"It wasn't my fault!" Blake retorted.

Morgan chuckled as he watched their little fiasco.

"Why did you not levitate?" he asked.

JD and Blake looked at each other.

To show them how much easier levitating would have been, Morgan began to rise, and when he was about three feet off the ground, he crossed his legs under himself. He appeared to be sitting on an invisible cushion and hovered at about ten feet before coming down to ground level.

JD folded his arms and let out an exasperated sigh.

"Are you saying we float over the metal fence?"

"I would not have a lump on my head if I levitated," Morgan said sarcastically.

"There's got to be a way to open the gates," Cassidy said.

"We have to be patient," Aristede said.

"Maybe there's a special phrase you have to say," Brianna said. And without so much as a thought, she shouted, "Open sesame!"

Cassidy giggled.

As soon as the words left her, Brianna wished she could take them back. While trying to be helpful, she had done it again. The boys' chuckles made her peach face turn red.

"What's *that* supposed to mean?" Blake said, giving Brianna an unkind look.

"I thought that would open the gates."

"Where did you hear something that kooky?" JD asked.

One of Brianna's favorite stories from the *Arabian Nights* included a tale of a treasure and how forty thieves had to say, "Open sesame," to get inside a hidden cave. Then the rocks moved, and the cave opened.

"How fortuitous for them," Morgan said, shaking his head. "The stories you Outsiders have about genies are absolutely absurd!"

As it happened, a heavy, deep voice interrupted him.

"There is a way in."

Two echoes followed:

"There is a way in."

"There is a way in."

"Who said that?" Blake asked. The faceless echo spooked him. *This must have been how Brianna felt when she first heard us,* he thought.

"I did, of course," the voice said.

"Of course."

"Of course."

Then an ugly-looking figure took shape from within the wall. It was a bald man, yet on either side of the head were two half faces. The eyes of the center face became one half of the set of eyes on the outer faces.

The deep-set eyes on the faces gave a harsh stare. This multifaced man was a bit frightening to look at. Before Aristede could tell the reason for visiting the gardens, the center face said, "You are here to return the box."

"The viziers informed us that you were coming," the face to the right said.

"We have been expecting you," the center face said. "We are the Three Faces of the Guardian."

"Three Faces of the Guardian."

"Three Faces of the Guardian."

"It is our job to make sure that all visitors to the Garden of Wegelius first check in with us before the gates open," the center face explained.

"We will call for the caretaker, who will escort all of you to the temple . . ." the left-side face said.

"So you can complete your mission," the face on the right added, finishing his brother's sentence.

Aristede, Cassidy, and the children clustered together near the guardians just as the center face pursed its lips, blowing a long, ongoing whistle. The face on the left then began to whistle, too, in the same high tone as the center face. A few seconds later, the face on the right began its whistle, matching that of the other two faces.

When the center face changed the pitch of its whistle, the sounds were melodic. The whistling began to soften, and by the time the sounds died off and blended into silence, the faces had pulled back into the pillar.

Nearby, there were sounds of leaves swishing on the ground. A hand pushed the branches aside, and then a short, heavy man appeared.

"The Temple of the Jinn awaits your visit. I am the keeper of the garden. My name is Fiesel."

The round-faced man looked at them through his deep-set brown eyes. Although his hair had thinned, there were still enough strands to pull back into a ponytail.

He twirled his fingers, and the gates slowly began to move. The heaviness of the metal rubbed the hinges together to make an irritating creaking noise.

"Follow me, please," Fiesel said. He gestured with his chunky finger for them to head into the gardens.

Flowering shrubs were in full bloom throughout the garden, dabs of color on a background of green. Slivers of light passing through the tall palm trees danced on the water cascading over a fifteen-foot-high rocky terrace. The lagoon was richly filled with lotus blossoms floating on the water's surface. Families of blue flamingos waded in the shallow end of the water garden.

A large footbridge crossed the water to a dirt path. The caretaker led them through the thick plantings to a clearing, where what looked like seven twenty-foot-tall giraffes were skimming through leaves on the acacia treetops, singling out leafy treats. Their stringy tails had dark hair at the ends.

The bodies of these giraffes looked like paint on artists' palettes, separated by light tan-colored hair. Some had red, yellow, and orange splotches, while others had ones of blue, green, and violet.

Two other men dressed in long white shirts tightly held the ropes around the giraffes' long necks and led the animals toward them at the edge of the clearing.

With a tug on the ropes, each giraffe spread its front legs, bending down in a clumsy stance. The first giraffe made a flutelike sound.

This would be their mode of transportation to the temple, since it was quite a walk otherwise.

"Everyone on a giraffe, please," the other man announced.

"Wouldn't it be quicker if we just vaporize?" JD asked.

"Now, there wouldn't be much fun in that, would there? Long ago, when the garden paradise was created, a rule of conduct required a time for meditation before one entered the temple. Traveling by giraffe allows time to think about one's place in the world," Mr. Fiesel said.

Blake pet his giraffe on the nose, and the creature suddenly gave off a blast of bad breath. What an introduction to giraffe travel.

Aristede helped Cassidy onto her giraffe and then checked to make sure the children were securely seated on the backs of theirs.

Once everyone had mounted the long-necked animals and settled into their saddles, one of the handlers went to each giraffe's behind and yanked on the tufts of the equally long tails. The giraffes made the same flute sounds as the first giraffe had.

One giraffe followed another as Fiesel led the caravan for about a mile south to another fertile garden.

"There it is: The Temple of the Jinn," he said.

The giraffe drivers brought the animals to a stop near two large shrubs shaped as elephants; then they made the animals kneel so the travelers could disembark. Behind the elephant topiaries were broad stone steps that guided them to the temple pavilion. Carved above the entry were the words, CHILDREN OF THE SULTAN, JINN OF THE WORLD, WELCOME! Fiesel bowed to welcome them to the temple as two hefty copper doors began to open.

Mr. Fiesel went no further. It was forbidden for the caretaker to enter the temple while others were inside. It was his job to feed and water the giraffes.

Aristede led his family under the archway. Pulling one of the many deep burgundy velvet curtains, he revealed a long, empty hallway with a faint orange glow at the end of the temple. The undying flame in a fire pit erased the darkness. Elaborately carved thrones on the north side circled the pit.

JD gasped.

Morgan swallowed.

And a cold, icy shiver shot down Blake's spine.

The genie family respectfully lowered their heads. Even Brianna felt required to honor the original jinn. It would be a sign of disrespect not to bow.

Only Aristede had been to the temple before. His father had brought him when he was a child. Everyone was silent. This was definitely a place where one whispered.

Cassidy stared at the embroidered wall hangings behind the high-back thrones. They were stitched to perfection.

As still as they could be, they stepped deliberately. Before a word was spoken by anyone, JD carried the box to the throne in the middle. He took one last look. Instead of the talon, it now contained Frassrand's severed hand with the manacle still there with it.

Without any fanfare, ghostly phantoms, pearly white in color, emerged on the thrones—the twelve jinn in all their nobleness.

"You have done well, my family," Mikayla said proudly.

"We all concur," Sundhar added. He was the one at the middle throne. "The evil one will not be able to enter the gardens! But you will need to be vigilant. You know much about him, and he may try to get revenge. Always beware."

Sundhar raised his palm. The other spirits rose again, and they clouded until, one by one, they vanished. Aristede led his family toward the door so that they could make a quiet exit from the temple.

Outside, they narrowed their eyes. The pounding light from the sun was not only very, very warm, but also blinding. They made their way down the steps and into the cooling shade that the tall trees provided. Fiesel had been waiting for them and quickly ushered them to another winding path littered with dried brown leaves.

"Before we take our trip back," Fiesel began, "there is something I want to show you. It is something all visitors must see."

Leaves swished under their footwear as they followed the trail.

Soon, lights caught everyone's attention. Fiesel led them closer to a grove of trees, and they became aware that sparking balls took the place of leaves. There was more to the lights, as inside each one was a portrait image.

"What is this place?" JD asked as his eyes moved up the unusually long rows of brightly lit trees.

"These are the Jinn Family Trees," Fiesel began. "Each family has a tree here."

"Which one is ours?" Morgan asked.

"If I remember correctly, it's over there," Aristede said as he pointed forward. "The one with our family's color. The tree with the purple lights."

Just when Brianna thought she had seen every unusual thing in this world, these trees amazed her. She walked into the grove and wandered from one tree to the next—each tree a different color from the one next to it. *How beautiful the trees must look at night,* she thought.

The lights moved around like a carousel. One of the purple lights had Aristede's face. He looked just like he did in real life.

There was a strange common characteristic to all the trees. Despite the different colors to show each line of the original jinn, every tree also had white lights on it.

"What do the white lights mean, Mr. Fiesel?" Brianna asked.

"The white ones are family members who are not genie-born," he said. "They are Outsiders!"

Footsteps flitted near her, and she soon saw JD, Morgan, and Blake coming toward her. Before she could tell them the meaning of the colorless lights, Cassidy's face soon came into view. Brianna stopped in her tracks, as what she saw was so unexpected.

"Miss Cassidy's light is white," she exclaimed. "She's an Outsider, like me. It all makes sense now. No wonder she knows so much about the human world."

The boys drew closer as the balls of light continued around the tree. Two other white lights passed that made Brianna throw both hands up. Brianna's fingers, arms, and even legs began to tingle. Her insides churned.

It couldn't be! It just couldn't be! It was impossible! None of them ever thought that these two people would be there.

"They . . . they are . . . the people from the outside world," Morgan said. "They are Brianna's grandparents."

"I don't get it," Blake said.

"Why are those Outsiders on *our* family tree?" JD asked.

Aristede took his wife's hand and gave a firm squeeze. His touch felt good. Cassidy squeezed back, and although she tried to be strong, tears trickled down her cheeks anyway. She wiped her face and then told them.

"Th-they're . . ." She hesitated before finally saying, "They're my . . . parents."

Chapter Twenty-Four

When Aristede Met Cassidy

> Dear Diary,
>
> I got one of the biggest shocks of all since I've been in this genie world. It happened while we were at the Garden of Wegelius when we took the riddle box to the Temple of the Jinn.

Brianna sat under the tree's overhanging branches, her back against the trunk for support as she wrote in her journal. The handwriting was very proper, each letter carefully formed and the words evenly spaced from one another. The pages were filling up quickly about the recent discoveries.

But the real surprise came when Mr. Fiesel took us to the Family Trees, where I learned that Miss Cassidy was not just an Outsider, but also my dad's older sister, who has been missing for many years. Gramma and Granddad have been worrying about her all this time, and she was only a few feet away from them in the amethyst bottle. I can't wait to let them know their "Casey" is alive and well (once I can get back home, that is).

I haven't been able to talk to her, because she has been in her bedchamber. Uncle Aristede has been taking meal trays to her. The boys and I have tried to keep busy, but no matter what we do to pass the time, we still have been wondering how Uncle Aristede met and married Aunt Casey.

I know I'm not the only one with a lot of questions to ask, especially why they never told me that she was my aunt. There was plenty of time, because I've been here for many weeks. They never even told JD, Morgan, or Blake she came from the outside world. I can understand that she couldn't go back and visit, because the portal was closed off, but what about when it was opened? Gramma and Granddad will be happy to know she's alive and well.

I hope we get some answers soon.

A few feet away, Blake sat pulling clumps of grass from the ground. When he was done shredding the blades apart, he plucked a wild dandelion from the earth.

With no warning, Sherbet pounced, knocking him over. The tiger playfully smacked at the boy with a powerful paw. Blake grabbed the fur on the side of the tiger's face and shook him like a large teddy bear. Sherbet enjoyed the play and let out a loud noise, sounding like a belch. The more Blake laughed, the more belching followed.

All that belching seemed to tire Sherbet. He moved to the pool and lapped at the water before taking a much-needed nap.

For a tiger, invisibility can come in handy, and for Tango, this ability added to his joyful play. He would disappear so that he could sneak up on his victim (in this case it was Blake) and nip at the young genie's fingers. When Blake was done playing, he took hold of two visible stripes and pushed Tango aside.

"Okay, that's enough," Blake said.

Tango took this brush-off as a challenge and began playing with Blake again by giving the boy several slobbery licks across his cheeks. Blake pushed Tango off him again.

This time Tango got the message and scampered to the lake, taking a sip of water.

Brianna watched as Tango and Sherbet began splashing each other. That was when she saw JD making his way toward them.

"Here you are," JD said. "What are you writing in there? About Mom and Dad, I'll bet."

"That's right." Brianna nodded. "Your mom must know how much Granddad and Gramma miss her. They're not sure if she's alive or dead. Why hasn't she ever gone back?"

"Because the portal's closed," JD replied.

"But it hasn't always been that way," Brianna said.

"True, but whatever the reasons, we're about to find out more. Dad wants everyone together when they tell us," JD said.

Blake briskly got up off the grass. Brianna closed her journal and stood up, too.

JD led Sherbet and Tango to the enclosure. He made sure both cats had plenty of food and fresh water and then hurried back to the house.

When he was close to the front door, Aristede was standing on the threshold, motioning JD over. The mood inside was mellow.

Cassidy's bloodshot eyes stared blankly across the chamber to the other side of the bottle, looking at nothing in particular. Blake turned to see what it was. What he and the others did notice was that her eyes were puffy and her red nose was raw, and she had been crying.

Cassidy had never expected to see Christian and Isabelle Carruthers on the family tree, so she had thought there was no reason to tell JD, Morgan, and Blake where she came from or about their relatives outside the bottle. Even when Brianna came, Cassidy had hoped her niece wouldn't be with them long. Could they forgive her for the deception?

"Let me tell you how I met your father." Cassidy brought her fingertips together. She was nervous, and her hands were so sweaty that she had to wipe her palms together to dry them. At last she said, "One day, when I was about eighteen . . . there was an antique store . . . it was on B Street. Mom's birthday was coming."

"Is that where you met Dad? He was there, too, looking for a present, right?" Blake said.

Aristede dropped his head next to Blake's and whispered, "Let her finish."

Cassidy closed her eyes as she composed her thoughts. She fought to find the right words to tell her story about seeing the purple bottle in the antique shop. There it sat, just on a shelf as customers walked in. Apparently it had been there for a long, long time and hadn't been cleaned in a while. There was so much grit on it that when the sun shone through the shop window, the amethyst glass could reflect only a lusterless glint.

"It certainly caught my eye, because it was so unusual," Cassidy said.

"You mean . . ." JD began, but Cassidy already knew the question he was going to ask.

"Yes. Ari was inside that bottle, although I didn't know it at the time. Anyway, I found an old lace tablecloth for my mom instead, and I bought the purple bottle for myself. I took it home, cleaned the dirt off, and set it on my dresser. It looked so pretty there."

"So that's where the amethyst bottle came from," Brianna said.

Cassidy nodded.

Then Aristede added softly, "I could see your mother, and I fell in love with her the instant I set eyes on her beautiful face."

Brianna clamped her hands together and swooned. "How romantic."

"Yuck. Sickening," Blake said as he scrunched his face.

"So, Dad, how did Mom open the bottle and let you out?" JD asked.

"I knew I had to get her attention," he started, "so I made faces."

A smile broke through Cassidy's sadness.

"Faces!" Morgan asked. "How did *that* get Mom's attention?"

"The bottle had been turned to a mirror on my dresser. Somehow, I didn't know why, Aristede could see his reflection and made faces," Cassidy said.

Aristede twisted his face, using his fingers to stretch his mouth wide. With his eyes crossed and his tongue sticking out to the corner of his mouth, he bobbled his head as he leered at them.

"Oh, Dad, you didn't," JD said. He squinted his eyes tightly and shook his head.

"It worked," Cassidy said. "I saw your father's face in the mirror, and it startled me. But as soon as I picked up the bottle, his face disappeared. I didn't know why, so I took the stopper out. I didn't know that a whole different world existed, let alone that you could get to it through the bottle."

Cassidy went to her husband and slipped her sleek arms across the back of his shoulders.

"I was master to a genie that not even my parents knew about. He became my best friend, and someone with whom I could share secrets. I kept quiet about Aristede, and soon I was in love with my genie. But the decision to marry him came at a very high price."

"What do you mean?" Blake asked. "I don't get it. You could leave when the stopper came out, couldn't you?"

She didn't say anything. How could she tell them that to have her life with Aristede *and* stay in the outside world was impossible? That was what Outsiders agreed to when they married a genie—another of the Jinn Codes. As a result she wasn't able to leave the bottle, and could see her parents only through the big window.

"Ever?" the foursome said at the same time.

She lowered her head, as if in shame, and nodded.

It dawned on JD, Morgan, and Blake just how deep their mother's pain had been, being separated from her parents and brothers.

"That's terrible," Brianna said.

"What about the viziers? Could they make it so Mom can go back to her home and visit her parents?" Morgan asked.

Although Aristede disagreed with the purpose of keeping their world secret, especially, he explained that he had never known them to grant such a request. But this was Cassidy's life now. She could see her parents once in a while.

The questions that had flooded Brianna's mind and that she had written about in her journal had been answered. But there was one more. It was probably the most bewildering one of them all.

"But as an Outsider, how is it that you can do magic?"

"I can answer that," Aristede said. "Another unusual aspect of being a genie is that when they marry mortals, their spouses gain the same powers and are near genie-like. That was what happened here."

Brianna jumped to her feet, jabbing Morgan in the ribs, when she suddenly saw Christian and Isabelle in the window. She edged her way to the glass and began tapping on the pane while shouting, "Granddad! Gramma!"

Brianna stared achingly. Cassidy slowly moved behind her. The perfume, the scent of lilac, was peppery, and the fragrance brought a twiglike smile to Brianna's face.

"I miss them so much," Cassidy finally said as she watched her parents.

Christian was sitting at his desk. On the computer screen was a website for missing children. He scooted his body forward when he saw Brianna's picture and began looking to see if there were any posts about the girl. He removed his glasses and rubbed his tired eyes.

Brianna remembered something. She reached beneath her blouse, grasped hold of the small locket at the end of a silver chain, and pulled it out for all to see. Then she reached behind her neck and unfastened the clasp.

"I almost forgot. I've had this with me the whole time I've been here," Brianna said. "This belongs to you, Aunt Casey." She handed the locket to her.

Cassidy took the silver heart and grinned happily. The light reflected off the dangling trinket.

"Gracious! My mother gave this locket to me when I was a young girl," Cassidy exclaimed.

"Gramma gave it to me. She said the locket belonged to someone named Casey," Brianna said as she put the chain on Cassidy's neck and closed the clasp. "Now I know that you are Casey. Cassidy . . . Casey. I should have made the connection sooner."

Her full name was Cassidy Lynn. Casey was what Christian had always called her since she was a little girl.

Cassidy conjured up a tall glass of lemongrass tea. A cherry floated on top of the drink. Sipping the tea soothed her somewhat, but she didn't know if she would be able to finish her tea and put the glass down without spilling its contents. Cassidy's lips quivered. She straightened her blouse nervously as everyone waited impatiently for her to continue her story. Finally . . .

"I couldn't bring myself to tell you that I was your aunt and the triplets were your cousins, because I was too afraid." Her voice cracked as she spoke. "It would have meant I had to face the truth, and that I would never get to go home, and if I couldn't get home, perhaps you couldn't either. I didn't want my parents to know where I was. They would try to get me back, and it would be so hard if they knew the truth."

She pressed the tiny clasp, which opened the heart-shaped locket that now hung gracefully from her neck. There were two photographs inside. There was one with her mother and daddy, and the other one was of Carson, Kyle, and her.

She shared the memories of growing up with her brothers. First there had been the one time when Kyle had taken one of her dolls and tied it to a homemade bottle rocket. Mrs. Beardsley, the doll, went twenty-five feet into the sky after Kyle pressed the launch button. He laughed so hard he had doubled over, arms wrapped around his belly to keep his insides from bursting, when it landed between the branches at the top of the large oak.

"Daddy had to use a ladder to get Mrs. Beardsley. When I got her back, her face was dirty, and her hair was burnt. I was so mad at Kyle for what he had done."

Next, Cassidy recalled that, as a teenager, she had a crush on a smooth-talking, handsome boy whom Christian and Isabelle had disliked. They had pointed out that he wasn't like any of the other boys that Casey usually dated. This boy was arrogant and moody, and he lacked manners. They even suspected that he was abusing their daughter. They had insisted that she stop seeing this *smarmy* punk (Isabelle's word for him), but Cassidy had refused.

"I knew more than them, or so I thought, and I continued seeing my boyfriend without their knowing it," Cassidy said. "Carson helped me sneak out of the house so I could be with him."

"Mother! You were bad," JD declared.

"My parents were right about him, though. He robbed a liquor store and tried to escape from the police on his motorcycle."

A liquor store? A motorcycle? The boys had no idea what these things were. It just served as another reminder for the triplets about their mother's life before she married their father.

"That goes to show you: parents always know best," Aristede said, proudly brushing his fingers across the fine hairs on his goatee.

"Yeah, right, Dad," JD said as he pushed at his father's shoulder affectionately.

Blake set his thin arms around Cassidy's waist and gave her a tight hug. He didn't care what others thought of him. His loving squeeze sent a feeling of peace through her that she hadn't felt in days. The anguish she had been feeling disappeared.

Cassidy took his head in her palms and looked directly into his eyes.

"And you are the best things that have ever happened to me."

"It's our fault, Mom," Blake said. If they hadn't baited Brianna into wishing to come into the bottle, Cassidy wouldn't be homesick now.

"No, no, Blake. Don't talk like that," Cassidy said. "I made the decision about my life long before you were born."

"Couldn't you talk to your mom and dad the way Brianna could with us?" Blake asked.

"I doubt that," Aristede said. "Remember, only Brianna was able to hear you, not your grandparents. In fact, I still don't understand how you could have talked to anyone the way you did."

Morgan's eyes widened as if he just recalled a chore he had forgotten to do. He had a fleeting thought as to why Brianna could hear him, JD, and Blake.

"It is because she is our cousin and the same age as us."

"It's as good an explanation as any," Aristede said.

"Too bad no one can hear me now. I would be able to tell someone to take the stopper out of the bottle. Then I could go home," Brianna said. Under her breath, she added, "If only I left the bottle *before* my granddad put the stopper back into place."

Aristede cocked his head, drew close to Brianna, and anxiously asked, "What did you say?"

"I-I said I should have gone back to my world before the stopper got put back into the bottle opening."

Aristede quickly began pacing the room for a moment, talking to himself about what sounded like mathematical calculations.

"The time loop. That's the way to get Brianna back to her home," he said, slapping the side of his hip.

"The time loop?" Cassidy asked.

"The time loop!" he repeated. "Traveling back in time. We go back to the moment before the bottle opening was closed off. Then we vaporize Brianna out just as quickly as she came in here!"

"You can do that?" JD asked.

"One of the powers we have is time travel. We don't do it often, but this time it just may be the answer," Aristede said. He was excited about this possible solution.

Cassidy, however, looked concerned. If they sent Brianna back right after she got here, might that change everything that had already happened?

"Not necessarily," Aristede said. "You see, by going back in time, there will be two of her. It will be the same for any one of us who goes back. The Brianna back there will still experience everything this Brianna already has."

It sounded complicated. There was so much to remember, and they would have to be extremely careful so that they would not come into contact with themselves. If they did, it could change all that had happened. Their timing would need to be precise if they wanted to keep everything the same during that time frame.

"Your mother and I were asleep until the bottle started to shake. Boys, show me where you were at the exact time Brianna vaporized into the bottle," Aristede said.

JD, Morgan, and Blake moved in front of the big window.

"There won't be much time to get Brianna out before the stopper is snugly in place. We have to be sure she's safely out before we get back to our time," Cassidy added.

"The lights were low that night. We could barely see the fireplace," Morgan said.

"That's good," Aristede said. "We will need you there, because you know when things happened. Let's do this quickly before anything else happens. Everyone ready?"

"N-n-now!" Blake stammered. His mouth dropped open. "W-w-we're g-going t-to go n-n-now?"

"Why not?" Aristede said as he led everyone behind the fireplace.

They stood in a circle. Aristede reached out his arms and said, "Everyone hold on to each other." He took hold of Cassidy's hand.

For a few hopeful moments, Brianna's fear about being forever trapped in the genie world was fading fast from her mind.

Aristede extended his finger, slowly turning it counterclockwise. The room began to blur, and they strained their eyes as a haze began to develop around them. The fireplace came back into focus a few seconds later, just as Aristede brought his finger to a stop.

The darkness covered their presence. This was a good thing, since it would be disastrous if they were seen. Across the center chamber, the *other* triplets were telling the *other* Brianna who they were and how she got into the amethyst bottle.

"This is strange, seeing ourselves," JD whispered.

"Shh. They will hear us," Morgan said.

That really was a bizarre statement to make, Morgan had to admit, but referring to their *other* selves like they were other people entirely was certainly weird.

JD moved to a shelf behind him and pulled something out from between the parchments. He thrust a hardbound book under Brianna's arm.

Brianna turned the book over and looked at the familiar cover illustration of *Chronicles of the Caretaker*.

"I wondered what happened to this," she exclaimed. "This book got me started with clues about the bottle. It was in one of the stories in here."

"We know. That is why JD took it, so it would not give you any more clues," Morgan told her.

"So you had it," she said. "It's been there all this time?"

JD nodded. His face showed a deep feeling of remorse.

Aristede took Brianna by the hand and pulled her aside. He crouched down to look in her eyes. "Now is your chance. Good-bye, Brianna."

Brianna took a few final minutes to say her good-byes.

Cassidy bent down and kissed her. Although the triplets probably wouldn't admit it out loud, deep down they all would miss Brianna.

"Give Mom and Daddy a kiss for me," Cassidy whispered.

"I will," Brianna said, smiling weakly. Her stomach rumbled as though there were several large birds flittering around. She desperately wanted to take her aunt with her.

"Wait," Cassidy said. "Your clothes! We can't send you home dressed like that, can we? I'll take care of it."

Cassidy took a step backward and strode around her niece, flicking her fingers up and down. Brianna's body tingled. When she looked down at her clothes, what she was wearing matched those of her counterpart. She had forgotten what her regular clothes felt like.

Suddenly the bottle began to tremble, and they knew why. It was Christian picking up the bottle, and they heard the other Morgan shout, "Hold on!"

Everyone reached out to grasp hold of anything solid. The shaking began to dwindle down until it stopped altogether.

"Now before the *other* Aristede and *other* Cassidy come down the corridor, we need to send Brianna back," Aristede said.

"Don't I have to wish it?" she asked.

"Remember, your power over a genie ended when you came here," Aristede said before turning to Blake. "You brought her here, so you're the one who has to send Brianna home."

Blake waved one arm around, and Brianna's physical body transmogrified into purple smoke. With another wave of the arm, this time pointing up, the mist spilled out and over the rim of the bottle.

But this was not any ordinary vapor. There was something very familiar about it. They had seen it before—when Brianna first entered the bottle. The curious purple vapor that came from behind the fireplace the triplets thought was a result of Granddad's breathing into the bottle and sucking it out again.

"That's the vapor—I remember it," JD said.

"That was us," Morgan said.

"You said it was the Outsider, I mean Granddad, who sucked air out of the bottle, Morgan," Blake reminded him.

"How could I know it was us sending Brianna home?" Morgan said.

"That's why we don't use the time loop often. Too many questions can create havoc," Aristede said.

The vapor brushed under Christian's nose. He blinked several times and put the stopper down on the shelf. Rubbing his eyes, he turned when he heard a one of the floorboards creak. It was Brianna.

"What the—" He stopped and needed a moment to gather his thoughts. "I came to check on you. I thought you might have fallen asleep."

He scratched Winston's head. Winston had fallen asleep in his arms, and Christian set him gently in his doggie bed. The puppy twisted his head to find the most comfortable sleeping position.

As he stood up, he noticed an object tucked under Brianna's right arm and said, "I see you found your book. You're still determined to find something, aren't you?"

"Nope. I found out everything I needed. There's nothing strange after all."

Christian pulled back a pajama sleeve to take a look at his wristwatch. It was past her bedtime, and she had to get to bed.

He put his arm around her shoulder and directed her to the hallway. Christian yanked the door opened and nearly crashed into Isabelle, who had been standing there in the door frame.

"I thought I heard something," she said, yawning. "What are you doing up so late?"

"I came to get Brianna. She was working on the computer and fell asleep," Christian said. "We were just going to bed."

"Thanks for worrying about me," Brianna said. She threw her arms around Isabelle and hugged her tightly.

"What's that for?" a startled Isabelle asked.

"Because I love you," she told her.

Christian turned out the light before the three started down the corridor to their respective bedrooms. With her grandparents in front, Brianna followed and in a low voice, she said, "That's for Casey."

Her grandmother turned and asked, "What was that, dear?"

Brianna's cheeks blushed as she smiled weakly. As much as she wanted to give her grandmother good news about her long-missing daughter, she knew she couldn't. It took a second before she replied, "Nothing, Gramma."

Back in the bottle, Cassidy whispered, "We did it. Let's get back to our time before your counterparts see us."

JD poked his finger in the air, obviously pointing up to the bottle opening. He mouthed something, too. When neither Morgan nor Blake knew what he was trying to tell them, JD grabbed hold of his brothers' hands. Seconds later, another stream of vapor came out of the bottle.

JD looked at the full moon hanging low in the sky. The moonlight covered the backyard. The same soft white light that shone on his face also produced a large shadow of the amethyst bottle into the back corner of the bookcase.

"Mom and Dad will be mad at us," Blake said, looking around to make sure none of the Outsiders was in earshot.

JD reached for the stopper. A look of complete satisfaction appeared on his face as he chucked the stopper up in the air once, caught it with his left hand, and pocketed it.

"Are you taking it?" Morgan exclaimed.

With the stopper tucked securely in JD's pocket, the bottle portal between the genie and the outer worlds would remain open.

"Now we can come and go whenever we want," JD said. "This is going to be fun!"

He waved his arm, and they vaporized again. Back into the bottle they went!

Meet the Author

Christian (Chris) Roulland Kueng had a deep desire to write, draw, and paint ever since he was a small child.

"Something I always wanted to do was write and illustrate a children's book," he says. "I had an idea, and it was fun using my imagination to create a magical place."

Chris grew up in Ontario, California, when there were orange groves and grape vineyards throughout the Southland. His parents, Robert and Margrit Kueng, came from Switzerland, and he is the oldest of their four sons. As a youngster, Chris loved going to school.

"The subjects I enjoyed most were art and creative writing."

Chris holds several university degrees. He studied fine arts at the California State University at Fullerton, during which time he worked as a freelance artist to supplement his income. He also obtained a master's degree in education from Azusa Pacific University, later adding a doctorate in educational leadership from the University of LaVerne. In addition, he is a graduate from the Institute of Children's Literature.

He has been an educator in the public school system for over thirty years, teaching elementary-school children and serving as a public school administrator. He works part time as an adjunct professor in the master's in education program at a local university.

Three Genie Brothers is Chris Kueng's first novel. He still lives in Ontario, where he divides his spare time between his family and his creative hobbies.